Evanly Bodies

Also by Rhys Bowen

The Constable Evans Mysteries

Evan Blessed
Evan's Gate
Evan Only Knows
Evans to Betsy
Evan Can Wait
Evan and Elle
Evan Help Us
Evans Above
Evanly Choirs

The Molly Murphy Mysteries

Oh Danny Boy
In Like Flynn
For the Love of Mike
Death of Riley
Murphy's Law

Evanly Bodies

Rhys Bowen

ST. MARTIN'S MINOTAUR 🙞 NEW YORK

 For information, address St. Martin's Press, 175 Fifth Avenue, New York, N.Y. 10010.

www.minotaurbooks.com

Library of Congress Cataloging-in-Publication Data

Bowen, Rhys.
Evanly bodies / Rhys Bowen.—1st ed.
p. cm.
ISBN-13: 978-0-312-34942-4
ISBN-10: 0-312-34942-4
1. Evans, Evan (Fictitious character)—Fiction. 2. Pakistanis—Wales—Fiction. 3. Arranged marriage—Fiction. 4. Serial murderers—Fiction. 5. Police—Wales—Fiction. I. Title.

PR6052.O848 E888 2006
823'.914—dc22

2006048380

First Edition: August 2006

10 9 8 7 6 5 4 3 2 1

This book is dedicated to my husband, John, who has championed my writing, been chauffeur, bodyguard, editor, chief cook and bottle-washer, put up with me through deadlines, bad reviews, signings to which nobody came, and rejoiced with me when things went right. May the next forty years be even better.

Acknowledgments

A heartfelt thanks to those who came to my aid on weapons questions: Harry G. Pellegrin, Jeff Poulin, Rus Morgan, Brent Kelmer, and, of course, my friend Robin Burcell.

Heartfelt thanks to Clare, who gave me the original idea for this crime, and to Jane and John for their helpful critiques.

Glossary

bara brith — speckled bread. Bread with mixed fruits in it (pronounced as it looks)

cariad — darling. Term of endearment. (pronounced *ca-ree-ad*)

Diolch yn fawr — thank you very much. (pronounced *dee-olch en vower*)

Escob Annwyl — literally, Dear Bishop. Good Heavens! (pronounced *escobe an-wheel*)

fach — little. Feminine of *bach* (pronounced *vuch* with the *ch* like the gutteral in *loch*)

Iechyd Da — Cheers. (pronounced *yachy dah*)

Ydych chi'n siarad Cymraeg? — Do you speak Welsh? (pronounced *idich-een sharad cumr-eye-g*)

Sut wyt ti? — How are you? Used as term of affection, same as "love" or "dear." (pronounced *sit wit tee*)

Evanly Bodies

Chapter 1

It was the postman who noticed it first. As he careened down Llanfair's one and only street, half in control of his motorbike and half not, he glanced at the small row of shops to his left. The village boasted three shops and a petrol pump. First in line of shops was a butcher, G. EVANS, CIGGYD, the Welsh word for "butcher" in large letters, and then PURVEYOR OF FINE MEATS in tiny ones; then R. EVANS, DAIRY PRODUCTS. These two had been known locally for years as Evans-the-Meat and Evans-the-Milk, respectively. Only the last store in the line, T. HARRIS, GROCER AND SUB–POST OFFICE, had spoiled the Evans's monopoly. But T. Harris was long dead, and his widow had finally given up the unequal struggle of trying to compete with the nearby Tesco's and had retired to live with her son near London. How she could want to spend her final years among foreigners had been a lively topic of discussion.

And so the corner grocery store had remained vacant for some time. The postman, yet another Evans, naturally nicknamed Evans-the-Post, had been modernized like most things in North Wales. He now made his deliveries by motorbike, enabling him to cover the outlying farms as well as the villages of Llanfair and Nant Peris. He had been riding the motorbike for at least a year now but was no nearer to mastering it. The look of wide-eyed terror in his eyes matched that of the pedestrians who were forced to scramble out of his way. One of them leaped aside now as Evans-the-Post turned to stare at what he had just seen, lost control, and almost mounted the pavement. It was Mrs. Powell-Jones, the minister's wife.

"Idiot! Fool!" Mrs. Powell-Jones shouted, as she reclaimed her dignity after the leap. "I'll call the postmaster about you! You'll end up killing somebody."

But Evans-the-Post was already well past her and out of hearing range. He finally wrestled the bike to a halt, extracted a letter from the mailbag, and loped toward the front door of a whitewashed cottage across the street. Instead of posting the letters through a perfectly good slot, however, he rapped on the door and waited until it was opened.

"Letter for you, Mrs. Williams," he said. "From your granddaughter, the one who's studying in London. She loved that jumper you knitted for her. And the *bara brith* you made."

The round, elderly woman smiled, not unkindly. "Thank you, Mr. Evans, although one of these days you'll find yourself in trouble if you keep on reading everyone's letters. You'll read something that's not good for you."

"I don't mean any harm," the man mumbled shyly.

"I know you don't. Go on then, off with you, or you'll be late checking in at the post office and that new postmaster will be after you."

Evans-the-Post went to leave, then swallowed hard, making a prominent Adam's apple dance up and down. "Somebody's moving into the old grocer's shop," he blurted out. "I've just seen them."

"No! *Escob Annwyl!* Are you sure it wasn't just the estate agent?"

"No, really moving in. I saw them doing carpentry in there, fixing things up."

"Well I never. I wonder who's taking it after all this time? I hope they're not thinking of turning it into something heathen. They turned one of the chapels in Blaenau Ffestiniog into a betting shop, you know. And remember that Frenchwoman who turned the chapel into a restaurant? I'm not surprised the Good Lord burned it down."

"A café wouldn't be bad," Evans-the-Post said. "Especially if they served fish and chips. We don't have anywhere to eat in the village, apart from the pub."

"Decent, God-fearing people should be eating in their own homes," Mrs. Williams said, folding her arms across a vast expanse of bosom. "I don't hold with all this eating fancy muck in restaurants. It isn't healthy. They say there's an obesity epidemic, and I say it's too much eating away from home." Since Mrs. Williams could never be described as slim, anyone else would have smiled at this remark, but Evans-the-Post nodded seriously.

Mrs. Williams leaned out her front door and peered up the street. A van was parked in front of the row of shops. Then she nodded to herself.

"I think I might make a custard today," she said, thoughtfully. "I'll just pop up to Evans-the-Milk and get an extra pint, just in case."

With that she put on her coat, tucked her basket on her arm, and started up the street. She hadn't gone far when she met Mair Hopkins on a similar journey.

"I'm putting Charlie on a diet," Mair confided, "So I thought I'd get some cottage cheese."

Together they walked in silence until they reached the shops, each knowing perfectly well the intention of the other, but each being too polite to mention it. The three shops were set back from the street on a broad stretch of pavement. The sound of hammering floated out of the former grocer's. Mair Hopkins's face lit up.

"So it's true what they were saying. There are new tenants in the corner shop. Thank the dear Lord for that. I'm that tired of having to catch the bus down the hill to Llanberis or sending Charlie out in the van when I run out of something."

"We don't know that it will be another grocer," Mrs. Williams said. "I'm just praying it won't be a betting shop, like that old chapel in Blaenau."

"A beauty parlor wouldn't be bad," Mair said. "Charlie told me it was about time I got my hair done more often."

"Well, I'd like to see the post office counter opened up again. You should see the line at the post office in Llanberis when I was there to pick up my pension."

"I know. It's terrible, just." Mair Hopkins shook her head.

The two women were about to cross the road to the shops when Mrs. Powell-Jones came flying toward them, seemingly out of nowhere, her pea green cardigan flapping as she ran.

"You've seen it then?" she said. "New people at the shop. I went in to welcome them to the village and to invite them to chapel on Sunday, as a minister's wife should, and you'll never believe it . . ."

"What?" The two women leaned closer.

"Heathens. Foreigners." Mrs. Powell-Jones almost spat out the words.

"You mean more English people?" Mrs. Williams asked. "Church not chapel?"

"Worse than that," Mrs. Powell-Jones whispered. "See for yourselves."

A man had just come out of the shop. He opened the back of the van and removed a long plank of wood. "Is this the size you wanted, Daddy?" he called.

"No, not that one, the thicker one," another voice called back, and an older man came out to join him.

"*Escob Annwyl,*" Mrs. Williams muttered, putting her hand to her heart. The men were dark skinned, and the younger one had a beard and was dressed in a white, flowing overshirt and leggings.

That evening Detective Constable Evan Evans was driving home from work when he noticed a light shining out from the formerly empty shop. Even though he was no longer a community policeman charged with keeping the peace in the village of Llanfair, his curiosity got the better of him. He parked and pushed open the shop door. Two brown-skinned men were bending over a sheet of paper. There were wood shavings on the floor, and sawdust floated in the air.

"Good evening," Evan said. "Doing some work on the place, are you?"

Both men looked up at Evan's voice.

"That's right," the older one said.

"We're trying to get this finished in a hurry," the younger one said in a dialect that came more from Yorkshire than Asia. "So I suggest you leave us in peace."

"I'm only doing my job, sir," Evan said pleasantly. "I'm a policeman and I live in this village so naturally I wanted to make sure no vandalism was going on in an empty building."

"A policeman?" The younger man still looked scornful. "Can't they even afford uniforms in North Wales, then?"

"I'm in the Plain Clothes Division," Evan said.

"Then it's not really your job to be checking up on us, is it? You're just plain nosy like the rest of them. In and out all day they've been, poking their noses in on some pretext or the other."

"That's enough, Rashid," the older man said. He wiped his hands on the apron he was wearing over normal street clothes, then held out his hand as he came toward Evan. "How do you do, Officer. I'm Azeem Khan. I've just bought this place."

"How do you do, Mr. Khan. Welcome to Llanfair then." Evan shook his outstretched hand.

Azeem Khan nodded for his son to do the same, but the boy was studying the building plan as if they didn't exist.

"Please excuse my son. He's going through a militant phase. It happens to most of us when we are students, doesn't it?" Unlike his son, his accent was still the lilting Pakistani of his forebears. He was clean-shaven, dressed in normal European-style clothes, and his black hair, now streaked with gray, was cut short and neatly parted. "Rashid, please stop acting in this manner and behave like a civilized human being."

Rashid Khan gave Evan a cold, challenging stare. "I've had enough encounters with the police to know that they don't like us, and we don't like them," he said.

"We're not in a big city now, Rashid," the father said. "We're in a small village, and it's important that we get along with everybody or we'll have no customers."

Evan smiled at the boy. "I suppose I should warn you that folks around here are suspicious of any strangers. It has nothing to do with race or anything like that. Any English person is considered a foreigner here. So don't take it personally. But I'll tell you one thing, if you're opening a new grocer's shop, everyone will be pleased. The older women in the village don't drive, and it's a long haul to take the bus all the way down to the supermarket."

"That's exactly what we thought when we first saw the place," Mr. Khan said enthusiastically. "A great opportunity, I told my wife."

"Did you have another shop before you moved?"

"For a while, yes, but the neighborhood went downhill so badly I was afraid to let my daughter out of the house. And now that my son is attending the university here in Wales, I said to my wife, 'Why not give it a try? Good clean air and peaceful surroundings.' She hasn't been well, you know. Her heart is not strong."

Evan turned back to Rashid. "So you are at university in Bangor? How do you like it?"

"All right so far. I've met other Muslim boys so at least I've got mates to hang out with."

"Good. Well, I'll let you get back to work then." Evan turned toward the door. "I live here in the village if you ever need me. Or at least not in the village anymore—just above the village. That little cottage just above the pub."

Mr. Khan beamed. "I was looking at that place when we first came by to see the shop, and I said to my wife, 'What a lovely view they must have.' And of course she said she couldn't imagine anybody living up that steep track."

"She's quite right, of course. That track is impossible on a rainy day. It's a sea of mud, but we're getting used to it."

"So you've just moved in too?"

"About a month ago. I just got married, and we rebuilt the cottage in time for the wedding. But I've lived in the village for several years. So has my wife. She was the local schoolteacher until they closed the school. Now she has to take the bus to the new school in the valley."

Old Mr. Khan nodded. "That's progress for you, isn't it? Everything changes and not always for the better."

"Are we going to get back to this, Dad?" Rashid demanded. "I've got a paper to write, you know."

"All right, all right." Mr. Khan gave Evan an apologetic smile and turned back to the blueprint.

Chapter 2

Evan was about to park his car for the night and make the ascent to the cottage on foot when he decided Bronwen wouldn't mind if he popped into the pub first. He was curious to know how much the inhabitants of Llanfair had gleaned about the newcomers during that first day. The Llanfair grapevine was so efficient that it could put the CIA to shame.

He crossed the street to where the sign of the Red Dragon squeaked as it swung in the evening breeze. The main bar was in full swing as he ducked his head to pass through the low doorway. Voices were raised in animated conversation. Through the smoke haze, Evan observed the usual group of men who assembled there most evenings.

"I never thought I'd live to see the day," Charlie Hopkins was exclaiming loudly. "When my Mair told me that one of them was dressed in those funny robes with a beard and sandals and all . . ."

"We don't want them here," a voice growled from a dark corner. "Why don't they go back where they came from?"

"Leeds, you mean?" someone challenged.

"Bloody Pakistan is what I mean. If God had intended dark-skinned people to live in Wales, he'd have made the sun shine here occasionally."

A chuckle ran around the bar.

"Well, I don't think it's all bad," Evans-the-Meat, countered.

Evan paused, on his way up to the bar, and listened in amazement. Of all the villagers, he would have labeled Evans-the-Meat as the most prejudiced, militantly Welsh, and antiforeigner.

"I think we'll get along just fine," Gareth Evans continued. "After all, Pakistan and Wales have something in common, don't they?"

"Similar accents when we speak English?" someone suggested.

"I'm serious, boyo. We both know what it's like to be dominated by a colonial power, don't we? We've both been occupied by the bloody English."

"So you're saying you'd rather have Pakis run that grocer's shop than, say, English people?" Barry-the-Bucket, the local bulldozer driver, asked.

"Absolutely," Evans-the-Meat insisted.

"Well, I don't agree with that at all," Betsy the barmaid leaned across the bar to join in. "I've been to Asian grocers before, and everything in the place stinks of curry. You'll probably go in for a can of baked beans and find you have to buy lentils instead. Great sacks of lentils everywhere, you wait and see. In fact—" She broke off as she spotted Evan waiting patiently behind the men at the bar. "Well, would you look who's here? Aren't you a sight for sore eyes. What will it be, the usual?"

"Yes, please, Betsy *fach,*" Evan said. "A pint of Guinness would go down a treat. I've been in meetings all day at headquarters, and I'm parched."

"Oh, poor boy, half starved he is these days. They say his wife doesn't feed him properly." Charlie chuckled and dug Evan in his well-padded ribs.

"I'm surprised she's letting you out so soon after the wedding," the butcher said. "You must have licked her into shape really quickly if she's letting you spend your evenings in the pub already."

"Oh, come on, Gareth." Evan chuckled. "I am not spending my evenings at the pub, and I certainly haven't attempted to lick Bronwen into shape. I just thought I'd pop in for a few minutes to see what everyone's heard about the people moving into the shop."

"They're Pakis," Charlie Hopkins said, as Betsy put a foaming mug of Guinness on the counter for Evan.

"I know. I went over just now. It's a father and son, doing the carpentry themselves."

"It's going to be trouble if you ask me," Barry-the-Bucket commented, between swigs from his glass. "You saw how the young one was dressed—like one of those Muslim priests you see on the telly. I wouldn't be surprised if they're not a terrorist cell hiding out here. You want to keep an eye on them, Evan."

"Give them a break, Barry," Evan said. "I'm sure they're a perfectly normal family. It's up to them how they choose to dress. They've got their religion, and we've got ours. That doesn't make them dangerous. I suggest we all work hard to make them feel welcome in the village."

"If they want us to make them feel welcome, then they've got to learn to be a bloody sight friendlier than they were today," Charlie Hopkins said. "My Mair poked her head around the door, just to exchange a friendly word with whoever it was, and they cut her dead. The younger one wouldn't even speak to her."

"Ah well, they're Muslims, look you, and she's a woman," Barry said. "Women don't count for anything in their religion. They'll probably start making all the women in the village wear veils when they go into the shop."

Evan laughed, a little uneasily. "Come on, Barry. They're as British as you or I. Give them a chance, all right?"

"I'd like to see anyone make me start wearing a veil," Betsy said. "I've got a good body, and I don't mind showing it off a little."

She smoothed down her T shirt, pulling the low neckline even lower, making every man in the bar look up from his glass.

"You get back to your pouring," Barry said firmly. He and Betsy had been dating for a while. "That's enough showing it off for one evening."

"Mind you"—Betsy gave him a teasing smile—"one of those see-through, filmy veils would be dead sexy. Like Salomé doing the dance of the seven veils." She wiggled her hips, making the men laugh.

Evan drained his glass and replaced it on the bar. "Thanks, Betsy love. I'd better be going, then. I don't like to keep Bronwen waiting, and I've had a tough day."

"Big case you're working on?" Charlie Hopkins asked.

"No, worse luck. Big meeting. It's the new Chief Constable. He's shaking up the whole police force. You want to hear the latest thing? New uniforms. He's going to have the poor blokes on the beat wearing black cargo pants and black turtleneck sweaters instead of the old shirts and ties."

"What? Cargo pants and sweaters? They'll look like a bunch of thugs. Where's the authority in that? People like a policeman to look like a policeman. They respect the brass buttons and the neat tie." Charlie Hopkins shook his head in disgust.

"I agree with you, Charlie," Evan said. "But the new Chief Constable says the ties are a liability during a scuffle, even though they're only clip on and come off easily, and he says the shirts only get crumpled when you wear them with body armor."

"Body armor?" Barry burst out laughing. "When have you ever worn body armor?"

"Never, personally, but some of the force has to, sometimes."

The rest of the men were laughing now.

"It's not as if you blokes are breaking up a gang fight or an international terrorist cell every day of the week now, is it?" Evans-the-Meat chuckled.

"There's nothing I can do about it, Gareth," Evan said. "I'm at the bottom of the pecking order. My opinion doesn't count for much. Unfortunately, I have a feeling that this new uniform is only the tip of the iceberg. We've got special meetings of the Plain Clothes Division going on for the next couple of weeks, and he's scheduled us for sensitivity training."

"For what?" Barry asked.

"We have to learn how to be nice to the public so that they don't regard us with hostility."

He broke off as the men around him were laughing.

"So when you catch a young thug you have to say, 'Oh no, you naughty boy. Please don't bash in that old lady's head and take her purse. It isn't nice,'" Evans-the-Meat said in high falsetto.

"You think it's funny, but that's just about what it's going to be," Evan said gloomily. "Oh well, there's not much I can do about it. I'd better get on home or Bronwen will worry."

Evan nodded to his friends and stepped out into the brisk evening breeze. It was quite a climb up the hill to the cottage. It had been easy enough during dry weather when the daylight lasted until after nine o'clock. Now, at the beginning of October, the evenings were closing in, and the valley was plunged into darkness by seven. Evan stumbled and slithered his way upward, wishing he had a car that could make the slope. But he still had only his old bone shaker, and in this weather the track really needed a four-wheel drive.

Light was streaming out of the cottage windows, sending a welcoming beacon down to him. As he approached the front door, Evan paused to savor the satisfaction of the moment—his own home built mainly by his own hands, his wife waiting for him with dinner on the table. What more could a man want from life?

He pushed open the front door. "Bron?" he called. "I hope I haven't kept dinner waiting too long, but I just had to pop into the pub . . ."

"Oh yes?" Bronwen appeared from the kitchen, taking off the apron she was wearing over her jeans and sweater. "Just had to pop in, did you?"

"I was only there a few minutes," Evan said, "and I just wanted to find out what the blokes in the village had heard about the Harris's old shop. Did you know it's been sold, and a Pakistani family has bought it? They're down there now, refitting the shelves and counters."

"I do know all about it," Bronwen said, "and I didn't have to pop into the pub to find out. It just so happens that we've got company."

"What?" Evan looked around the room for the first time. Perched at the edge of one of the kitchen chairs was a young girl, dressed in a navy blue-and-white school uniform. She looked to be in her midteens, with light brown skin and one long, luxurious dark braid of hair down her back. She rose awkwardly to her feet and smiled shyly. "Oh hello," Evan said. "Sorry, I didn't see you there."

"Evan"—Bronwen took his arm—"I'd like you to meet Jamila. She's the daughter of the new people at the grocer's shop. We met on the bus coming home from school and got talking, and she very kindly offered to help me carry my shopping up the hill. So I thought the very least I could do was invite her to stay for dinner with us. Our first dinner guest."

"Nice to meet you, Jamila. This is all right with your family, is it?"

"Oh yes. I asked Mummy, and she it would be fine to stay and help Mrs. Evans, especially when she found out that Mrs. Evans was the schoolteacher. I'd only be in the way at the shop while Daddy and Rashid are working anyway."

"So has your family moved in yet?"

"We're in the process of moving in. We had the van bring up some things today, and the rest is coming tomorrow. Daddy says they'll have the shop opened on Saturday." She spoke, like her brother, with a slight Yorkshire accent.

"Where are you living now then?" Evan asked.

"We've been renting a couple of rooms in Bangor so that Rashid and I could start the school year here. But now we'll be living in the flat over the shop. It's going to be rather crowded, but I expect we'll survive. Rashid wants to move into student housing at the university as soon as they can find a suitable place."

"That shouldn't take long, should it? I thought the university would find housing for students."

"Well, there is plenty of housing, but not what Rashid wants. He'll only live with other Muslim students, you see, so they're trying to find a house to rent—and not everybody is too keen to rent to a group of Pakistani boys, as you can imagine."

"That's illegal, isn't it?" Bronwen said angrily.

"I'm sure it is," Evan agreed, "but you're not surprised to hear that an old Welsh landlady finds an excuse not to let out rooms to anybody who looks so different, are you? It's very hard to prove a discrimination case. But I'm sure the university will have to come up with something if your brother perseveres."

"Oh, he's good at pushing to get his own way, believe me." Jamila smiled. "Rashid is a great one for his rights."

"Well, don't just stand there, Evan," Bronwen said. "Dinner's all ready, and I'm sure you're starving as usual. Let's eat, and we can continue our conversation at the dining table." She put a hand on Jamila's shoulder. "I hope you don't mind eating in the kitchen, Jamila, but we decided the living room would be too cramped if we tried to fit in a dining table."

"Oh no, I think what you've got here is just lovely," she said. "So warm and friendly, like something out of a storybook."

"That was the idea," Bronwen said. "Sit down, you two. It's a chicken casserole tonight. You don't have any dietary restrictions about chicken, do you, Jamila?"

"I'm not like my brother, Mrs. Evans." Jamila rolled her eyes. "I'm not particularly religious. I don't eat pork because my family never cooks it, but I've eaten a sausage at a friend's house before now. I mean, it made sense not to eat pork when people lived in a desert and had no means of refrigeration, but now pigs are as safe as any other animals, aren't they?"

"Well, I'd agree with that," Bronwen said, ladling out a generous helping of casserole onto Jamila's plate and putting it in front of her, "but many people feel passionately about it, don't they? Wars have been started over less."

"I know. My parents were never particularly religious either. My father has always behaved like a good Muslim—going to the mosque, saying his prayers, that kind of thing—but he was never fanatical about it. But now my brother has gone off the deep end. He's been bullying me to wear a *hajib*—you know, a scarf around my head. I've refused flatly. I mean, I live in the UK, don't I? And I think it's insulting to women to tell them to make themselves invisible. If it was up to Rashid, he'd make Mummy and me be hidden under burkas and never go out." She looked at their faces and laughed. "No, I'm serious. He's been going on at my father not to let me go to any parties or anywhere apart from school where I'm not escorted by a male family member. That's so silly, isn't it?"

"Well, I say stick to your guns, Jamila," Bronwen said.

Jamila beamed. "Oh, thank you, Mrs. Evans. You don't know how encouraging it is to hear that. Luckily I've already made some good friends at school, and they're supportive too. I'm trying hard to learn Welsh quickly; then I can talk to my friends on the phone, and Rashid won't know what I'm saying."

"You can come up here and practice with us," Evan said. "I'm a policeman and I often work long hours. Bronwen would enjoy the company, wouldn't you, love?"

"That would be lovely," Bronwen said. "I'll help you with your Welsh if you like. And since I'm an old married schoolteacher, even your brother couldn't object, could he?"

Jamila gave them both a happy smile.

Chapter 3

The room was full by the time Evan entered. Sun streaming in through the south-facing plate-glass windows had made it too warm and stuffy. He looked around and saw his fellow detective constable, Glynis Davies, sitting next to DI Watkins in the back row. Evan went over to join them, pulling up a stackable chair beside them.

"We wondered where you'd got to, boyo," Watkins said. "We thought you were going to incur the wrath of God by coming in after He'd started talking."

"It rained all last night, didn't it?" Evan muttered. "It took me ages to get down the hill."

"You drove your car up that track?" Glynis asked. "Wasn't that asking for trouble?"

"Not the car—me. The car was parked down below, but it took me awhile to get down to it. It was so slippery, and I didn't want to risk sitting down on my rear end and arriving here covered in mud."

"So what do you think you're going to do all winter?" Watkins asked. "In case you hadn't noticed, it does rain a lot up here, and snow, too. Is this going to be a recurrent excuse for showing up late?"

Evan grinned. "We're going to have to do something, I know. Bronwen's father promised us his old Land Rover when he gets a new one, but he doesn't show any signs of doing so. And we can hardly keep nagging him, so it's a case of taking the track carefully at the moment."

"Well, luckily you haven't missed anything," Glynis whispered. "The great man is running late too."

"What is this for now?" Evan asking, looking at the other officers assembled in the room. "It looks like the whole Plain Clothes Division is here this time. Who exactly would be holding the fort if there's a major crime?"

"Don't ask me," Inspector Watkins muttered. "I'm as much in the dark as you are. I'm too lowly to have been invited to the brainstorming sessions among the top brass."

"What can't we have covered already?" Evan asked.

"Maybe it's to tell us that the Plain Clothes Division will now be wearing uniforms. Plainer plain clothes, so to speak." The detective constable sitting in front of Evan turned round to him with a grin.

"Let's hope they're not as ugly as the uniforms he's planning to make the poor blokes on the beat wear," someone else chimed in.

"No, I bet it's nothing to do with uniforms. My bet is that it's more sensitivity training." Glynis said.

"Oh God, please no," the first DC rolled his eyes. "Where did they find him, anyway?"

"He's just done a stint in America."

"As if they know anything about sensitivity training there. They just shoot first and then show great sensitivity to the corpse."

A general chuckle ran around the room. Evan noticed that DI Watkins tried not to smile but couldn't quite manage to keep a straight face.

"Now, come on, lads," Watkins said. "That's not the spirit. We may not find his methods easy at first, but he is our new boss and it's up to us to learn to love and appreciate him."

"Providing he's sensitive enough," someone quipped.

This time there was loud laughter.

At that moment the door opened and the new Chief Constable Mathry came in. He was followed by the division commanders of the three regions, Chief Superintendents Morris, Talley, and Jones;

and behind them the various chiefs of operations, including Evan's own boss, DCI Hughes.

The Chief Constable looked around the room, beaming. "That's what I like to see, lads, positive team spirit. That's the ticket. I know we're all going to get along splendidly. What we need is more meetings like this, more chances for the entire division to interact. There has been too much compartmentalization and not enough cooperation between the regions." He perched on the edge of the desk at the front of the room. "I've been taking a look at the logs on that recent mugging on Mount Snowdon. It was originally reported to Colwyn Bay HQ, who referred it to Caernarfon as the national park was within their jurisdiction. However, it was then handed back to Colwyn Bay because they had more manpower. Precious time lost with haggling back and forth."

"With all due respect, sir," DCI Hughes rose from his chair. "As senior detective of the Caernarfon Station, I have to point out that we had only five men on the roster."

"Five people," Glynis muttered, loud enough for Evan to hear.

"This mugging happened on a Sunday when two of my men had days off after working ten days straight, and one was still on leave of absence for his honeymoon."

"Awww," several men teased.

"Should have called him back, lazy bugger," someone else commented.

"Gentlemen, please." Hughes held up his hand. "As I was saying, we were undermanned that day. It made sense to call in a bigger unit."

"Excuse me, sir." Glynis rose to her feet. "I don't wish to sound like a raving feminist, but I should like to point out, for the record, that there are two women officers present. To hear only the male members of the force being addressed is somewhat insulting."

"Quite right, young lady." The Chief Constable nodded. "Hit the nail on the head. That's exactly what I was getting at in our session on sensitivity the other day, being aware of those around you, watching that you don't offend unintentionally. Now would you like to rephrase what you were saying, Hughes?"

DCI Hughes turned slightly pink. "My apologies, sir. Just a slip of the tongue, I assure you. Now, as I was saying . . ." he cleared his throat before repeating what he had just said, using nongender-specific language with great care.

"You'll be put on shoplifting detail forever after this," Evan whispered to Glynis. "Making your boss blush in front of his fellow officers."

"I know, but I couldn't sit there and hear him address the assembly as 'gentlemen.'"

"You all know the old proverb, a new broom sweeps clean," the Chief Constable said, as DCI Hughes sat down again. "I've been studying the running of this division, and I've decided the only thing to do is a complete overhaul. Superintendents Morris and Talley have been working with me all weekend, and we've decided to avoid miscommunications and holdups like the one I just referred to by instituting a Major Incident Team to be kept on call at headquarters here in Colwyn Bay. We have selected officers from each division to rotate onto this team. My hope is that by working together with officers from all three divisions, we will create a better spirit of cooperation throughout the force."

"How's this going to work, sir?" A detective inspector in the front row asked. "Who's going to decide what's a major incident?"

"A 'major incident' is something a local division isn't equipped to handle at any given moment. A murder, a kidnapping—any crime that would need to coordinate with our forensics and specialist teams. Local stations will call us in when they need us, and the next available team will be dispatched."

"Excuse me, sir?" a tentative hand went up, "but do I understand correctly that you've selected officers from all three divisions to take their turns operating out of Colwyn Bay?"

"Quite right. Absolutely."

"That will mean rather a long drive for some of us. I live close to Wrexham. That will be an hour's commute for me."

"Yes, I do appreciate that this will be a problem for a few officers. We're working on a feasibility study to see if police accommodations can be provided for those officers who genuinely live too far away. How many men would be seriously inconvenienced?"

A good number of hands were raised.

"Ah yes, well that is a considerable number. If you'll meet with us after the meeting, we'll take commuting distance into consideration when forming our first teams."

"And what about the female officers?" Glynis asked in her clear voice. "You can't expect us to bunk down with the men."

There were several muttered comments along the lines of "we wouldn't mind a bit."

"Good point, Miss—uh?"

"Detective Constable Davies, sir."

"We'll definitely include your concerns in the feasibility study, DC Davies." The big man gave her an encouraging smile.

"They just don't get it, do they?" Glynis muttered to Evan.

"This will require further study, I can see. Obviously an officer is of no use to us if he's going to take over an hour to respond to a crime scene. Chief Superintendent Morris, would you like to tell everyone where we are so far?"

"Right, sir." The older man rose to his feet. "We are setting up response teams within the Major Incident Division. Teams will be composed of a DI, a detective sergeant, and two detective constables to each unit. When a call is received, the next available team will be dispatched. We're going to start with three teams and see if this is sufficient for our needs. We want to have all situations covered, but we don't want officers sitting around drinking tea and doing the crossword all day either."

"Sounds all right to me," a voice muttered.

"A roster of the first teams to be selected will be placed on the notice board after the meeting. Now if you'll—"

He broke off as the door to the room opened and a young female dispatcher came in, looking distinctly embarrassed as the attention of all the senior officers was suddenly on her. "Excuse me, sir, but we've just had a call from Bangor. They are reporting a homicide. The Bangor duty officer says he needs their detectives back on the job right away."

Chief Constable Mathry clapped his hands together delightedly. "Our first test, men. Superintendent Morris, whom have we assigned to the first response team?"

The superintendent glanced down at the sheaf of papers he was carrying. "We had DI Bragg from Central, DS Wingate from Eastern, DC Pritchard from Central, and DC Evans from Western. Let's have you four lads up here right away for briefing."

The Chief Constable was still beaming. "I realize this will be a baptism of fire, men, throwing you together like this before you've had time to get to know each other; but I have great confidence in your abilities, and I know you'll be a credit to the force."

It took Evan a moment to stand up.

"Good luck, Evan." Glynis gave him an encouraging smile.

Watkins leaned close to him and grabbed his wrist as he began to make his way to the front of the room. "Watch out for Bragg. Word is that he's a right bugger to work for. Likes all the credit for himself."

Evan nodded. He gave Watkins and Glynis Davies what he hoped was a confident grin as he moved forward to join the other men.

Chapter 4

The house was a big Victorian, set back from the road amid spacious lawns. The garden sloped downhill, giving glimpses of a view over the Menai Strait and the Isle of Anglesey. The water in the strait sparkled in morning sunlight as a small fishing boat chugged out toward the Atlantic. It looked most peaceful and inviting. Evan had always been shaken by the contrast between a violent crime and life going on peacefully around it. He noticed that late roses were still in bloom along the driveway as they walked up to the house. The garden was immaculate, obviously tended with a loving hand.

As they approached the front door, a uniformed sergeant came out to meet them.

"What's this then?" he asked, looking at them suspiciously. "Where's our lads? Where's DI Lewis?"

"There's been a reorganization at headquarters," Inspector Bragg said, in what sounded like confrontational tones. "And you are?"

"Presley, sir. But Ifan, not Elvis, even though I've got the looks for it."

The other men grinned, but no muscle moved on DI Bragg's face. During the high-speed ride from headquarters, which had taken place in almost complete silence, Evan had already decided that he wasn't at all happy with this assignment. If someone thought they were giving him a bump up the career ladder, he wasn't especially grateful. He rather suspected that DCI Hughes, his former boss, had had a hand in it. Hughes had not appreciated being outsmarted by Evan on a couple of occasions. Evan suspected that this new DI would like his toes being trodden on even less.

Bragg was built like an ex–Royal Marine: lean, middle aged, close-cropped grizzled air, a body that looked as if it was chiseled from rock. He wasn't particularly tall, however, probably no more than five foot ten. He stepped forward until he was standing eyeball-to-eyeball with Sergeant Presley. "I'm DI Bragg, in charge of the Major Incident Team that will be handling this case from now on. Your men should report any findings to me and only to me. I want an interview room made available at your station immediately, and I want the report from those men who handled the first response right away."

"Right you are, sir," the sergeant said. Evan thought he put a little too much emphasis on the word "sir." The sergeant looked around the group, and his face lit up when he spotted Evan. "Hello, Evans. I'm glad to see you're here, at least."

"DC Evans is the junior member of this team," Bragg said. "His role will be confined to taking notes and running errands for the senior officers. Now what exactly do we have here?"

"He was found lying sprawled across the breakfast table, apparently shot."

"Who was?" Bragg snapped.

"The man's name is Rogers, Professor Martin Rogers. He's head of the History Department at the university."

"It's his house?"

"Yes sir."

"We've had a positive identification? It wasn't an intruder?"

"Who broke in to eat Professor Roger's boiled egg for breakfast?" Sergeant Presley quipped, saw the steely look in Bragg's eyes, and added, "Not an intruder, sir. His wife identified him. She was the one who found him when she came back from walking the dog."

"Where's she now?"

"With a female PC. She resting upstairs in her bedroom."

"How's she taking it? Hysterical?"

"No sir. Very calm really. One of these upper-class ladies who's brought up not to make a fuss, I'd say."

"So it was the wife who made the nine-nine-nine call?"

"Yes sir."

"Anyone else in the house? Servant of any kind?"

"Not in evidence, sir. We just secured the crime scene and called in the plain clothes branch."

"Very good." For once Bragg sounded almost pleased. "Has the doctor been summoned, and forensics?"

"The doctor's here now, sir. It's up to you blokes to ask for forensics. Outside of our jurisdiction, you know."

Evan thought he looked rather smug when he said this, as if he was enjoying this encounter with DI Bragg.

"Right. Evans, get on to it. Use the squad car radio. We want the full Forensics Incident Team here right away."

"Very good, sir," Evan said. His feet felt like lead as he walked back to the car. After working for so long with DI Watkins and then with Glynis Davies, people he had come to know and trust, this was a bitter blow. From the few words that had been exchanged, he suspected that Bragg was well aware of his past successes and was determined to keep him firmly in his place: a junior officer, whose role was confined to running errands.

He made the calls to headquarters, then let himself into the house through the open front door. The house looked immaculate, as if it was ready for a photo shoot for *Better Homes and Gardens.* From the central hall Evan could see a drawing room and dining room full of good quality antique furniture, absolutely glowing with high polish. No clutter. Not a thing out of place. There were vases of fresh flowers on side tables, and exquisite, hand-embroidered cushions on chairs and sofas. Not at all the sort of place where anything as sordid as a murder should have happened.

DI Bragg glanced up briefly as Evan entered the kitchen: Detective Sergeant Wingate was standing close to the window with an older, harried-looking man beside him. Evan recognized the police doctor, with whom he had worked before. Wingate was obviously from an upper-class background, dressed in well-cut slacks and sport's jacket. His hair was a little longer than Evan would have worn it. There was no sign of the other DC. Evan suspected he'd also been sent on some menial errand.

At first glance the kitchen matched the other rooms he had seen—understated good taste and money at work: white wood, glass-fronted cabinets, blue-and-white Delft tile, blue-and-white china on the shelves, a vase of yellow crysanthymums as decoration, and a red Aga discreetly nestled into a corner. Then his eyes were drawn to the table by the window. It had been set for breakfast with a white cloth and the same blue-and-white china he'd seen on the shelves. Only now the scene was marred by a body, wearing a checked shirt and tweeds, sprawled across the table. From where he was standing Evan couldn't see the face, but he could see the red stain that had soaked into the white cloth around where the head lay.

"Ah, Evans. Got in touch with forensics then?" Bragg asked. "Good man. Now watch your step in here, won't you? Don't touch anything until forensics has given the place a good going over. We don't want you mucking up the crime scene with your fingerprints."

As if I would, you berk, Evan thought.

"Anything you'd like me to do now, sir?" he asked.

"Just hang around, observe, learn," DI Bragg said. "Do you have your notebook handy? I'll need you to take notes when I conduct interviews."

"Yes, sir." Evan produced a notebook and pen, rather wishing that he'd gone over to a handheld computer, which would have definitely scored points.

"Right, Doctor, as we were saying." Bragg turned back to the man standing by the window. "Time of death?"

"I can't give you to the minute," the doctor said, looking at Bragg with the same distaste Evan himself felt. "He was in the middle of eating a boiled egg. His wife can tell you at what time she served breakfast, I'd imagine. So it would be the interval between her serving the egg and his having a chance to finish it."

"And if the scene was staged, and the egg put on the table just to confuse the investigation?" Bragg asked.

"All I can say is he hadn't been dead long when I arrived. No more than an hour probably. Of course he was lying in a south-facing window with the sun shining full on him. That would have helped keep the body warm. But there was no sign of rigor mortis when I first saw him."

"And cause of death?" Bragg asked.

A bloody great hole in the side of his head, Evan was dying to say. He thought the doctor remarkably patient when he answered evenly, "A gunshot wound to the left temple, fired at fairly close range, I'd surmise."

"Any chance it could have been suicide?" Bragg asked.

The doctor glanced from Bragg to the body and back again. "Not unless somebody removed the weapon afterward. I'm no ballistics expert, but I would estimate the shot came from a few feet away. Your spatter experts will tell you more accurately than I."

"In which case where did the shooter stand, I wonder?" Bragg asked. "The table's close to the window, and yet the shot is in the left temple—unless he turned around and then back again as he fell."

"The shot could have come in through the window, sir," Evan said.

Bragg turned on him with a patronizing smirk. "Through the window, Constable? The window, in case you haven't noticed, is closed."

"Somebody could have closed it," Evan said.

"He's not wrong, sir," Detective Sergeant Wingate said, looking out into the garden. "Those bushes would offer splendid cover, and someone standing right beside that yew would have a perfect line of fire at a person seated at the table."

"And after he'd killed the poor bloke, he then went into the house and calmly shut the window, did he? Rather risky, wouldn't you say?" Bragg said smugly.

"Not if he knew the house was empty. He'd probably observed the wife going out with the dog and knew there were no live-in servants."

"In other words, he'd cased the joint first?"

"Well, it's clearly not a murder committed in the course of a burglary, is it?" DS Wingate said. "I've taken a look in the other rooms downstairs, and nothing whatsoever has been disturbed. They've some nice silver, too."

"Until we have gone over the whole house with Mrs. Rogers, we have no way of knowing whether a burglary has or has not occurred. The man's a professor. Important papers could be missing. You young officers are great at jumping to conclusions. All in aid of the hasty arrest and your picture in the paper, is it?"

"No sir. Just trying to talk our way through the various scenarios."

"I'll decide what we talk about, Wingate. At your former station I'm sure you were all mates together; but I like to run a tight ship, and I'm the captain, got it?"

"Aye, aye, Captain," Wingate said dryly. He caught Evans's eyes, and Evan realized with gratitude that he had at least one ally in the camp.

"So you'll leave us your report then, Doctor?" Bragg asked.

"I'll have it typed up and sent over to you," the doctor said.

"We'll be setting up shop at the Bangor Police Station. That's where you can find us. Thanks for showing up so quickly. Evans will show you out."

"I can find my own way, thanks," the doctor said, picked up his bag, and departed.

"Right, Constable, take this down," Bragg said. "Plan of attack: Interview wife. Go over house with her. Locate the weapon. Search outside for footprints. Possible eye witnesses. Question neighbors. That should get us started until we've got a forensic report and a possible motive. Wingate, you take Pritchard and search the grounds. Watch where you tread so that you don't disturb anything. We'll need casts of any footprints. Evans, you can come with me, and we'll talk to Mrs. Rogers. Ten to one she did it herself. Cherchez la femme. That's what they always say, isn't it?"

"Do they, sir?" Evan said, and noted a grin from Wingate. "If she did it herself, don't you think she might have taken longer to call the police so that the time of death wasn't so obvious? And don't you think she'd have removed the boiled egg and established a better alibi than walking the dog?"

"What did they teach you during detective training, Constable? Didn't they tell you 'always start with the obvious'? So until the wife is ruled out, she's logically the number-one suspect. The majority of murders are committed by family members or close friends. You should know that. It's very rare you come upon a murder among strangers, outside of the drug scene, of which, I suppose, you've had little experience in your sheltered corner of North Wales."

"We've had a couple of cases, sir," Evan said, "now that they're shipping in drugs from Ireland through Holyhead. There are drugs pretty much everywhere these days, aren't there?"

"I suppose there would be the odd case of drugs among the students at the university here. This man was a professor, wasn't he? The next step will be to speak with his colleagues. There is sometimes bitter rivalry among academics, so I hear. I don't think it should take us long at all to have this case wrapped up."

"No sir," Evan said, and followed Bragg up the thick Axminster carpet of the staircase.

Chapter 5

DI Bragg tapped on a bedroom door then entered without waiting for a summons. Evan followed. The room was in the same good taste as the downstairs had been—pale, striped wallpaper; Regency chest of drawers; built-in, white-painted wardrobes; a good nineteenth-century watercolor of Mount Snowdon on the wall. A sewing basket and a half finished tapestry lay on the bedside table. A slim, gray-haired woman sat stiff and upright on the bed, staring away from them, out of the window, while a policewoman perched awkwardly in a white wicker chair.

It took the woman on the bed a moment to react to the sound of the door opening and turn her head toward the men who had just come into her bedroom. She looked at them with neither interest nor surprise, her face a mask of composure apart from lips pressed firmly together.

"I thought you were supposed to be resting, Mrs. Rogers," DI Bragg said.

"The doctor prescribed a sedative, but she wouldn't take it," the WPC said, as if this had personally offended her. "I've tried to get her to lie down at least and drink some hot tea for the shock."

"As if I could rest at a time like this," Mrs. Rogers said. Her voice was soft but smooth and cultured. "My husband's body lying downstairs, blood all over my kitchen, and you tell me to rest?"

"I understand what you must be going through. I'm Detective Inspector Bragg. I'll be handling this case. This is Detective Constable Evans, who'll be taking notes as we talk. You do feel up to talking, don't you?"

"Yes. I can talk. It's better than sitting here and thinking," she said.

"Good. Let's start at the beginning then. Your full name is?"

"Madeleine Jane Rogers. I'm usually called Missy. It's a childhood nickname that stuck."

"And you've been married to Martin Rogers for how long?"

"Twenty-nine years, almost thirty. Our anniversary would have been this November."

"Any children?"

"Unfortunately no. We couldn't have children. It's always been my great regret."

Bragg cleared his throat. "Right. Let's get to this morning then, shall we?"

"Yes. Very well. It was just the same as every other morning. I always get up first. I lay the table and prepare the breakfast; then I take the dog for a walk."

"No servants in the house?"

"Servants?" She made a sound that was half laugh, half cough. "How much do you think university professors earn, Inspector? When Martin's father grew up in this house, there was a pack of servants, but we're now down to a cleaning lady, once a week, and a gardener who does the heavy jobs for me."

"I see. You don't usually eat breakfast with your husband then?"

"No. I'm always up at six or six thirty. Martin never rises before eight. I—I don't sleep too well."

"And this morning you were up at your usual time?"

"Yes. I got up at about six thirty, made myself a cup of tea, ate a slice of toast and marmalade, and read the paper. I took Martin up a cup of tea about seven fifteen. Then I went outside and did a spot of gardening. Then about seven forty-five, I boiled him an egg and called up the stairs to say it was ready. He said he'd be down right away. I put the egg and the toast on the table, poured him a cup of tea, and then shouted up the stairs again to remind him not to let the yolk get hard. He hated eggs with hard yolks. Then I took the dog for a walk, the way I always do."

Evan looked around the room. "Where is the dog now?" he asked.

"I shut him in the summerhouse. He's a highly strung animal. I thought he'd get terribly upset with what would be going on here."

"Good idea," DI Bragg said, glancing across at Evans. Evan couldn't tell from the glance whether the DI was annoyed that he had spoken up. "So your walk started when?"

"I always leave at eight o'clock, and I'm out for about an hour."

"When you went out this morning, did you notice anything suspicious? Something that caught your eye as not quite right?"

"You mean did I glimpse someone lurking in the bushes? I'm afraid I didn't. And Lucky would have growled if he'd sensed somebody was in the garden. He has a wonderful sense of smell."

"Do you always take the same route?"

"It depends on the weather. On nice days I like to walk as close to the water as possible and enjoy the view across the strait to Anglesey. When the weather is not so fine, I stick to the town route, past the park, so that Lucky can have a bit of a run. I take a tennis ball for him. He loves retrieving balls."

"This morning was fine, so you did the water route then?"

"Exactly."

"Did you pass anybody along the way?"

She frowned, as if digesting this request. "Cars passed me. A boy on a bike, on his way to school. I don't recall any people—" She broke off as the full implication of the question came to her. "You want to ascertain that I really was on a walk with my dog when Martin was shot? Surely you can't think that I had anything to do with his death?"

"This is all purely routine, Mrs. Rogers. We have to examine every option."

"Yes, I suppose you do," she said. "Very well, I did say good morning to a man as I passed his garden. He's out there most mornings, and he has a little white dog who has become Lucky's friend. They always exchange a sniff and a tail wag through the gate."

"Do you happen to know the name and address?"

"I'm afraid I don't. Isn't that terrible? You pass the time of day with somebody for years, and you never take it to that next level and find out their name. I can take you and show you the house. It's very easy to find. It's black and white, pseudo-Tudor, and there's a white, fluffy dog in the garden most of the time."

"Pseudo-Tudor. On which street?"

"Ffordd Telford," she said. "Or Telford Road if you prefer it in English—which it always used to be, of course."

Bragg glanced at Evans again. "Got that, Evans?"

"Yes sir."

"Right, let's get back to your account of the morning. So your walk lasted the usual hour, did it?"

"More or less. I never time it to the minute. I came back and got Lucky a drink in his bowl outside. Martin doesn't like him eating or drinking in the house. Then I hung my jacket in the hall cupboard. The radio was on in the kitchen, and it was playing a Beatles' song. 'She loves you, yeah, yeah, yeah.' It made me remember happier days. Then I went through to the kitchen, and it took me a minute to notice Martin lying there, sprawled across the table, and the pool of blood on the tablecloth . . ." She put her hand up to her mouth and fought to compose herself. "It was a terrible shock. I'm sorry," she said at last.

"Did you try to move him?"

"No. I didn't touch him. It was so obvious that he was dead, you see. I walked around him and his eyes were open, staring at me. It was horrible. I ran to the phone and dialed nine-nine-nine, and then I went and locked up Lucky and waited for the police to arrive. That's about it, really. I'm afraid none of it seems real, almost as if I was describing a film I'd seen last night."

"Do you have someone to go to for a few days, Mrs. Rogers?" the WPC asked. "Family close by?"

"I've no real family anymore." Missy Rogers shuddered as she said it. "My parents died some years ago. I've a sister, but she lives in the south of France now. We see each other once a year at the most."

"Close friends living nearby?" the WPC insisted.

"We have plenty of friends among the faculty, and there's the altar guild at church."

"Any of them you'd like me to call to come and fetch you?"

Missy Rogers shook her head emphatically. "No. I'd prefer to be alone at the moment, thank you. I don't think I could stand other people's pity. I—I don't like being fussed over, I'm afraid. You'll be taking Martin's body away soon, will you?"

"As soon as the forensic boys have done their job and gone over the crime scene. If I were you, I'd stay up here until they're done."

"Would you like me to bring your dog up to you, Mrs. Rogers?" Evan asked. "He can't be too happy, shut away by himself all this time, and animals can be very comforting."

Missy Rogers's face lit up. "Yes. Thank you. I would like that. Would you mind? Would it be all right, Inspector, if the dog was brought straight up here?"

"No problem at all, Mrs. Rogers. I'll have Evans bring it to you as soon as we've finished our little chat."

"What more can I possibly tell you?" she asked.

"Well, the obvious question is whether anybody would have a reason to kill your husband."

Missy Rogers stared up at Bragg. "My husband wasn't an easy man, Detective Inspector. You have to understand that. He liked things done his way. He had strong opinions, so naturally he clashed with people from time to time. This isn't to say that he annoyed anyone enough to want to kill him."

"So what's your take on this, Mrs. Rogers?" Bragg asked. "Who do you think might have killed your husband? Some sort of suspicion must have entered your mind when you saw him lying there."

"Absolutely not. I was flabbergasted. Completely in shock."

"And now you've had some time to think. Anyone we should be looking at? Anyone who had quarreled with your husband recently or bore him an ongoing grudge?"

For the first time Evan noticed a spark of reaction in her face. "I don't know about you, Inspector," she said, "but when I have a disagreement with somebody, I don't rush out and shoot them afterward. It needs much more than that to make you want to shoot somebody."

"Like what, Mrs. Rogers?"

"A deep-seated, primal emotion, I should think. Intense hatred or fear. There has to be no other way out."

"So if you had to make a guess, is there anyone who might possess such a deep-seated emotion in regard to your husband?"

"Nobody I can think of."

"Then who might have waited for you to leave and then shot him?"

"I wish I could tell you that, Inspector, but I can't. A burglar, maybe, who saw me go out and was sure the house would be empty? There have certainly been plenty of robberies in this neighborhood recently. Our neighbors have alarm systems. We never had one installed because of Lucky; he's a wonderful watchdog."

"Would you be kind enough to take a look around the house with me to see if anything has been taken or disturbed?"

"Certainly." She got to her feet, brushed down her tweed skirt, and nodded that she was ready to begin. At the doorway she hesitated. "I—uh—won't have to go into the kitchen again, will I? I don't think I could bear to see . . ."

"No, not unless you kept the family secrets hidden in a safe in the kitchen floor."

"No, there's no safe," she said. "I have some good jewelry at the bank; Martin has a rather valuable coin collection and some rare stamps, but they're at the bank too. What little silver we have is on display. It seems such a shame to have beautiful things and not enjoy them. Beautiful objects make life bearable, don't you think?"

They walked from room to room. The ground floor contained a dining room, drawing room, and a library, its walls lined floor to ceiling with books. There were two spare bedrooms on the same floor as the master, as well as a former bedroom now turned into a study, with walls of yet more books, filing cabinets, and a desk with papers stacked neatly on it. Then up a flight of stairs to what had once been servants' bedrooms. One of these was now a room used for sewing and ironing. The other was stacked with boxes. Nothing appeared to have been touched.

"Is it possible that your husband had any valuable papers in his study?" Bragg asked.

"Papers worth stealing?" She half smiled. "He was a well-respected man in his field, but I don't think his work was so unique or outstanding that anybody would want to steal his papers. It's not as if he was a scientist developing a new bomb, is it? He was a historian, specializing in the eighteenth century. I don't think any of his work was earth-shattering enough to steal—or to kill him for."

She swayed suddenly and grabbed onto the banister. "I'm afraid I really do need to sit down for a while. This has been all too much for me."

"Quite understandable," Inspector Bragg said. "I think I've got everything I need for now, Mrs. Rogers. Of course the forensic team will need to take your fingerprints when they get here, but for now I suggest that you go back to your room and lie down. We'll have Constable Evans fetch your dog for you."

"Thank you. You're most kind."

Evan took her arm and escorted her back to the bedroom.

"Just one last thing, Mrs. Rogers," DI Bragg called after her. "Did your husband own a gun?"

"He had several antique guns. He used to use them as visual aids for his lectures. I don't know if any of them actually work anymore."

"And where would we find them?"

"He kept them in one of the drawers of the bureau in the library. I don't think it's locked. I'll show you." She led them down the stairs again, into the library, and pulled open a drawer. Several ancient firearms lay on a velvet backing—what looked like a dueling pistol with a mother-of-pearl handle; a colt revolver, an ancient musket. And one gap, with the imprint of a gun that had lain there.

Chapter 6

"We'll show that gun imprint to the ballistic technician when he gets here," Bragg said, as Evan followed him out of the house and they stood together on the driveway. Bragg glanced out into the street. "They're taking their time, aren't they?"

"The traffic's terrible these days," Evan said. "It sometimes takes ages just to get out of Colwyn Bay."

"So what do you think, Evans?"

Evan was surprised at the question. "What do I think, sir? She certainly loves her dog, doesn't she? The only time we saw any emotion at all was when I brought that dog into the room."

"In the case of a tragedy, you cling to anything familiar, don't you? And dogs are supposed to be a wonderful comfort, aren't they, although I can't see it myself. Peeing and pooping all over the floor and shedding hair wherever they walk. Got a dog yourself?"

"No sir. It wouldn't be fair. My wife and I are out of the house all day. Besides, we're newly married."

"Wouldn't want half her attention going to a dog, eh?" Bragg chuckled.

"Are you married, sir?"

"I was. Nor ready to take that plunge again in a hurry. Let's go and see where Wingate and Pritchard have got to."

He set off ahead of Evan with determined strides.

They found the other two officers in the garden shed.

"I hope you haven't been putting your paws over stuff in here," Bragg said, as he stood in the doorway. "This might be important. A good place to hide out and watch what was going on in the house. There's a clear view from here of the front door."

"We touched a pair of gumboots," Wingate said. "We needed to match them up with a couple of footprints we found. They're lady's size, obviously Mrs. Rogers's."

"Any other prints that don't match these?"

"A couple, sir. Great big boot in some of the flower beds."

"That would probably be the gardener. When we interview him, we must remember to get a print of his boot sole."

Bragg stepped into the shed and sniffed. "Smells like someone's been using an engine of some kind in here. Hot oil smell."

"That's right, sir," Pritchard said. "The lawn mower has been used recently. It was still a little warm."

"Mrs. Rogers said she did a spot of gardening this morning, didn't she?" Evan said.

"So she did. Well, that explains that then. No luck with finding the weapon?"

"No sir. We searched the bushes pretty thoroughly. There's a garden pond. We fished about in it a little, but we didn't find anything. You might want to have it searched more thoroughly if you think that the perpetrator might have got rid of the weapon and not run off with it. If it had been me, I'd have taken it away with me."

"He probably did, but people don't always behave rationally when they've just killed somebody. Sometimes they panic and want to get rid of that weapon as quickly as possible. You'd be amazed where I've found weapons before now. Stashed in the most obvious of places, almost as if the killer wanted to be discovered."

They came back out into the fresh air.

"So what's next, sir?" Sergeant Wingate asked.

"We'll know more as soon as forensics get here," Bragg said, staring with annoyance in the direction of the road again. "And we'll need to do a detailed search of the house once forensics have taken fingerprints. We need to find out if that antique weapon is really missing or just moved somewhere else."

"And if it's been recently fired," Evan added.

Bragg gave him a withering look. "Obviously we'd like to know if it's been recently fired, Constable. That goes without saying."

"Oh, have you found the weapon, sir?" Constable Pritchard asked.

"Possibly. Rogers has an antique gun collection. One of them is missing."

"I see." Wingate nodded. "It would be good if we knew the type of weapon we were looking for. What sort of bullets do antique guns use?"

"They just used to melt lumps of lead and pour it into a mold, didn't they? I've no idea if any modern bullets would fit. Let's hope the ballistics bloke knows the answer to that one," Bragg said. "Right, let's get on with it. We're wasting precious time standing here chatting."

"I think we should interview the neighbors as soon as possible, while the whole thing is still fresh in their minds." Wingate stared at the tall Victorian house next door that could be seen above the high hedge.

Bragg looked around. "It's hardly likely the neighbors will have seen anything with all these bloody trees and bushes in the way. The houses are too far apart."

"But someone would have heard a shot, surely," Evan said. "And there always seems to be somebody who just happens to be looking out of a window and notices who comes and goes from neighboring houses."

"Thus speaks the expert detective," Bragg said. "How long have you been on the force, Evans? How many months is it?"

"Not many, sir." Evan laughed it off.

"But that's a valid observation," Wingate commented. "There usually is one nosy neighbor on every street. Even if they saw nothing this morning, they might be able to offer us some insight into the dynamics of the Rogers's household."

"'Insight' and 'dynamics.' My, we are into big words this morning, aren't we, Wingate? Are you planning to ram your university education down our throats?"

"I'm sorry, sir. I'll choose my language more carefully in future."

Evan stifled a smile. As an insult, it could not have been better.

"Don't get me wrong," Bragg went on, as if nothing had happened. "I fully intend to interview the neighbors. And it will be worth asking for the public's help through the media too. Evans, this comes under Western Division, doesn't it? You'd be familiar with the local media. I'm leaving it to you to get it onto this evening's news and into tomorrow's paper. Can you do that?"

"Yes sir. I think I can manage it."

"Good lad."

Bragg really had no appreciation of sarcasm, Evan decided.

"Be careful how much you tell them. A suspicious death—don't call it a homicide until we're sure of our facts. You can tell them the street name and the approximate time of the incident. Anyone who was passing and noticed suspicious or unusual activity is requested to call the Bangor Police Station, got it?" He looked up as a white van turned into the drive and scrunched over the gravel. "Ah, finally forensics have got off their arses. It's important that I stick around while they're here, but I think I can send you off to interview the neighbors, can't I, Wingate?"

"Yes. I think that may be within the realm of my capabilities, sir," Wingate answered.

This time the sarcasm was not lost. "There's no need to be smart, Wingate. We're a brand-new team, and I'm the fall guy if anything goes wrong. I have to make sure my officers know what they are doing."

"I assure you that I am quite capable of interviewing the neighbors, sir, as I suspect are Pritchard and Evans."

"Yes, well, I'll need Pritchard with me while Evans is away. You can bugger off now, Evans, and you too, Wingate."

The two men walked down the driveway together, passing the forensic crew as they opened up the back of their van.

"Hello, Evans. Having fun, are we?" the young police photographer asked in Welsh. "He's a right bugger, so they say, that Bragg." He saw Evan's face and grinned. "And his Welsh isn't too hot either."

Evan turned to Wingate. "How is your Welsh?"

"Not a native speaker like you. My family farms in border country, and we were raised to speak English."

"That's too bad."

"In the current circumstances, I'd have to agree with you," Wingate said. "I'm Jeremy, by the way, and you are?"

"Evan."

"No, your first name."

"That's it. Evan Evans. Parents lacking in imagination, I'm afraid."

Jeremy Wingate grinned. "We'll get through this somehow, although I don't know what we've done to deserve this form of cruel and unusual punishment."

"He may not be so bad when we get to know him," Evan said.

"On the other hand, he may be a bloody sight worse." Wingate leaned closer as Evan opened the squad car door. "I'll keep you posted on what I find out from the neighbors. I have a distinct feeling this chappy isn't too bright. We may need to do his work for him."

Evan drove away, catching glimpses of the bright waters of the strait on one side of him and the Snowdon range, bright crisp outlines in the clear air, on the other. The local Bangor Police Station would have been nearer to look up media contacts, but Evan headed for Caernarfon instead. At least he knew his way around there.

Evan felt a pang of regret as he entered through the familiar swinging glass doors. Why did they have to choose him of all people for this assignment? What if this new setup was so successful that it became permanent? A bleak future stretched ahead of him, starting every day at the soulless redbrick-and-glass headquarters and ending with a long drive home. He was on his way down the hall, when a man came out of the duty office to his right and almost mowed him down. It took Evan a second to realize who it was.

"Sorry, Sarge. I didn't recognize you. What are you wearing? Is it dress down Friday or something?"

The beefy sergeant Bill Jones scowled. "It's the new bloody uniform. I've been selected as one of the guinea pigs, and if you make any cracks about it—"

Evan examined the black roll neck sweater and the black combat pants. "Well, you'd blend in well at a rock concert or a skinheads gathering," he said.

"I think it's bloody terrible," Sergeant Jones said, "and I can't stand the feel of this around my neck. Makes me itch all the time. And too hot when I'm in the office like today."

"You tell them what you think. If enough of us do, they won't go ahead with it."

"Some of the younger men like it, unfortunately," Sergeant Jones said. "They think it makes them look cool." He pulled a disgusted face. "So what are you doing here then, boyo?" he asked. "I heard you'd been called to higher things." He put his hands together as if in prayer and looked toward heaven.

"Give over, Bill," Evan said. "You don't think I wanted this assignment, do you?"

"Major Crimes Team? I'd say it was a step up the ladder for you. The local boys are livid because it means that all we'll get here will be the petty stuff—the nicked wallets and the drunken brawls—while you blokes get all the juicy crimes."

"Yes, but at what price?" Evan said. "Have you run into DI Bragg ever? He's a right son of a you-know-what."

Sergeant Jones grinned. "I expect it's good for you. You've had it too easy here." He reached across and thumped Evan on the shoulder with a meaty hand. "Don't let it get you down, boy. You're a good cop, and he probably knows that. He's just trying to establish a pecking order."

"Thanks, Bill," Evan said. "I came here because I've got to contact the local radio and TV stations about this morning's murder, and I know where to find the list of media contacts here."

"A murder, is it?"

Evan nodded. "A university professor in Bangor shot to death at the breakfast table."

"Likely as not it's one of his students, disgruntled about the marks he got on his exams. They tend to go to extremes these days, don't they? Too much pressure and some of them crack."

"Interesting thought, Bill. We'll look into that." Evan continued down the hall and into the room that housed a couple of computers. He had just logged on when Glynis Davies came in, looking fresh and elegant in a dark blue pant suit.

"I certainly didn't expect to see you," she said. "Has Bragg kicked you off his team already?"

"No, worse luck." Evan looked up at her with a smile. "Hey, maybe you're onto something there. If I'm clueless enough, maybe he'll ask to have me replaced."

"You might find yourself out of the force or back in uniform. Not worth the risk," Glynis said. "No, Evan, whatever you may think, this is a career opportunity for you. You have to make the most of it. So what are you doing here?"

"I have to contact the local media to ask for the public's help on this murder case. I know how to find everything here, although . . ." he looked up appealingly. "I know what a computer whiz you are. You wouldn't like to—"

"No, I bloody well wouldn't," Glynis said. Then she paused and smiled, "Or as it's been drummed into us during our sensitivity training: thank you for asking, but I respectfully decline."

Evan laughed. "Oh well, it was worth a try."

"I tell you what I will do for you," Glynis said. "I'm off to get some lunch at the Greek place across the street. Do you want me to bring back a sandwich for you?"

"Glynis, you're an angel. I'll love you forever."

"You better not let your new wife hear you saying that. She might not understand." Glynis tossed back her striking red hair and flashed him a smile as she headed for the door.

Chapter 7

Evan had just worked his way through the warm gyro by the time he arrived back at the Rogers's house in Bangor. As he got out to open the front gate, he saw Jeremy Wingate coming up the street toward him. Wingate glanced at him, then scowled. "You've got onion on your chin. Don't tell me you stopped for lunch, you sly bugger?"

"I went to make my calls from my old station. A very kind young lady offered to fetch me a sandwich. I could hardly refuse."

"Some people have all the luck." Wingate said. "The very least you could have done was to have her bring one for me too."

"Next time I will. For all I knew, Bragg might have decided to take a lunch break."

"Not him. Works till he drops, I fear."

"Are the forensic boys still in there?" Evan looked at the white van still beside the front door.

"Yeah, still at it. It will probably take them twice as long with Bragg breathing down their necks. I can't tell you how glad I was to get out on my own for a while. I expect you felt the same."

"Pangs of regret, I have to confess," Evan said. "Still, it's hard when everyone keeps telling you it's a step up the ladder."

"Hopefully a quick step." Wingate grinned.

"So did you learn anything from the neighbors?"

"Not much. As you'd expect, you don't have a good view of the street from most of these houses. And there must be several professional couples. Nobody was home at either of those houses across the street, which is annoying, as they'd be the only ones with a clear view of who was going in and out of this gate."

"What about next door?" Evan indicated a large, redbrick house, half hidden by large evergreens.

"Crusty old bugger—an ex-colonel from the south of England. He lives alone since his wife died. It seems that he and Professor Rogers have had their run-ins over the years. He thought she was pleasant enough, but as they both like to keep themselves to themselves, they only exchanged the odd word when they were gardening."

"And he hadn't noticed anything unusual this morning."

"He had a gripe about the fact that someone was out there mowing before eight. He said the noise disturbed his breakfast. He couldn't hear the news properly. He was about to come out and complain when the sound stopped."

"I wonder why she was mowing?" Evan said. "If they have a gardener, you'd have thought she'd have left that to him. Heavy work, lugging a mower, even a power one."

"She's obviously a fanatic where her garden is concerned. You look at all those beds. Not a weed in sight. Maybe she found a few blades of grass that the gardener missed, and she couldn't stand to see them."

"Maybe." Evan nodded, pushing other, more disturbing thoughts to the back of his mind. "So what's next, do you think?"

"We have to wait until the great man emerges and pronounces judgment, I suppose. Well, talk of the devil." They looked up at the sound of feet scrunching on gravel and saw DI Bragg coming toward them.

"Finished already?" he called, looking at Wingate.

"Yes sir. Nothing much to report from the neighbors. Several houses unoccupied at this time of day. Some of the neighbors I spoke to knew the Rogers. Thought he was a pleasant chap. She was rather standoffish. Said 'good morning' but not much more. The man next door complained about the lawn mower being used this morning, but he didn't see or hear anything unusual."

"So no strange cars parked on the street?"

"No sir."

"And anyone hear a shot?"

"No. One woman thought she heard an engine backfire while she was upstairs getting dressed, but the shower was running in the bathroom and she didn't think any more of it. Most of these houses have double glazing installed, and the traffic on the Holyhead Road is quite noisy at that time in the morning."

"That's too bad. Let's hope someone will come forward after they hear about it on the news. You contacted all the local media, did you, Evans?"

"Yes sir. All done. It will be on this evening's news and in tomorrow's papers."

"Good man. Well, I can report that forensics are getting along nicely. They've located the bullet. Dug it out of the wall."

"Out of the wall?" Evan blurted out.

"That's right. It went in through one side of the head and out the other apparently. This is particularly lucky because now they can work on an exact trajectory and be able to tell us where it was fired from. The ballistics chap is inclined to go along with our theory of firing through the open window, by the way."

Evan thought he remembered that Bragg had discounted that theory when he presented it. Now, suddenly, it had become "our" theory.

"What about fingerprints?" he asked.

"They've finished dusting for fingerprints, and there is one set of prints we can't yet identify. I suspect it will turn out to be the cleaning lady's because they are all over the house."

"What about on the window latch?" Evan asked.

"Nothing. Just his and hers."

"Maybe the killer wore gloves," Evan suggested.

"You can't shoot very well in gloves. He'd have had to take them off to fire the gun."

"Unless they were latex. I expect you can shoot just as well in those," Sergeant Wingate said.

"True. In which case he departed wearing them. We didn't find any in the rubbish bin. And you didn't find any dumped in the bushes outside, did you?"

"No sir. Nothing dumped in the bushes. The whole garden is meticulously neat."

"What about the cartridge?" Evan asked. "If the shot really was fired through the window, wouldn't the cartridge have been ejected outside?"

"Again, unless he looked for it and took it with him," Wingate said.

"A thoughtful, well-organized murderer." Bragg said the words slowly. "Maybe we can start to put together a profile. What have we got so far?"

"He must have observed the Rogers's morning routine," Evan said. "He knew when Mrs. Rogers left to walk the dog. He knew Professor Rogers sat at the window to eat his breakfast and that the window was likely to be open."

"So a carefully planned crime. Nothing impulsive about it."

"And someone who knew the victim," Wingate added, "ruling out any kind of burglary or home invasion."

"Right." Bragg looked up as two members of the forensic team came out to the van. One of them came up to the detectives.

"We're off for a bite of lunch," he said. "We should have you cleared to move the body this afternoon. We'll schedule the morgue pickup and the clean-up crew so that the widow can use her kitchen again by tonight. I don't suppose she'll want to make herself a cup of tea with blood spatters on the walls."

"So we're definitely dealing with a homicide?" Bragg said. "No possibility that he shot himself?"

"Blew his brains out and then went to dispose of the weapon?" the technician said with a chuckle.

"The wife could have disposed of the weapon."

"And why would she do that?"

"She was ashamed that her husband killed himself?" Bragg suggested.

"Usually it would be the other way around. They kill somebody and then stick the gun into his hand to make it look like suicide. But no, in this case the victim was definitely shot by someone standing about six to eight feet away. Small-caliber weapon."

"Will you have any way of knowing if the bullet was fired from an antique weapon? The one missing from the collection?"

The technician shrugged. "You'll have to ask Freeman; he's the ballistics expert. But judging by the imprint left on the velvet in that drawer, the missing gun looked identical to the dueling pistol beside it. And that would be logical, wouldn't it? You always had dueling pistols in pairs—one for each party." He grinned. "And if my memory serves me correctly, they didn't fire bullets in those days but round balls. Whether they could be adapted to fire modern bullets, I don't know. As I said, ask Freeman. I have to go now, or Huw will leave without me. He's like a madman if he doesn't get his nosh on time."

He didn't wait for an answer but ran to hoist himself into the rapidly reversing van.

The woman police constable appeared at the front door. "It's past lunchtime, and I really think Mrs. Rogers should have something to eat," she said. "Is it okay to take her to a café? They're still working in the kitchen, and the body's still there."

"That's fine with me," Bragg said. "Take her out if she'll go. It might be a good thing. You could try chatting to her in the car and see if she opens up at all. I get the feeling she knows or suspects more than she's letting on. Someone must have hated her husband enough to have wanted him dead. It might even have been her."

"Oh surely not, sir," the WPC said. "She's in shock, poor woman. Ashen gray."

"Not exactly showing grief though, is she? Or surprise? When we opened that drawer and saw a gun was missing, I was watching her face. No surprise registered at all. It was almost as if she knew it wouldn't be there."

"But why on earth would she want to murder her husband?" the WPC asked.

"That's what we've got to find out."

DI Bragg showed no indication of wanting to take a lunch break, and Evan silently thanked Glynis again for the gyro. When Pritchard and Wingate muttered about needing at least a cup of coffee, Bragg relented and sent Pritchard off for fast food.

"Bunch of pansies," Bragg said. "Obviously never been through army training."

"Oh, so you served in the army, did you, sir?" Wingate asked, giving Evan a knowing look.

"I did. Seven years. Saw action in Kuwait and then in Bosnia. I tell you boys, I've seen stuff that would make your hair curl. There's no crime you'll encounter here to compare with some of the attrocities I've seen."

That explained a lot, Evan thought. He tried to think more kindly of DI Bragg. Anyone who had seen atrocities in Bosnia would have to have come back a changed man.

"Right, don't hang about here doing nothing. Just because someone's gone on a food run, doesn't mean the rest of us can take a break. Evans, you can drive. We're going to talk to the charwoman. Wingate, you can see if the gardener's home. He only lives around the corner."

"Anything particular you want me to ask him, sir?" Wingate asked innocently.

"Use your initiative man," Bragg snapped. "I presume you must have shown some resourcefulness in the past or you wouldn't have been promoted to sergeant."

"Right you are, sir." Wingate set off.

Evan suspected that Wingate was going to get his kicks by baiting their senior officer. While it might be amusing to watch, it made for an atmosphere of tension and that would be no way to work in the long run. It was probably as Sergeant Jones in Caernarfon had suggested—they were jostling for pecking order at the moment, testing each other's strengths and weaknesses.

Chapter 8

"You're lucky to have caught me at home." The bony little woman wiped her hands on her pinny as she faced the detectives at her front door. Her house was in the middle of one of those grimy rows that once housed slate quarry workers. Some had now been gentrified, with bright painted flower boxes at the windows and a sports car parked outside. This one hadn't. "I usually work for Mrs. Thomas on Thursdays," she went on, "but she was feeling poorly today and didn't want me to come. She gets migraines something terrible, poor dear. *Ydych chi'n siarad Cymraeg?*" she asked hopefully.

"I do, but Detective Inspector Bragg here prefers English," Evan said.

"Detective Inspector? Dear me—what on earth is this about? Nothing's missing from any of the homes I clean, is it? I'm always so particular about locking up after me." She glanced up and down the street to see if any neighbors were watching.

"No, I'm afraid it's more serious than that, Mrs. Ellis. Do you mind if we come inside?"

"All right," she said, after a moment's hesitation. "Come on, then." She led them into a small, dark living room at the back of the house. There were two well-worn armchairs facing a television set, but she indicated the straight-backed chairs on either side of a Welsh dresser to the policemen. She herself did not sit but stood in front of an electric fireplace, her bony arms folded.

"I believe you work for the Rogers on Oak Grove Road?" Bragg asked.

"Oh yes, I do. I have done for years. A very nice lady, Mrs. Rogers. Very refined."

"I'm afraid we have some bad news for you. Professor Rogers was found dead this morning."

"Found dead? Well, I can't say I'm really surprised. I've seen it coming."

"What do you mean?" Bragg asked sharply.

"Well, that man was working himself to death, wasn't he? And always strung up, like a rubber band ready to snap. I always thought he might end up having a heart attack."

"So tell me about him, Mrs. Ellis. He was always 'strung up,' as you put it? Was he ever at home when you worked there? What was he like?"

"Well, he wasn't easy to please. He liked everything just so. And if everything wasn't how he wanted it, he'd fly off the handle. If I dusted his desk and moved one of his papers, he'd let me know it. But then if I didn't dust, he'd point that out to me, too. 'You missed a spot here, Gwladys,' he'd say."

"So why did you keep on going there if he was so unpleasant?" Bragg asked.

"I wouldn't say he was unpleasant, just hard to please. He was the perfect gentleman most of the time. Ever so polite, you know. He'd always open the door for me if he saw me coming, that sort of thing. But he was a perfectionist, you know. Everything had to be arranged in the exact order he wanted it, or he wasn't happy. His food had to be just right too. Poor Mrs. Rogers—if she over- or undercooked something, he'd let her have it."

"'Let her have it'?" Bragg looked up sharply. "You mean he hit her?"

"Oh no, sir. Nothing like that. Like I just said, Professor Rogers was a gentleman. But he'd yell a lot. 'Missy, where are you? Come down here right away. I thought I told you I wanted my eggs cooked for three minutes.' That's the way he spoke to her."

"And how did she speak to him?"

"She was always polite and calm. 'I'm sorry, Martin. I'll pay better attention to it next time.' That was the way to calm him down. If she got upset and cried, it just made him shout louder."

"So he wasn't what you'd call an easy man to live with?" Bragg asked.

"No sir, I'd say definitely not."

"So you'd say it was a difficult marriage then? A strained marriage?"

She thought for a moment. "I'd say he was fond enough of her in his way. He could be quite affectionate if he was in a good mood. The trick was keeping him in a good mood."

"Tell me about Mrs. Rogers," Bragg said. "What does she do with herself? Does she go out much?"

"No sir. Very much the homebody, Mrs. Rogers is. She loves her garden and she's always working on the house—polishing, cleaning, to make sure everything is just perfect. She does do the flowers for the church. She takes great pride in her flowers."

"What about friends? Do friends drop in often?"

"Not when I'm there, sir. I can't say what happens on the other days."

"Has she ever worked outside the home?"

"Not since I've been going there," Mrs. Ellis said. "I gather she met Professor Rogers when they were both students at the university, and she worked while he was still studying for his higher degrees. But then old Mr. Rogers died, and they inherited a fair bit of money and the house, so I understand, and she didn't need to work after that."

Evan thought of how many women would love to be in Missy Rogers's shoes—enough money, beautiful house, time to do whatever she wanted. And yet he sensed that Missy Rogers didn't see it as a blessing at all.

"Don't you want to know how Professor Rogers died, Mrs. Ellis?" Bragg asked.

"I presumed it would be a heart attack. That kind of man, who gets upset so easily, they always say is prone to heart trouble, don't they?"

"Actually he was murdered, Mrs. Ellis. Someone shot him while he was eating breakfast this morning."

"Dear Lord." She put her hand up to her mouth. "Who could have done such a terrible thing?"

"Any ideas, Mrs. Ellis?" Bragg asked. "You say that Professor Rogers tended to fly off the handle easily. Did he have any particular people he feuded with? Any rows with the neighbors?"

"He didn't get along with old Colonel Partridge next door, but that was over silly, petty things. The colonel complained if the dog barked or if they played music with the windows open. And, of course, Professor Rogers wasn't going to let the old man get the better of him so he complained right back. The colonel was getting deaf, and he'd started to turn his radio up loud enough to hear. Professor Rogers would telephone him and tell him to turn down the noise." Mrs. Ellis played with the edge of her pinny, twisting the fabric nervously in her fingers. "But you don't go killing somebody for trifling little things like that, do you?"

"What about his work at the university? Did he clash with any of his colleagues there?"

"I couldn't tell you that, sir. I only go there one morning a week. I've no idea what the Rogers do with the rest of their lives. Mrs. Rogers is not one to gossip, so I really don't know much about them apart from what I see with my own eyes."

Inspector Bragg stood up. Evan followed suit, giving the old lady an encouraging smile. "Thank you, Mrs. Ellis. You've been most helpful."

"I must telephone poor Mrs. Rogers," she said, as she escorted them to the door. "I expect she'll need some help with the cleaning if there have been policemen all over the house. She'll be so upset with all that mess, I shouldn't wonder."

"This Rogers sounds like a right sod," Bragg commented as they got into the squad car and drove away. "It's looking better by the minute that it was the wife who pulled the trigger. She had enough motive, didn't she? Bad-tempered bastard of a husband and enough money and a nice house if she was rid of him."

"Yes, but . . ." Evan began. He instinctively liked Mrs. Rogers. He admired the well-bred way she was handling her pain.

"But what?"

"If Mrs. Rogers did it, why not set up a better alibi for herself? After all, we've only got her word for it that she took the dog for a walk and her husband was killed while she was away. Why call us so soon? Why not shoot him and then be gone for several hours, or plan an overnight trip to a relative so that it would be harder for us to determine the actual time of death?"

"Lucky for us, criminals aren't always too bright," Bragg said. "She probably didn't think it through well enough. She may even have thought we'd take her at her word that she was out walking the dog. Well, I suppose we should hear what Wingate has to report on the gardener, and then it's on to the university. If he behaved like that to his wife and his cleaning lady, I don't suppose he was a saint to his colleagues. Someone there might have had an even better motive than his wife for wanting him out of the way."

The gardener, it turned out, went to the Rogers's once a week. He did all the heavy work; turned over the beds, clipped the hedges, and mowed the lawns.

"Mowed the lawns, you see." Bragg sounded triumphant. "So why did she decide to get the mower out this morning?"

"I suppose the noise of a mower would muffle a shot pretty well," Wingate voiced what Evan had been thinking, "especially a temperamental mower that was hard to get started, according to the gardener. It probably coughed and backfired a few times, so that nobody would notice the sound of a shot."

Bragg nodded as if he agreed with this theory. "So she started the mower, called her husband down to breakfast, shot him, put the mower back in the shed, and then took the dog out for his walk as if nothing had happened," Bragg said. "Cool customer."

"One more thing," Evan said. "If your scenario is right, she went inside to close the window."

"And to make sure he was really dead, I should think."

"But this is all supposition," Evan said. "We've no real evidence.

We can't jump to conclusions like this until we know more about Professor Rogers and his life. If Martin Rogers really was that annoying to live with, she could always have left him. She's still young and able-bodied. She could start a new life easily enough, and he'd have to have paid her alimony."

"I suppose you've got a point there," Bragg said. "As she said herself, you only kill somebody when there is no other way out."

Chapter 9

The University of Wales in Bangor was perched on top of a steep hill, with spectacular views toward the Snowdon range in one direction and the Island of Angelsey in the other. The town of Bangor huddled directly below, in its shadow. A fierce wind was blowing off the Menai Strait as Evan emerged from the squad car, and there was promise of rain in the bank of clouds out beyond Anglesey. DI Bragg started up a flight of steps to what was obviously the main building, a tall Victorian monstrosity, complete with towers and turrets.

University campuses always evoked strange feelings in Evan. He had certainly been bright enough to win a university place, even before universities sprouted up everywhere like mushrooms. But he had been the dutiful son and did what was expected of him by following his father into the police force. In truth, in those days his only passion had been rugby, and he had no great desire to prolong his academic studies. But every time he crossed a quadrangle like this one, and saw young people deep in discussion, clutching armfuls of books, he felt a gnawing sense of regret that he had missed out on that carefree step in his life. He had also missed out on expanding his horizons. Bronwen, who had gone to Cambridge, could talk easily on almost any subject and throw in words like Descartes and Kant, making Evan realize just how well-read she was. He found himself thinking that he should start reading again, maybe even check out night school classes.

"Lazy lot of unshaven buggers, aren't they?" DI Bragg brought Evan out of his reverie. "It's too bad they did away with conscription. I'd love to get this lot into uniform and shape them up." He shielded his eyes from the sun as he looked around him. "Do you know your way around this place? Any idea where we'd find Rogers's colleagues? Some kind of faculty building?"

"He was a professor in the History Department," Evan said. "I'm sure one of the students can direct us there."

He stopped a pair of young girls, who seemed remarkably underdressed for the chill of early autumn, with bare midriffs and low-slung jeans. They pointed to a smaller building set in its own grounds, as the wind whipped their long hair across their faces. One of them gave Evans a flirtatious smile as they continued on their way.

"History," Bragg commented, setting off in the new direction toward the building that housed the department, "now that's a bloody waste of time for a start. Ten sixty-six and all that. Magna Carta. Lot of useless dates. What's the point in it, Evans? We never seem to learn from history, do we?"

"We can always hope, sir," Evan said.

"You're too much of a bloody optimist, boyo," Bragg said, but in not unfriendly fashion.

Inside the building they located an office and were told they'd probably find Dr. Skinner in his office, if he wasn't in the SCR.

"SCR?" Bragg asked.

"Senior common room. Where the professors hang out," the girl said. "But I think I saw him going down the hall to his office, and he's got a lecture at four."

Evan led the way and passed an office door with Professor Martin Rogers, Ph.D., written on it in neat script. They found the next door half open and a man sitting at a desk.

"Enter!" he called in theatrical tones, in response to their knock. Then he registered surprise at two strange faces. "Yes, gentlemen? What can I do for you?"

"North Wales Police." DI Bragg produced a warrant card. "I'm

Detective Inspector Bragg, and this is Detective Constable Evans. And your name, sir?"

"Dr. Skinner."

"How do you do, Dr. Skinner. We'd like to talk to you about Professor Rogers."

"Rogers? What's he done?" The look on his face was half astonishment, half joy. He was, Evan thought, a caricature of the absent-minded professor—old tweed jacket, frayed cuffs, tartan tie with various things spilled on it, hair not properly combed, and thick-lensed glasses. But a second glance at him made Evan realize that he wasn't quite as old as he had first thought. A relatively young man still, in fact.

"I'm afraid he was found dead this morning," Bragg said.

"Good God." Skinner lapsed into silence, staring down at the papers in front of him. "I presume he didn't die of natural causes, or you wouldn't be here," he said at last.

"You don't think he'd have killed himself?" Bragg asked.

"Martin Rogers kill himself? Good God, no. Last person on earth to do that. He had a very high opinion of himself, Inspector. No, I'd be most surprised if you told me that Martin had killed himself."

"But not surprised if I told you that somebody else had killed him?" Bragg asked.

"Well, yes, actually I would be surprised. We all had our differences with Martin. He wasn't always easy to get along with, but he could be highly entertaining, too. And as for someone killing him—was it some kind of home invasion, some kind of young thug? There have been too many of those around town these days."

"We can't tell yet, sir. Our forensic team is still working on the crime scene. We're just here asking preliminary questions, trying to get some idea of the man's life and whether anyone might have had a motive for wanting him out of the way. You worked closely with him, did you?"

"Yes, we're a tightly knit bunch in the History Department. We work closely together."

"And do I understand correctly that Professor Rogers was head of the department?"

"Yes, he was. Not to everyone's satisfaction, I might say."

"Meaning what? He wasn't good at his job?"

"Oh no, he was a first-rate historian. Meticulous researcher. Really knew his stuff. But our department is now called the School of History and Welsh History. Professor Rogers isn't a native Welsh speaker, you see. He's quite fluent, but it's different if you're not born to it, isn't it?"

"And you are a native Welsh speaker?" Evan couldn't resist asking.

"Not me. Good Lord, no. I can barely stammer through *Iechyd Da!* He pronounced it *Yacky da*. I'm an archeologist and I'm currently digging up a Roman camp nearby, so luckily language doesn't matter in my case. No, it's Dr. Humphries who really cares. She's been in the department as long as Rogers, you see, and Welsh history is her speciality. She's very bitter that the chair went to Rogers."

"Bitter enough to want him out of the way?"

Dr. Skinner gave an embarrassed chuckle. "No, I don't see Gwyneth as the killing sort. How was he killed, by the way?"

"Shot through an open kitchen window."

"I see." He paused, considering. "So anyone could have done it. It would be easy enough to slink into that large garden, hide out in the bushes, and wait for the perfect chance. If one believes the papers, some young people do it for sport these days, just for the fun of watching someone die." He looked up as if the thought had just crossed his mind. "Presumably Missy knows he's been killed. How is she taking it?"

"Very calmly so far," Bragg said.

"Yes, she would. What a trouper. She's a saint, that woman."

"What makes you say that, sir?" Bragg was quick to ask.

"As I said before, Martin wasn't the easiest man in the world. He liked everything his way, all the time, and heaven help the person who upset him. I don't imagine that Missy had an easy life with him. In many ways he was like an overgrown child. He was sent off to boarding school at seven, you know. It's my personal belief that they stunt one's emotional growth. Martin was emotionally frozen at seven. If he didn't get his own way, he'd have a temper tantrum. But from what I saw, Missy was quite good at handling him—like an efficient nanny, you know."

Evan had been watching Skinner's face as he spoke. He was making a supreme attempt to stay calm, casual, and disinterested. He's sweet on her, Evan decided. And if she was secretly sweet on him, they'd have a perfect motive for doing away with Martin Rogers right there in front of them.

"Did you have much chance to observe Professor Rogers at home?" Bragg was asking.

"We went round there quite often, as a matter of fact. Martin liked to hold faculty meetings there. Most of the rest of us aren't married, you see, and Rhys Thomas's wife is a God-awful cook, so it made sense. Missy always puts on a wonderful spread for us, and Martin likes to hold court in his own castle. We call him "God" behind his back. You know, God has spoken, let no one contradict. Only joking, you understand, the way one does."

Bragg nodded. "The way one does. You say that Professor Rogers wasn't easy to get along with, that he wanted his own way. That sort of attitude leads to conflict, doesn't it? Had there been any major clashes recently?"

"Life with Martin is a series of ups and downs," Skinner said. "The amazing thing is that when everything is going smoothly, he's the most amiable chap in the world. Entertaining, witty. One can go out for a pint with him and have the best of evenings. Then something goes wrong, and you realize that you can't stand the bastard."

"Where would I find the rest of the History Department faculty?" Bragg asked.

"The rest of the department? What time is it? Oh my God, quarter to four. I'm due to lecture in fifteen minutes so I'm afraid I have to get going. Dr. Humphries will be coming back to her office from a tutorial. Rhys Thomas has already gone home, I think. The office will have his address. Jenkins and Sloan—they'll probably be having a cup of tea in the common room. And Badger is out with a group of students at a dig."

"Badger?"

"Yes. Badger Brock. He's our historical anthropologist. Very dedicated, almost obsessed. He was furious when Martin slashed his budget for—"

He broke off, realizing what he was saying. "I'm not telling tales out of school," he said. "I'm late for my lecture, and think you'd better talk to them all yourselves."

Skinner had only just left when Dr. Gwyneth Humphries came flying down the hall, with various loose garments trailing out behind her. She wore a stole of Welsh tartan, clasped with a Celtic knot, and Birkenstocks on her feet. Her hair was twisted into a bun and held in place with a stick pin, also finished with a Celtic knot. She may have been close to fifty but looked younger, with a makeup-free, unlined face and clear blue eyes.

She expressed horror and shock at the news. She couldn't think of anyone who might want to kill Martin Rogers. He could be damned annoying, she admitted, but every faculty had its academic differences. It was part of living in a closed community like a university. Personally she admired Professor Rogers's dedication to scholarship. Try as Bragg might, he couldn't get her to say anything negative nor to offer any opinions on who might have wanted Rogers dead.

"Just one last question, Dr. Humphries," Bragg said, as they prepared to leave. "Where were you between seven and nine this morning?"

"What a ridiculous question," she said, her fair Celtic face flushing red. "If you must know, I was at home, breakfasting with my two cats until seven thirty, then I walked to work because I live here in town only ten minutes away. I was here, in my office, by eight thirty because I had an appointment at eight forty-five with a student who is having academic problems."

"She would have been cutting it fine if she was in her office by eight thirty," Bragg muttered, as they came out of the dark building into late afternoon sunlight. The bank of clouds had crept in and was threatening to swallow the setting sun at any moment. "But if she had nothing to hide, then why did she go red when I asked her?"

"Maybe one does not talk to a spinster lady about her morning toilette," Evan said.

"Breakfast with her cats—you don't think they'd vouch for her, do you?"

"You should have asked her if she owned a car," Evan said. "The Rogers's house is quite a distance from the town center."

"Are there really people in the world who don't own cars these days?"

"There are plenty of old ladies up in the villages where I live who have never learned to drive," Evan said. "Then their husbands die, and they have to rely on public transportation. I just thought that Dr. Humphries looked like the sort of woman who'd get around on a bicycle."

Bragg grinned. "Yes, she does look the type, doesn't she? I should have had you interview her in Welsh. She might have opened up more. In fact, why don't you go back tomorrow for a chat with her. Go and ask her the car question and take it from there. Let's go and find that common room and see if the other faculty members are there. I could do with a cup of tea myself."

It was a first confession of weakness from him.

The common room contained the two younger lecturers, Paul Jenkins and Olive Sloan. They answered the rapid questions fired at them politely enough, but both were newly arrived at the university and seemed to know little about their department chair, except that Rogers seemed a pleasant enough chap and their colleagues also pleasant enough people. They both looked surprised at being asked to say where they were that morning. Jenkins had a live-in girlfriend who breakfasted with him at eight, and Olive Sloan was dropped off by her husband on his way to work at the hospital in Prestatyn.

Owen Rhys Thomas hadn't arrived home when they called at his house nearby. His wife said he often stopped off at the fitness center after a long day. As to what time he left the house in the morning, Ann Rhys Thomas said that he did the morning school run, leaving the house at seven forty-five to drop off two children at two different schools.

This seemed to rule out all three of them, and Evan was glad when Bragg finally admitted he'd had enough for one day.

Chapter 10

It was after seven when Evan parked his car on the gravel strip beside the pub in Llanfair and set off up the track to his new home. The promised rain had begun—that fine, misty rain that seems peculiar to Wales and Ireland and is described by locals as "a soft day." From the gusts of wind that buffeted his back as he scrambled up the steep slope, Evan suspected that worse was to come tonight.

The sun had long set, and Evan was grateful for the lights that shone out of the cottage windows through the mist. It was a good feeling to know that this place was home, that Bronwen was there, and that supper would be waiting for him. He reached the front door, wiped the worst of the mud from his shoes, and brushed the rain from his jacket before he entered.

"Hello, *cariad*. One husband dying of hunger," he called, as he stepped inside. There were good cooking smells coming from the kitchen, and a fire was crackling in the grate.

"About time." Bronwen rose from the sofa in front of the fire. "I'd just about given up on you. I thought it was supposed to be more meetings today. Don't tell me they kept you at a meeting this late?"

"The day started off in a meeting and ended in a murder investigation," Evan said. "I've been put on a new Major Crimes Team out of HQ, and we were sent out right away to cover the murder."

Bronwen had come to meet him and threw her arms around his neck. "Evan, that's wonderful. I'm so proud of you." She kissed him firmly on the lips.

"I'm not so sure how wonderful it will be," he said. "The DI is going to be an absolute bugger to work with, but if I get that kind of reception every time you're proud of me—" He drew her to him and started to kiss her hungrily.

"Evan!" She pulled away from him. "Hold on a minute before you get carried away. We've got a visitor."

"What?" Evan looked around the room for the first time. Jamila rose from the low chair on the far side of the fire where she had been sitting.

"Oh hello, Jamila," Evan said. "Sorry, I didn't see you there. *Sut wyt ti?*" he asked in Welsh.

Jamila attempted a smile. "Not so good, Mr. Evans."

"Jamila's had some startling news, to say the least," Bronwen said. "She came straight up here to tell us."

"Bad news, Jamila?"

"Terrible, Mr. Evans. Absolutely terrible." He could see now that she had been crying. "I've just found out something really awful is going to happen to me."

"What is it?"

Jamila gave a hopeless glance to Bronwen.

"Jamila's family plans to take her to Pakistan to marry her off to a man more than twice her age," Bronwen said. "A man she's never even met."

"Surely not?" Evan shook his head in disbelief. "I could believe that your brother might want to do something like that, but your father seems like a sensible man, perfectly westernized in his ways."

"You'd have thought so, wouldn't you?" Jamila pressed her lips together to prevent herself from crying again before she went on. "But now he's turned into the worst kind of old-fashioned Muslim father, practically overnight. Rashid was spying on me, you see. I stayed at my friend Rhian's house to work on a school project, and some boys from our class stopped by to say hello. There was nothing wrong with it. They're nice boys. We just had some soft drinks and chatted. But Rashid made it sound as if I'd tricked our parents and gone there deliberately to drink with boys. So now I overheard Daddy and Mummy talking, and they have been in touch with relatives in Pakistan and these relatives have found a suitable man for me."

"But they can't marry you off against your will," Evan said. "You're underage to get married anyway."

"Not in Pakistan," Jamila said. "They force girls to get married when they are eleven or twelve there."

"But surely your parents can't think that you'd go to Pakistan to get married. If you refuse to go, they can't drag you there, kicking and screaming, can they?" Evan asked, glancing at Bronwen.

"They were going to trick her, Evan. That's what's so horrible," Bronwen said. "They were going to make it seem like a family holiday over Christmas. And then, when Jamila was there, it would be too late and she'd be helpless."

"And are they planning to just leave you in Pakistan with this man?"

Jamila spread her hands in a hopeless gesture. "I don't know. I don't know any details or what they're planning to do. I just heard Daddy say, 'Don't tell her anything, just that it's going to be a lovely family holiday.'

"And Mummy said, 'But the poor child. It's not fair to her.'

"And Daddy said, 'You and I had an arranged marriage, didn't we, and I'd say it turned out well enough for both of us. He's a good man and he's rich. She'll have plenty of clothes and a chauffeur to drive her around. What more should she want?'

"'But she's so keen on her education,' Mummy said. 'Shouldn't she be allowed to finish that, at least?'

"'And wind up running with a bad crowd or pregnant or on drugs? Is that what you want for her?' Daddy shouted. I crept away. I didn't want to hear anymore."

Bronwen put a comforting arm around the girl. "I'm sure they're just upset at the moment, and they're overreacting, Jamila. If you like I'll go and talk to them tomorrow. I'll tell them that you've found out what they have planned for you, that you are extremely upset, and absolutely refuse to go. I'll make them see that this is blighting your future, and that they are not behaving in a reasonable manner."

Jamila's face lit up. "Oh, would you do that for me? That would be so wonderful. I can't thank you enough."

Bronwen squeezed her shoulder. "Who else would I have to help me carry my shopping up the hill?"

Later that night, after Jamila had gone home and the meal had been cleared away, Evan sat with his arm around Bronwen on the sofa in front of the fire. Fierce rain peppered the windows, and wind moaned in the chimney. Bronwen gave a sigh of content and rested her head against Evan's shoulder.

"This is the first time I've really appreciated our little cottage," she said. "A haven of peace, shutting out the horrible world."

"Is the world so horrible?" Evan asked. "I thought you were the one who always saw the glass half full."

"I did. It just seems that everything is difficult at the moment. Poor little Jamila. I feel so angry when I think of those stupid people, that I'll have to be careful I don't let them have it."

"I think you need to be very tactful when you talk to her parents," Evan said. "If they feel too threatened, they'll just send her away from here out of our reach. On second thought, it might be best if you spoke to someone at her school. They might be able to intervene for her legally and declare her a ward of the court if necessary."

"But that would mean taking her away from her family, which I'm not sure is the best idea," Bronwen said. "Making the parents see reason is obviously what I want to achieve. I think it's the brother who is the big problem in the family. He's probably putting a lot of pressure on the father to act like a Muslim patriarch, and the father doesn't want to lose face by having his daughter defy him."

Evan stroked Bronwen's hair. "I'm glad we don't go in for arranged marriages in Wales," he said, "or your parents would have had you hitched to some gentleman farmer or boring solicitor."

"And yours would have married you off to a policewoman." Bronwen laughed.

"Oh no. My mother would have never come up with anyone good enough for me. She'd have kept me at home."

"She thought that Maggie girl was pretty special," Bronwen reminded him of an old flame in Swansea.

"Only when it was clear I was already interested in you. When I was dating Maggie, Ma never had a good word to say for her. I don't suppose either set of parents is too happy about us right now."

"Don't say that, Evan. Mummy really likes you, and Daddy had to be impressed after you rescued me. Of course, when it comes to your mother . . . I've come to realize I'll never be good enough. But luckily, Swansea is a long way away." She turned and brushed his cheek with a kiss. "Look at the time," she said. "There were so many things I wanted to talk to you about this evening, and now it's bedtime already."

"What did you want to talk about?" Evan asked. "I'm not sleepy yet."

"Well, for one thing, you've got a new murder investigation, and you never got a chance to tell me about it."

"I suspect the actual investigation will be fairly straightforward," Evan said, and gave her basic details. "It's going to boil down to someone who had a grudge against Professor Rogers."

"One of his colleagues, do you think?"

"I can't say yet. We only just spoke to them for a few minutes today. They all seemed normal enough people. If they killed Rogers, then they all came straight in to work as usual and put in a full day with students. That would take a cool head, wouldn't it? Tomorrow I hope Bragg will listen to my suggestion and start interviewing some of the students. We can find out from them if any of their professors seemed particularly stressed or distracted that day. Also, Sergeant Bill Jones in Caernarfon suggested it might be a disgruntled student who took a potshot."

Bronwen looked up and nodded. "Quite possible. They do seem to take grades as a matter of life or death these days, and so many of them can get their hands on guns too." She paused, thinking, and sat up. "You said you hoped Bragg might take your suggestion? Why don't you go and interview the students yourself?"

"Oh dear me, no," Evan said. "I've come up against the ultimate dictator. I've been told I'm the junior officer, and my job is to run errands. I've been with him to interview people all day long, and if I open my mouth I get frowned at. It's not easy, I can tell you, especially since he has this unfortunate, pushy manner. He flings out one question after another and doesn't wait for the full answer to come out or to watch the reaction."

"Evan, that's terrible. Doesn't he know how successful you've been? Didn't you tell him that you've solved cases on your own before now?"

"I rather think he's heard rumors about that and is determined I'm not going to step into his limelight. After all, there must be a reason I was selected for the first team in this new Major Crimes Unit. It must have been a recommendation rather than a punishment, although it feels like the latter."

"Poor Evan." She swiveled around to him and stroked back his unruly dark hair. "We all have our crosses to bear, don't we?"

"I haven't even asked you about school recently, have I? Is that a cross to bear?"

She sighed. "I'll get used to it, I expect. It's just that after twenty students in my own little village school, it's quite a shock to be in a great big, modern classroom. And everything regulated by the bell, and town kids are certainly different from village kids. We've got a mixture of races. Most of the teaching is in English not Welsh, and some of those kids are hopelessly behind in their reading and writing. I seem to spend all my time helping the stragglers and dealing with the problem kids, and the bright, well-behaved kids are left to fend for themselves. It doesn't seem fair, does it?"

"You'll learn how to handle it. You're a brilliant teacher, Bron. I've watched you."

"And you're a brilliant detective. We both need to assert ourselves before we're walked over." She yawned. "I don't know about you, but that extra hour on the bus just about does me in. I'm going to have to go to bed if I'm to catch that bus in the morning." She stood up, then took Evan's hand. "You're not going to let me get into that cold bed all alone, are you?"

Evan needed no second urging.

Chapter 11

The next morning dawned bleak and wet, with the wind snatching brown leaves from tree branches and sheep huddled miserably against the stone walls. The mountain peaks had been swallowed up into cloud that came down to the cottage itself. Bronwen looked out of the window and sighed as the village below appeared and disappeared in the swirling mist. "Now I'm beginning to have serious second thoughts about this place," she said. "It's on days like this that I realize just how isolated we are up here."

"Generations of shepherds survived perfectly well," Evan said.

"Yes, but they didn't have to get down the hill to catch the bus, did they? If it goes on like this, I'll have to wear my anorak and hiking boots to school. There's no way I'd make it down that hill in ordinary shoes and not lose them in the mud."

"I'll run you to school in the car," Evan said. "That way you can change out of your boots and look presentable when you get to school."

"Are you sure it won't make you late? I don't want you to start off on the wrong foot with your dictator."

"He wants us to meet at the Bangor Police Station at eight thirty. I can do that easily. Come on. We'll slither together."

Hand in hand, they picked their way down the track, while the wind whipped at their raincoats and sheep scattered in alarm at the sight of them. By the time Evan arrived in Bangor, the storm had subsided to a steady, unrelenting rain. Evan had dried off and was making a cup of tea when the other officers came in, looking windblown and miserable.

"God-awful weather," Bragg complained. "I forgot how much worse it gets the further west you go, but I expect you're used to it, aren't you, Evans."

"Born with webbed feet, sir," Evan said.

Wingate and Pritchard chuckled, and even Bragg managed a smile. "Right. I stopped by HQ on my way in, and they should have a forensics report for us by the end of the day. I hope they took all the pictures and casts they needed of the footprints because any evidence in that garden will be washed away by now."

"So what's on the agenda for today?" Wingate asked.

"We go back to the university and have another chat with those history professors," Bragg said. "We need to find one of them who is ready to dish the dirt. They were all far too polite and well mannered yesterday, didn't you think, Evans?"

"Absolutely," Evan said. "I got the feeling they might have been ready to tell us a whole lot more if there had been more time to chat."

It was the closest he could come to letting Bragg know that his rapid-fire approach might not always be the best. Bragg nodded.

"Right, especially that Humphries woman. Evans, I'd like you to go back and speak to her in Welsh. She may say things to you that she'd not say to the rest of us. And I think I'll go and speak to the widow again. There's a lot more we need to find out about the rest of Rogers's life: what relatives he had living close by; whether there might have been any disputes with family members—over a will, for example; whether he belonged to the darts club or the golf club or the County Council."

"Whether he had a mistress," Wingate suggested.

"Oh yes, and you think Mrs. Rogers would tell me that, even if she knew?" Bragg chuckled. "She's definitely a proud woman, Wingate. I get the feeling she's not going to tell us anything she doesn't want us to know. And if she did it, I reckon she's going to be a tough nut to crack."

"You don't really think she did it, do you, sir?" Pritchard asked. Then he flushed as Bragg stared up at him. He had fair, sandy hair and a boyish face that made him look even younger than he was, and he was clearly still ill at ease with his new boss.

"Why do you think that, Pritchard? I'd say she was still the most obvious suspect."

"If you were going to kill someone, would you call the police right afterward?"

"If I thought I could get away with it, I would. An innocent person would obviously call the police immediately, and she'd want to appear innocent, wouldn't she? I'll take another crack at her today, see if I can rattle her at all."

"Vee have vays of making you talk," Wingate said, in a fake German accent. "So what do you want Pritchard and me to do?"

"Let's see. What else should we be doing right away?" Bragg looked around the group.

"If I may make a suggestion about something we shouldn't overlook, sir?" Evan began.

"Oh, and what is Hercule Poirot going to tell us to do now?" He grinned, then realized that Wingate and Pritchard weren't smiling. "Okay, Evans. What is it?"

"The students, sir. I don't think we should overlook them. They'd know if one of their professors was not acting normally yesterday. And if one of them carried a grudge, felt that Professor Rogers had failed him unfairly perhaps, or was going to fail him, he might have taken matters into his own hands."

"That's a good point, Evan," Jeremy Wingate said. "I was thinking along the same lines."

"Of course. That goes without saying." Bragg waved a dismissive hand. "We were always planning to get to the students in good time. But what do they teach you in basic training—always start with the most likely suspects, and they are the people closest to the victim. His wife, his colleagues, his relatives, if he has any. So Wingate, why don't you go with Evans and you can chat to your students and professors, then Pritchard can come with me to see how the widow is holding up today."

The storm might have died down in the middle of the town, but up on the hilltop where the university was perched, it was a different story. Rain buffeted the car windows and wind whipped the bare trees into a crazy dance as Evan drove up the steep road. He parked on a double line as close as possible to the History Department building.

"For once it's good to be on official business," He commented to Jeremy Wingate, "but we've still got a good hike. The students here must be tough."

The full force of wind hit them as they opened the car doors, and it drove them up the hill as if an invisible hand was pushing them. They were drenched and out of breath as they stepped into the warmth and quiet of the building foyer. From the receptionist in the office they learned that Dr. Skinner was giving an early lecture until ten, but nobody else would be teaching until that hour. If they'd already come in, they'd be in their offices or making a cup of coffee in the staff common room.

They went along the hall and found Dr. Gwyneth Humphries in residence in her office, Dr. Rhys Thomas in his.

"You have your chat in Welsh with the Celtic witch lady," Wingate said in a low voice, "and I'll talk to Rhys Thomas. I don't see why we should waste time by having two of us present at each of these interviews, do you?"

"Of course not," Evan said. "I think Bragg only wanted to have one of us standing behind him to make him seem more important. He asked me to take notes, but he's never once asked to see what I've written. It was just to keep me in my place."

"Yes, he's got a thing about you, I've noticed," Wingate said. "He perceives you as a threat. Why is that, do you think?"

Evan shrugged. "I got some publicity for a couple of cases I helped solve, I suppose. Not that I've ever sought out publicity."

"Of course not. No, I've already spotted that our Bragg has a very fragile ego. One has to tread carefully around him. And you know damned well that we'll do the spade work on the case, and he'll take all the credit."

"Probably." Evan chuckled. "Well, it's good for the soul, isn't it?"

"I've no particular wish to improve my soul." Wingate slapped him on the shoulder. "Meet you in that little staff common room in half an hour then."

Gwyneth Humphries looked startled to see Evans at her door and even more taken aback when he spoke to her in Welsh.

"I suppose I can manage to spare you a few minutes," she said, hastily tidying up papers on her desk, "but I can't think what else I can possibly tell you that hasn't already come out. And why didn't you tell me you spoke Welsh yesterday? I much prefer using my own language in my own country, if you please."

"Inspector Bragg, who is my boss, isn't fluent enough to conduct his interviews in Welsh," Evan said.

"He's not that effective in English either, is he?" There was a twinkle in her eye as she sought to guage whether Evans was on her side or not. "Rather a rude and unpleasant man, I felt."

"Not the greatest social skills in the world, I'm afraid; but I'm sure he's a good policeman, or he'd never have been given the job," Evan said.

"No? In our world, inadequacy on the job results in being shoved upstairs," she said dryly.

"In your particular department?" Evan asked.

"Well, no, I wasn't trying to infer . . ." She was flustered now, playing with the long, knitted scarf she wore today. "Martin Rogers—well, he knew his subject all right. He was quite a lively lecturer. But he only got the professorship because he was a man, and it's all old-boys together, as usual. He was at school with members of the board, you know. But he knew nothing about Welsh history, which, after all, is what the department should be all about."

Evan let her trail off into silence. After a moment she shifted uncomfortably and said, "That doesn't imply that I resented him enough to want him dead. I was actually quite fond of Martin in my way."

And she blushed again.

"You must have had time to think about his death by now," Evan said. "And maybe you've come up with your own suspicions. Can you think of anybody at all who might have wanted Martin Rogers dead?"

She hesitated for a while. "Martin wasn't always an easy man," she said slowly. "We've each had our little run-ins with him over the years. I've had to fight for increased visibility for the Welsh side of the department. Paul Jenkins clashed with him immediately upon his arrival over politics. Paul's a rabid socialist you see, and Martin was staunchly conservative. Martin sat in on Paul's first lectures and accused him of coloring history with his own brand of politics. Hot words were exchanged over freedom of speech."

"And the others?" Evan asked. "Dr. Rhys Thomas? Sloan?"

"Olive has managed to glide under Martin's radar so far. She's definitely the type of person who avoids conflict at all costs. But Rhys Thomas—Martin accused him of plagiarism in an article he published. Sparks flew about that."

"How long ago was that?"

"Last academic year."

"And David Skinner?"

"Poor old David. He's too meek and mild to stand up to anybody. Martin walked all over him—swapped his classes around, downplayed the findings at his dig."

"And what about the other chap out at the dig? Badger something?"

"Brock. Dr. Ernest Brock. They nicknamed him Badger. Well yes, Martin couldn't stand him and, in fact, has been trying to get rid of him. Dr. Brock's a good man actually. Enthusiastic. The students like him. But he's hopelessly messy and undisciplined. He has cardboard boxes stacked with potentially valuable finds. His records are so fuzzy that nobody but he can understand them. Martin was the world's neatest human being, so naturally Brock drove him mad."

"If he was trying to get rid of Brock, might that not have provided a good motive for murder?"

She burst out laughing. "Dear me, no. If you knew Badger . . . he took great delight in baiting Martin. If anything it would have been the other way around. I'd have believed that Martin might have taken a potshot at Badger." Then she shook her head violently so that her long earrings danced. "This is all ridiculous. Of course we argued from time to time. Of course there were hurt feelings and thoughtless things said. But nobody decides to murder another human being for those reasons."

Evan nodded. "I tend to agree with you," he said.

Dr. Humphries started to gather up papers. "I really have to go," she said, "I lecture on the Black Death at ten. It's one of my most popular classes. Amazing how ghoulish the young are, isn't it?"

"Speaking of the young"—Evan followed her out into the hall—"what about students? Can you think of one of them who might have had a particular grievance against Professor Rogers?"

"Not that I know of. Students have always got some kind of grievance, but I'd have heard if it was anything big. They are not shy about expressing their opinions these days, you know."

"Tell me one more thing." They were almost at the front door now. "Was Professor Rogers one for the ladies? What did the female students think of him?"

"Martin was—could be—very charming." She paused to toss her scarf over her shoulder. "He was, however, devoted to his wife. And you'd never have found him making a grab for a female student. Such behavior was just not in his character. I really have to go now." And she fled.

Again there was just the hint of embarrassment. Had she and Martin Rogers ever had an affair? Evan wondered. And what about the meek and mild Dr. Skinner over whom Rogers habitually walked? Didn't such people eventually snap?

He made his way back down the hallway, deep in thought. Wingate was in the small staff room, nursing a cup of instant coffee with Paul Jenkins and Olive Sloan.

"How did it go?" he asked.

"Interesting," Evan said.

Paul Jenkins looked up from his coffee. "Has Gwyneth been spilling the beans about the rest of us? About David's sordid affair with Martin and Badger filching the department funds to bet on the horses?" He looked at their faces and laughed. "Just kidding," he said.

"Not particularly funny," Wingate said, "given that a man is lying in the morgue with a hole through his head because he represented such a major threat that somebody had to kill him."

"Sorry." Jenkins made a face. "Actually, I think it's pretty beastly, but I think you're barking up the wrong tree if you're trying to find some deep, dark secret here. We're just a typical university department, and our biggest squabbles are about whether a certain document dated from 1257 or 1258."

He stopped talking as Rhys Jones and David Skinner came in to join them. Skinner reacted to the presence of two policemen again. "Christ, not more interrogations," he said. "Are we to be browbeaten until one of us confesses? I thought I'd told you everything yesterday."

"One thing we forgot to ask you, sir," Jeremy Wingate said easily. "It's about your movements yesterday morning."

"My movements?" Skinner looked bewildered.

"Yes. Where were you between about seven thirty and eight thirty?"

"That's easy enough. Snoring my head off. I don't have a class on Thursdays until eleven, so I don't surface before nine. Sinful, I'm sure, but true."

"And you have no one to vouch for that?" Wingate asked.

"He wishes," Jenkins quipped.

"No, no one." Skinner shot him a look.

Suddenly the door burst open, and a young man barged in. He made a dramatic picture with his leather jacket and shoulder-length black hair that had been blown every which way in the wind. "Have you heard the news, chaps!" he shouted. "Somebody's finally done it! They've put old Martin Rogers out of his misery!"

Chapter 12

"I'm not sure whether that was an exercise in futility or not," Sergeant Wingate said to Evan as they came out of the History Department building. The wind had subsided and the weather was brightening from the west, revealing the odd patch of blue between the strands of cloud. "Did you find out anything interesting?"

"Gwyneth Humphries made it clear that every one of them had clashed with Martin Rogers at one time or another. Maybe that was to throw us off the scent and not have us focus on one of them."

"Could be. Rhys Thomas said pretty much the same thing to me."

"And Brock seemed to think it wasn't even surprising that Professor Rogers had been murdered," Evan went on. "But then he was the one who had a perfect alibi for yesterday. He was out at his dig with a bunch of students."

"I'll tell you one thing," Evan added, watching the steady stream of students making their way down the hill like a column of ants. "Gwyneth Humphries was sweet on Professor Rogers."

"No kidding? Do you think something was going on there? A liaison on the side?"

"I don't think so. She took pains to tell me how morally correct Rogers was."

"So it was unrequited love on her part—pining from afar. Maybe her theory was, if I can't have him then nobody else can. Hell has no fury, and all that."

"I can't see her shooting somebody," Evan said. "She's a dramatic woman, I grant you, but shooting is too cold and calculated for her. I can picture her stabbing him with a Celtic dagger, perhaps."

"So what do we tell Bragg?" Wingate asked.

"Let's wait and hear what he's come up with this morning. And we haven't spoken to any students yet."

"I'd imagine there are several hundred students who attend history lectures. Rather a tall order to interview them all. Where do you suggest we start?"

"I think we're like Mohammed," Evan said, looking down the hill. "I think the mountain is coming to us." And indeed students were suddenly streaming out of buildings all over the campus, some of them now heading in the direction of the History Department building. At the same moment there were noises in the hallway behind them, and another group of students was coming down the stairs.

Jeremy Wingate stepped out to meet them as they came through the doors.

"Excuse me a minute," he said. "Are any of you students of Professor Rogers?"

The young man who was leading the group looked around uneasily. "We all are," he said. "Everybody gets the head of department at one time or another."

"I know what this is about," a girl said. She had that startlingly red hair found in the true Celt and bright green eyes. "He's been killed, hasn't he? I saw it on the telly last night."

"That's right, I'm afraid," Wingate said. "We're police officers; and if you've got a moment, we'd like to ask you some questions."

"Fire away," the first boy said. "I'd love a good excuse to be fifteen minutes late for Humphries."

"The 'Black Death'?" Wingate asked with a grin. "I thought that class was supposed to be fascinating."

"The subject is, but she's boring as hell. She drones on and on and on. Half the people who signed up for that class have already dropped it. So what did you want to know about Professor Rogers?"

Wingate glanced at Evan.

"We wondered whether any of you knew if he might have had a recent run-in with any of his students," Evan said.

"He was a miserable old sod," another boy commented, putting on his anorak hood against the wind. "He was one of the faculty members on the site council, and he was always vetoing anything he didn't approve of. You know, the gay/lesbian dance, that kind of thing. Very old-fashioned and prejudiced."

"He was really stodgy," a girl agreed. "Totally behind the times. If you showed up at one of his lectures in a skimpy top, he'd make you put your jacket on."

"But you don't kill your teacher because he makes you put your jacket on, do you?" Wingate asked.

They looked at him with wide-eyed horror. "Who said anything about killing?" the first girl asked. "He was annoying. My dad's annoying sometimes, but I don't think about killing him."

"Exactly," Evan said. "It has to be a life-or-death situation to make you want to kill someone in my experience. So I wondered, has there been a case where Professor Rogers might have pushed a student to the edge. Maybe he had failed somebody or was going to fail somebody?"

They looked at each other, considering this.

"There was Simon last year," the red-haired girl said at last, checking with her friends for confirmation in voicing this opinion.

"Simon?" Evan asked quietly.

"Simon Pennington. He graduated in June. He was very bright, probably one of the best students in his year. He thought he should have got a first, but he only got an upper two. He was really angry, and he thought it was all Professor Rogers's fault. Apparently Professor Rogers had assessed his special project as competent but not original. His family went to the dean and demanded a reassessment, but the dean wouldn't do it."

"He came back here to see old Rogers a couple of weeks ago, after term had started," a boy said. "He was yelling that Rogers had ruined his life, and he was never going to get into the Diplomatic Corps now."

"And where would we find this Simon Pennington?"

They looked at each other and shrugged.

"The registrar would have a contact address. He lived near London, didn't he?"

"I think so. He was definitely not Welsh anyway."

This got a laugh from the Welsh members of the group.

Evan left the university with an address in Surrey for Simon Pennington, but a phone call to that address indicated that Simon was currently traveling abroad and wouldn't be back for another month.

"Great alibi, don't you think?" Wingate asked Evan, as they headed back to the station. "There's nothing to stop him from popping back into the country, shooting the professor, and then going back to the Continent again. They never really check EU passports these days, do they?"

"We should definitely keep him in mind," Evan agreed. "Should we find more students to interview or get back to Bragg?"

"Much as I hate to face him this early in the day, I think he'll probably be expecting to see our keen and eager young faces sometime soon."

They made their way down the path to the waiting car.

"At least the university meter maids didn't have the nerve to ticket us," Wingate said.

"I bet they don't even set foot outside in this weather." Evan smiled.

A call to Bragg revealed that he was still at the Rogers's house.

"I want you two over here right away," he said. "We're giving the place a thorough search."

"Looking for what in particular, sir?" Evan asked.

"That missing weapon, among other things. I've got nothing new out of Mrs. Rogers. According to her, Martin Roger had no family nearby. He didn't belong to a golf club. He didn't attend a church, unlike her. No close ties at all or interests outside of the university.

Doesn't she realize if she can't come up with a likely suspect, the suspicion is all going to fall on her?"

"I think Bragg operates rather like the medieval ducking stool," Wingate said dryly, as they sped through deserted wet streets toward the Rogers's house. "If he holds her underwater long enough, she's going to confess."

Missy Rogers, still accompanied by the same woman police constable, was sitting on the sofa in the drawing room working on a tapestry. The dog, Lucky, lay at her feet. It rose with a deep growl as they came in.

"It's all right, Lucky." She put a comforting hand on his head. "He knows something isn't right," she said, by way of apology for his behavior. "He's such a sensitive animal."

"Is Inspector Bragg here?" Wingate asked.

"I think you'll find your inspector in Martin's study," she said. "I can't think what they hope to find. Martin received no threatening letters, no blackmail, nothing that might be filed away in a study."

"What about a student called Simon Pennington?" Evan asked. "Did your husband mention him to you?"

She frowned, then shook her head. "I can't say that he did. He dealt with hundreds of students, and he rarely discussed his work at home. His research yes, but not the petty problems of the university. He liked his home to be his haven."

"Evans? Is that you?" boomed the voice down the stairs. "I want you up here right now. And Wingate."

The two men gave Missy Rogers a commiserating smile as they heeded the call from above.

"I don't remember giving you permission to question Mrs. Rogers," Bragg said.

"We were just following up on a lead we'd got at the university," Wingate said quickly. "A student who believed Professor Rogers was responsible for his failing to get a first-class degree."

"Then he'd already have left the university last summer, wouldn't he?"

"But he came back a couple of weeks ago and had a shouting match with Professor Rogers," Evan said.

"Have you tried to contact him?"

"I called his home in Surrey," Evan said. "Apparently he's gone abroad."

"How convenient."

"That's what we thought."

"Well, I suppose it's the only credible lead we've got so far, apart from the widow," Bragg said. "Right, let's get on with the job in hand and see what turns up, and Wingate, you can retrace the steps of Mrs. Rogers's dog walk yesterday and see if anyone can vouch for seeing her. Of course, that proves nothing. It would only take a minute or so to shoot her husband and then walk the dog as if nothing had happened."

He was speaking in his usual loud, strident voice, and Evan looked at the open study door.

"I don't think you should give her any idea that you suspect her," he said.

"Of course I should. Make her good and nervous. When you've been in the force as long as I have, Evans, then you can start giving suggestions. Until then you sort through that filing cabinet and keep quiet."

Evan bit back the anger and went over to the filing cabinet. Everything was in meticulous order, ranging from household accounts to historical papers published. Years and years of receipts, bank statements, letters written to the water board to complain about water pressure. Martin Rogers's whole life was documented here, neatly filed to be resurrected if needed. Evan flicked through the household accounts. For every month there was a handwritten sheet stapled to a typewritten sheet. Evan realized that the writing on the first sheet was not Martin Rogers's. It must therefore be Missy's. Account for the week ending September 21. Then beside some of the items, in Martin's small, neat script, some comments: 'Wasteful. Why not buy larger size?' And even against one item: 'Not necessary. Amount not allowed.' On the typewritten sheet was a reconciliation—the amount of money paid into the housekeeping account that year, compared to the previous year. Evan wondered if Martin gave his wife any money for herself. He certainly vetted what she spent on keeping the house running and queried her over trivialities.

He put the accounts back and went on looking. Under letters he found copies of every letter Martin had written. Evan read through the last year or two but came up with nothing inflammatory. Then he pulled out a bundle of envelopes, tied with a string. Old love letters? He wondered and hesitated to open the bundle. Then he noticed that some of the postmarks were quite recent. He pulled out the first letter and was surprised to see it was addressed to Missy Rogers, not Martin. It was from her sister in France. "I haven't heard from you in a while so I hope you are well," she wrote. Just a chatty, ordinary letter. There were more letters from her sister, letters from what appeared to be an old school friend, even from her parents, dated five or more years ago. Had Missy asked Martin to keep them in the filing cabinet for her? Evan retied the string uneasily. Now was not the right time to confront her with them. He'd wait and see how things developed.

In the bottom drawer of the filing cabinet, he came upon a folder marked WEAPONS. In it was a detailed list of all the antique weapons Martin Rogers owned, date purchased, from whom, history, when used as a visual aid in a class. Evan read through the list slowly, then double-checked.

"Have you got something there, Evans?" Inspector Bragg called.

"I think I have." Evan looked up. "This is a list of the weapons in that drawer. There never was a second dueling pistol."

"What exactly are you saying?" Bragg asked.

"That there doesn't appear to be a missing weapon. The ones in the tray downstairs are all accounted for."

"So someone laid the same gun down on the velvet to give the impression of a missing weapon?" Bragg nodded. "Now who would have had the opportunity to do that?"

"Only the widow, I suppose," Evan had to admit.

"It's looking more and more likely, Evans. And yet she's sitting down there doing her embroidery, not blinking an eyelid, knowing that we're up here. Pritchard?"

Pritchard jumped up from where he was squatting at the bottom drawer of the desk. "Yes sir?"

"Leave that and start looking for another weapon," he said. "We know that none of those antique pistols has been fired recently. So the real weapon has to have been hidden or disposed of."

"Maybe Mrs. Rogers dropped it into the shrubbery on her dog walk," Pritchard suggested, "Or threw it into the Menai Strait."

"Both possible. Evans, call HQ and have a team of men sent out to search. We may also need frogmen."

"Shouldn't we wait for the ballistics report?" Evan said cautiously. "It would make more sense if the men knew what they were looking for."

"I suppose so," Bragg reluctantly agreed. "Let's have the WPC take Mrs. Rogers out for a walk or a cup of coffee, and then we'll give this whole place a proper going over. Maybe she's stashed it under our noses."

But a thorough search of the house failed to turn up the weapon. Evan felt most uncomfortable rummaging through neat drawers of underwear and nightclothes. On Missy's bedside table there was a faded photograph of a couple taken in wartime, the man handsome in his army uniform, the woman looking coy in one of those 1940s suits with the big shoulders. Beside it another photo of the same couple, their faces now wrinkled but still handsome. Beside it a photograph of Missy, her arm around another woman in what looked like the south of France. Her parents and sister, Evan surmised. They were the only photographs in the house.

His search was interrupted by the arrival of DS Wingate. He had retraced the route of the dog walk and had spoken to the old man Missy had mentioned, the one with the little white dog of whom Lucky was so fond. The old man remembered seeing Mrs. Rogers go past at her usual time the previous morning, but she had seemed more hurried and preoccupied. She'd just given him a perfunctory "Good morning" and dragged Lucky past without giving the dogs time to greet each other in their usual way.

"She was stressed," Bragg said delightedly. "What did I tell you?

She was in a hurry to get back on schedule after she'd taken the time to shoot her husband and then put the lawn mower away."

"Did anyone else see her?" Evan asked.

"The woman at the corner shop was just putting out the trays of apples and saw her walk by, but that was about it. At least we know she stuck to the route she had described to us."

"Right, lads, back to searching for that weapon," Bragg said. "Given the amount of time she'd have needed to complete that walk, she wouldn't have had much chance to hide a weapon before she called us."

"Unless she'd dropped it in the bushes along the way," Evan reminded him.

He didn't look pleased to be reminded. "Right. Yes. We know that," he said.

But another hour's searching revealed nothing. Mrs. Rogers had returned from her outing with the policewoman and was now out in her garden, pulling the dead heads off chrysanthemums while the policewoman threw a ball for Lucky. It was a peaceful, everyday scene. Someone had lit a bonfire in a neighboring back garden, and the pleasant smell of burning wood and leaves floated toward them as they piled back into their vehicles.

"I get the feeling she's a smart cookie, and she thinks we're rather slow and stupid," Bragg said. "She probably thinks it's really easy to outwit us."

"Well, she has, so far," Wingate said. "We've got nothing on her that would stand up in court."

"We'll get it," Bragg said. "I have a good feeling about this one."

As soon as they arrived back at headquarters in Colwyn Bay, they went first to the forensics lab.

"I was just about to call you lot," they were greeted by Owen Jones, one of the members of yesterday's team. "I think we've wrapped up all the preliminary findings on your crime scene yesterday."

"And?" Bragg demanded.

"What do you want first? Ballistics report?"

"Fire away," Bragg said. Pritchard smirked. Evan couldn't decide whether Bragg was intending to be witty or not.

"Right." Jones picked up a piece of paper from the table beside him. "Interesting size bullet—eight millimeter. You don't come across that often in modern weapons. Nine is more common. Our ballistics chap suggests it might have come from a Nambu Type 14, a Japanese handgun used by their officers in World War II. I take it nobody's been able to come up with the casing yet? That would confirm it."

"No casing," Bragg said. "We've given the house and grounds a pretty thorough search, and we've come up with nothing."

"There was a photo of a bloke in a WWII uniform on the bedside table," Pritchard said. "Her dad, do you think? Left her the weapon?"

"I bet he did," Bragg said excitedly. "Tell me, do you think it was a weapon that a woman could have fired easily?"

"Absolutely,' the technician said. "If it's a Nambu, it's a light little thing. In fact it was always a source of amusement that Japanese officers were issued something so flimsy. Most of them chose to carry swords instead, so I understand. More chance of killing somebody with those."

"And yet it seems to have done an efficient job this time," Bragg said.

"Five feet away—you can't very well miss, can you?"

"True. So what else have you got for us, Jones?"

"Fingerprints—no obvious fingerprints that we can't identify. Especially significant from your point of view, the only prints on the lawn mower were Mrs. Rogers's and the gardener's. Mrs. Rogers's were the clearest. And on the window latch, only Mrs. Rogers's fingerprints show up, apart from a few indistinct ones."

"And if the killer had worn gloves?" Bragg asked.

"If he'd worn gloves, he'd likely have smudged the nice clear set of prints we got. As it was, we didn't see any evidence of smudging or attempts to wipe anything clean."

"If Mrs. Rogers really is the killer, surely she'd have thought of that," Evan blurted out. "The first thing she'd have done is to wipe away her fingerprints."

Bragg smirked. "As I've said before, it's lucky for us that most perpetrators aren't too bright. And they're in panic mode. They don't always stop to think." He clapped his hands together. "Right, lads. I think we're finally getting somewhere. Let's have the uniform boys bring her in."

"Are you charging her, sir?" Wingate asked. "Isn't that a little premature?"

"I'm not charging her officially, Wingate. As of now she's helping us with our inquiries. However, I think we're going to be too busy to get to her before tomorrow morning. Let's just see whether a night in a cell will make her more willing to tell us what she knows."

Chapter 13

Evan felt uneasy as he drove home in the fading light. The storm had blown away, leaving stripes of deep blue cloud across a pink sky. The setting sun glowed on the west-facing slopes, turning the granite dusky pink and even tingeing the fleeces of the sheep. Water cascaded down the hillsides in ribbons and danced in the ditches beside the road. The sounds of splashing water and bleating of sheep floated into the car through the open window, over the noise of the engine.

Earlier in his career Evan would have parked the car and gone for a brisk walk up the hill to savor the sunset. Now he felt burdened with too much on his mind. He was still uncomfortable with Inspector Bragg's decision to bring in Mrs. Rogers. The thought of that genteel woman spending a night in jail was repugnant to him. He admired her quiet dignity, and he wanted to believe in her innocence. He knew from past experience that a few obvious clues do not necessarily a murderer make. And yet he had to agree with Bragg that she did now seem the likely suspect. Would anyone else have thought of coming back into the house to close the window? Would anyone else have put away the lawn mower? He had to admit he was rather glad he wasn't in charge of the case.

He parked his car and climbed up the track just as the last rays of sun vanished, leaving the valley in deep gloom. Ahead of him the slopes of the Glydrs still glowed brightly, and the windows in his own little cottage winked back the sun's dying rays. He quickened his pace and took the last part of the hill at a run.

"Bron?" he called, flinging open the door. "Bron, do you feel like coming for a walk before it's quite dark? Have you seen the sky out there? It's a lovely evening."

Bronwen came out of the bedroom, brushing the wisps of fair hair back from her face.

"Oh hello, Evan," she said. "Sorry, I haven't started supper yet."

He took a long look at her. "What's wrong?" he asked. She'd clearly been crying.

"I've just had a really horrible experience," she said.

He went over to her and took her into his arms. "What is it, *cariad?* Tell me all about it."

She buried her head against his shoulder. "I went to see the Khans, like I promised," she said. "I thought we could talk like reasonable people. I was doing okay with the parents at first. I told them that Jamila was a bright girl and had a good future ahead of her, and if they loved her they should think what was best for her. And her best future was obviously here. Then the brother arrived, and he went ballistic on me. He screamed that it was all my fault that his sister had turned into a loose slut with no morals. He accused me of turning her against her family and her religion. She'd never have dared to answer her father back before she met me, he said. He got right in my face, and he said if I ever dared to speak to her again, I'd be sorry."

"Oh, he did, did he?" Evan started to move toward the door.

Bronwen grabbed at his sleeve. "No, Evan. Don't go down there. It wouldn't do any good."

"I'm not having anyone threatening my wife," Evan muttered.

"But more fighting won't solve anything. I just feel like such a failure." She let out a big sigh. "I guess I'm not the wise schoolteacher I thought I was. I really thought I was going to be the voice of reason, and they'd listen to me. But the moment Rashid came on the scene, the two older ones sided with him. Even the father told me I was interfering in private, family business and would I please leave his house immediately. Then I suppose I lost it too. I told them that my husband was a policeman; and if they tried to take Jamila out of the country, they'd find that British law wouldn't allow them to behave in that barbaric way."

"Not the wisest thing to say," Evan said. "There's nothing we could do to stop them from taking their daughter where they like. You know that."

"I suppose so." Bronwen nestled her head against him again. "I just felt so angry and hopeless. Now I'm afraid I'll have scared them into taking some sort of action sooner than they'd intended to."

"You might be right," Evan said.

She pushed him away from her. "Stop sounding so damn smug and reasonable!" she shouted. "I suppose you'd have handled it perfectly! You were just about to go down there and beat up Rashid."

Evan had to smile. He pulled her close again and stroked her cheek. "I'm sure I'd have done no better than you, sweetheart. You're not going to change a mind-set that has been formed through the culture of generations."

"So what can we do now, Evan?" Bronwen demanded. "We can't just let them take her to Pakistan and marry her off to some old man."

"I suppose you could speak to someone at her school," Evan said. "They may have the power to intervene, although, I warn you, Jamila may not thank you for it if she's forcibly taken away from her family. And I suspect that this is such a delicate cultural issue that the school will stay well clear."

Bronwen paced the room. "I feel so angry and so powerless," she said.

"There is something you might do," Evan said. "Talk to Jamila herself and ask her what she wants. Would she really rather be put in foster care?"

"I don't think that's going to happen easily," Bronwen said. "From now on her brother is going to be driving her to school and back, so that she doesn't have a chance to meet with us corrupt non-Muslims." Her face brightened as she came up with an idea. "I know. Perhaps we could tell everybody to boycott the shop until they promise to keep Jamila here with them."

Evan shook his head, smiling. "You really are riled up tonight," he said. "I've never seen you like this before. What good do you think that would do? They'd up and move away, and then you wouldn't even know what happened to Jamila." He took her face in his hands. "What you don't seem to realize is that you can't force these people, Bronwen. They're proud of their culture. Any attack on their way of life and they are going to resist you, however sane and logical you think you are being."

"I suppose you're right."

"Jamila's a bright girl and she's made some friends. She may well figure this one out for herself," Evan said. "In fact there's only one thing to do now."

"What?" she looked up hopefully.

"I'll open a bottle of wine, and you start cooking the dinner."

At that she laughed. "That does seem the only sensible thing to do. Did you have a horrible day as well?"

"It wasn't bad," Evan said, "but we wound up arresting Professor Rogers's widow."

"The wife did it?"

"My boss seems to think so."

"But you don't?"

Evan shrugged. "I don't know. All the physical evidence does seem to point in her direction, but she's such a restrained, dignified woman, Bron. One of the old school, brought up to keep all her emotions in check and always to do the right thing. I just can't picture her shooting somebody."

"I'm sure you'll find out the truth, Evan. You always do," Bronwen said.

"I hope so. It's not as if he's going to let me say a word when he interviews her, and his interviewing style is such that anyone would clam up."

"Then you're going to have to do a little extra sleuthing on your own."

"Go behind my inspector's back?"

She laughed. "When has that ever stopped you before?"

. . .

The next morning Evan woke Bronwen with a cup of tea.

"Well, this is really nice," she said, giving him a sleepy smile. "Breakfast in bed and a nice day ahead."

"Not for me, love, I'm afraid." Evan bent to kiss her. "I've got to go to work. Don't look at me like that. I know it's Saturday, but we don't get days off when we're on a case. We keep going as long as it takes. You know that."

Bronwen sighed. "Yes, I suppose I did know that. You drummed it into me before we got married. You told me being a policeman's wife wasn't easy."

"I gave you enough chances to back out." He ruffled her hair.

"I should have listened. Now I'm stuck with you, I suppose."

"Unless you want to divorce me and live the high life on my assets."

"Half this cottage, you mean?" she laughed. "I can't decide which is the better half."

"I have to go." Evan turned to the door. "We're interviewing Professor Rogers's widow at nine. When I say we, I mean Bragg, of course. I'll be in the back, taking notes."

Bronwen sat up. "Don't let that man walk all over you, Evan. Sometimes you're too nice. He should be damned grateful to have you on his team. And if you don't tell him, I'll come down and do it myself."

"Bronwen the belligerent," Evan said. "You used to be such a tranquil little thing."

"It's all the good sex," Bronwen said dryly. "It's got me fired up."

Evan laughed as he let himself out of the front door.

Mrs. Rogers looked as if she had come to a meeting with her bank manager when she was ushered into the interview room the next morning. Her hair was in neat waves, she wore a touch of makeup, and she looked smart in her gray wool dress. Yesterday there had been some kind of pearl broach on the dress; Evan remembered. Sharp objects had obviously been removed before she was put in a holding cell.

"Please sit down, Mrs. Rogers." DI Bragg motioned to a chair with unexpected civility. He leaned across and pressed the record button on a tape recorder. "Saturday October third. Nine thirty a.m. Detective Inspector Bragg interviewing Mrs. Madeleine Jane Rogers. Also present in the room: Detective Sergeant Wingate, Detective Constables Evans and Pritchard. Sorry about that, Mrs. Rogers. Just a little formality to make sure this is all conducted by the book." He smiled at her. Evan had to admit he was being unnaturally charming.

"I must apologize for keeping you here overnight. I trust it wasn't too unpleasant."

"Thank you, but everyone was very kind," she said. "I was treated well, and the breakfast was quite edible. In fact it was rather nice to have my breakfast brought to me on a tray for once." There was a hint of a twinkle in her eyes.

"You do understand that we couldn't arrange this meeting until this morning," Bragg said.

"I understand perfectly, Inspector. I wasn't born yesterday. You thought a night in jail might frighten me into a confession. However, I'm afraid I have nothing to confess."

"You have the right to having a lawyer present, you know. That has been made clear to you?" Bragg said.

Her eyes challenged him. "Does that mean that I've been charged with this murder?"

"No. Not yet."

"Then don't you have to charge me or release me? You can't keep me here indefinitely, can you?"

Bragg leaned forward in his seat. "Mrs. Rogers, there's nothing I'd like better than to let you go. You give us some proof that you did not kill your husband, and you can leave anytime you want to."

"I'm afraid I can't do that, Inspector," she said calmly. "I have no proof at all, no alibi really, except for anyone who may have spotted me on my dog walk. My only proof is logic—why would I want to kill Martin? What could I possible gain from it? I have no close family anymore, apart from a sister I rarely see. My life was Martin. We did everything as a couple. By taking him away, I've had my whole life taken away from me."

Bragg continued to lean forward. "Mrs. Rogers, am I right in thinking that your father was in the war?"

"Yes, he was."

"And he served on what front?"

"The war in Asia. He was in Burma and captured by the Japanese. He was lucky to escape with his life. Most of his friends died building the Burma railway."

"And he brought back a Japanese officer's pistol as a souvenir?"

"I believe he did."

"And you own that pistol now?"

"Certainly not. I have no interest in weapons. I didn't even like those gruesome things that Martin collected."

"Your husband didn't have a Japanese pistol in his collection then?"

She smiled at this. "My husband's specialty was eighteenth-century Europe. A Japanese pistol would have been little use in his lectures."

"Did he ever own a pair of dueling pistols? There's only one in his collection at the moment."

"Unfortunately no," she said. "He's been trying for years to complete the pair; but they are much sought after these days, and when they've come up for auction, they've been at a price we couldn't afford."

"So the missing gun in the tray was what?"

"As I told you, Inspector, I have no interest in weapons. Martin never allowed anyone but himself to touch his collections."

"Let's move on. What made you decide to mow the lawn early in the morning when the gardener usually does it?"

"Mow the lawn? When?"

"On Thursday morning, when your husband was killed."

"I most certainly didn't mow the lawn."

"You said you went outside to do a spot of gardening."

"Yes. I weeded a bed, and I took the heads off some late roses."

"Your next-door neighbor heard the lawn mower around eight o'clock and was going to complain when it stopped."

"How strange. I can assure you it wasn't I, Inspector. If somebody used the mower, it was after Lucky and I had left on our walk."

"Who's looking after your dog at the moment, Mrs. Rogers?"

"I asked a friend who does the flowers at church with me to come in and feed him last night. Then I had to have somebody phone her to do the same this morning. I expected to be back home by now, you see. It's really not fair on poor Lucky. First he loses his daddy and then his mummy." For the first time she pressed her lips together, and turned her head toward the wall.

"Coming back to that lawn mower. So you didn't touch it, then?"

"I said I didn't."

"But it has your prints clearly on the handle. Yours and only yours."

"Extraordinary," She frowned and then nodded. "How silly. I remember now. The gardener was here on Tuesday, and he left it out. He's getting old and forgetful, I'm afraid. It was going to rain, so I wheeled it into the shed."

"And if somebody used it yesterday, why didn't they disturb your nice set of prints on the handle?"

"I can only presume that they used gloves or they took pains not to touch the handle."

"And speaking of fingerprints," Bragg went on, "we come to the latch on the kitchen window. That window was closed when we arrived, and yet the forensic team has determined that the shot was fired through an open window. Somebody closed it after your husband was shot."

"Not I, Inspector."

"And yet yours were the only prints on the latch."

"Again then all I can say is that somebody thought this through very carefully and closed the window holding a cloth or a tissue and tried to avoid touching the latch."

Bragg looked back at the other officers. Wingate was sitting behind him. Evans and Pritchard were standing, leaning against the back wall, about as far from the action as was possible in that small room. Any questions you'd like to add, Wingate?" Bragg asked.

"Yes. Thank you, sir." Wingate nodded to Mrs. Rogers. "When you took your dog for a walk that morning, you seemed preoccupied and in a remarkable hurry. Why was that?"

"May I ask who told you that?"

"The old man with the little white dog you mentioned to us. He said you barely grunted good morning to him and dragged Lucky past before he could stop and greet his little friend."

"I have no idea what made him say that. We only ever exchange a brief good morning. It's not as if I stop and gossip with him. In fact, I—" She broke off as there was a tap on the door, and it opened to reveal a uniformed constable.

Bragg bent forward and switched off the tape recorder that had been running. "What is it, Constable? Can't you see we're in the middle of an interview session?"

"I was sent to fetch you, sir. Important information my boss thinks you should have right away."

Bragg got to his feet.

"We'll have to continue this later. I do apologize, Mrs. Rogers. Pritchard, would you please arrange to have Mrs. Rogers escorted to the cafeteria and get her a cup of coffee."

As soon as she had gone, Bragg followed the uniformed constable along the echoing vinyl-tiled corridor. The others followed in his wake.

"This better be good," Bragg snapped to the constable. "We were just getting somewhere with her. Just getting her flustered, don't you think, men?"

"I believe it's very important, sir, or my sergeant wouldn't have sent me to get you."

There were several uniform branch members standing in the incident room, as well as a senior uniformed officer. The latter stepped forward and held out a hand to Bragg.

"DCI Neath. How's it going, boys?"

"We were just interviewing the widow, sir. It's looking promising. We've got her prints on everything."

"Yes, well you would have, wouldn't you? She lived there," Neath said dryly.

“What is this, sir?” Bragg demanded. “Don’t tell me that some kind of old-boy network is trying to get her off.”

“Nothing like that, Bragg. We’ve had an interesting development that may well affect your case. There was another murder last night. An Italian café owner was shot through the open window of his kitchen early this morning. It appears to have been done with the same weapon.”

Chapter 14

DI Bragg blinked, as if digesting this. "The same weapon, sir? Are you sure?"

"The bullet's been recovered. Again it went in one side of his temple, out the other, and stuck in the wall. Identical bullet to the one that killed Martin Rogers."

"Well, this is a turn up for the books, isn't it?" Bragg turned back to his team, who were standing behind him. "An Italian restaurant, you say?"

"I think restaurant would be a flattering name for it. It's more like a little pizza and spaghetti place called Papa Luigi's at the not-so-good end of Llandudno, next to an Indian take-away."

"And is the dead owner Luigi?" Jeremy Wingate asked.

"That's right. Luigi Alessi. Found by his wife, Pamela Alessi, when he hadn't come to bed when she woke around three a.m. She went down to the kitchen and found him slumped over the table, just like Martin Rogers."

"And he's really from Italy?" Evan asked.

"The genuine article. Been here twenty years, but apparently still spoke with a thick accent."

"A university professor in Bangor and an Italian café owner in Llandudno." DI Bragg ran his fingers through his close-cropped hair. "What on earth could they have in common?"

"That's what you blokes get paid to find out." DCI Neath grinned.

"Unless it was like you said," Evan suggested. "Missy Rogers threw the gun away when she was out walking her dog. Then the second gunman found it in the bushes."

"And only decided to kill Papa Luigi because he'd fortuitously found a weapon?" Bragg asked scornfully.

"No, I didn't mean that at all." Evan said. "He was planning to kill Luigi anyway, but finding a weapon with bullets still in the cartridge was too good an opportunity. It meant that he couldn't be tracked down by the weapon."

"That's not bad thinking, Evans." DCI Neath nodded as he digested what Evans had said. "But the odds of it happening must be astronomical. The right person was walking down a street at the right time to find a weapon at the very moment he was planning to shoot somebody." He went around the table and pulled out a chair for himself. "That really is the ultimate in coincidence. I'm not saying that I haven't seen such extreme coincidences in my career, but we can't risk working from that starting point. We have to assume that one person is out there with a gun, and he's already shot two people."

"Well one thing, we'll have to let Mrs. Rogers go now, won't we?" Wingate said. "You have to admit she's got the perfect alibi for the second shooting. And I can't see her having a vendetta against a pizza parlor owner ten miles away. What could he have done to her—not put on enough olives?"

"Don't be flippant, Wingate," Bragg snapped. It was clear that this latest development had really thrown him. He'd been like a dog, homing in on its quarry, and now suddenly to be denied was a bitter blow.

"Yes, I rather think you'll have to release Mrs. Rogers," DCI Neath said. "But if I were you, I wouldn't let her know about this second murder yet. At least not until we know what we're dealing with."

They made their way back to the interview room in silence and had Mrs. Rogers brought to them. She looked wary, clearly wanting to find out what this new piece of information might be and how it affected her case.

"Mrs. Rogers," Bragg said slowly, "you'll be pleased to know that you can go home to your dog."

Her face lit up. "You're letting me go? Oh, that is good news. It's been such a strain. First finding Martin like that, and then knowing that you thought I might have done it. I can't believe it's over." She pulled a lace-edged handkerchief out of her sleeve and pressed it to her nose and mouth. "I'm sorry," she murmured. "It's all been so terrible. And my poor dog. I've been so worried."

"One thing before you go, Mrs. Rogers," Bragg said. "Do you eat Italian food?"

"Italian food?" Her eyes registered her surprise. "What an extraordinary question. And the answer is no thank you. Martin was very conservative in his food tastes. Nothing with garlic or olive oil, no strong spices. Strictly a British meat and two-veg man, although he did enjoy the occasional curry."

"So you'd have no reason to visit a pizza parlor in Llandudno?"

"A pizza parlor in Llandudno? What on earth is this about? We very rarely go to Llandudno. The shops there are no better than in Bangor, and it's one of those seaside places with day-trippers. Martin couldn't stand that sort of thing."

"So the name Luigi means nothing to you?"

For a moment her eyes lit up. "Does this mean you've found the man who shot my husband? He was Italian?"

"No, Mrs. Rogers. We haven't found the person who shot your husband, but we may be closer to doing so. And if you could have provided us with any kind of link to a pizza parlor in Llandudno, we'd know better what direction to take."

She spread her hands in a gracious gesture, still clutching her handkerchief in one of them. "There's nothing more I'd like than to help you, Inspector," she said, "but I can't think of any possible link. I'm sure Martin's students eat pizza, of course. It seems to be a mainstay of the student diet these days, doesn't it? But I don't think you'd have got Martin to touch a slice."

Bragg nodded. "Thank you, Mrs. Rogers. You've been very helpful. You're free to go, only please don't leave the area without notifying us. We may need to ask you more questions as this inquiry progresses."

"Thank you, Inspector." She nodded to the officers then left the room.

For a moment there was silence, then Bragg sighed. "Back to square one," he said. "Damn. I was so sure it was the widow. Damn and blast that bloody pizza parlor. Oh well, I suppose we better get down there and see for ourselves."

Papa Luigi's was in a row of shops behind the train station. The others were a laundromat, a corner grocery, Yvette's Beauty Salon, and the Taj Mahal Take-out Curries. It was in the old part of town that had been built in Victorian times and probably seen better days. Now it had a seedy air about it. The larger houses opposite were all divided into flats, and some looked in desperate need of a coat of paint. News of the murder had obviously leaked to the population because there was quite a crowd loitering with interest—boys on dirt bikes, mothers with prams, and some scruffy-looking youths with various facial piercings.

"The couple lived over the shop," Bragg informed the others as they parked on a double yellow line and emerged from the car.

"Then you'd think the wife would have heard the shot," Evan said.

"Yes, you'd have thought so. And so should the people above the other shops." He pointed out several brown-skinned faces peering down from above the curry take-out.

"Perhaps gunfire is so usual in this neighborhood that nobody thinks twice about it," Pritchard ventured.

"This is Wales, boy, not Chicago," Bragg said dryly. "I don't know where you live, but I've yet to find a corner of Wales in which gunfire is a usual occurrence." He looked around at the youths, lounging against a betting shop on the other side of the road. "I'm not saying a place like this won't have its share of drugs and violence and gangs. Hello—" he broke off. "It looks like forensics have beaten us to it this time."

Evan spotted the white police vehicle tucked in behind a delivery van. There was crime scene tape across the front of the shop.

"Let's take a look around first, to get our bearings before we go inside," Bragg said. He led them across the street. The crowd watched with interest. Beside each of the shops there was a front door. The one beside Luigi's was open, presumably leading up to the flat over the shop. The curtains upstairs were closed, however. Bragg led them down the side street to the alley that ran behind the block of shops. It was wide enough to take deliveries, and, indeed, there was a van parked behind the laundromat. Each of the shops had a back door that opened onto the alley. On the far side of the alley was a high wooden fence, concealing the small back gardens of the houses beyond. And the toot of a diesel horn and then the approaching rumble was a reminder that the railway lay just on the other side of those houses.

There was tape across the alleyway. Bragg was about to duck under it when a man in a dark, roll neck sweater stepped out to block him.

"Where do you think you're going?"

"Who the hell are you?" Bragg demanded.

"Police Constable Parry, and this is a crime scene. You need to step away."

"Police Constable Parry, are you? What's this then?" Bragg pointed at the black combat pants and sweater.

"New uniform," Parry said. "Now if you'll just go back the way you came."

Bragg whipped out a warrant card. "I'm Detective Inspector Bragg, son."

"Inspector Mostyn didn't tell me you were coming." The young policeman stood his ground.

"Inspector Mostyn?"

"In charge of this case."

"The hell he is. Wasn't he told we'd be taking over?"

"Taking over?"

"We're the Major Crimes Unit from headquarters. Where is he?"

"In there with the forensic team. Shall I tell him you're here?"

Bragg's ears had turned distinctly red. "What you can do is get out of the bloody way," he said. "Come on, men. Let's get in there. I knew this was going to happen."

He pushed up his sleeves as if he anticipated a real fist fight and stomped down the alley. One by one Evan and the others ducked under the crime scene tape and headed for the back door of the pizza parlor. The door was ajar and in the wall beyond it a good-sized window opened onto the alleyway. An arm was hanging out over the sill.

"At least they haven't moved him yet," Bragg said, and stalked inside.

The back door led to a narrow hallway with stairs going up. On one side an open door led into the restaurant kitchen. One wall was taken up with a pizza oven and a stove top. A stainless steel table ran along the front of the kitchen. The wall above it was open with a glimpse of vinyl-topped tables and chrome chairs beyond. Pots and pans were neatly stacked on shelves. On one of the shelves there was also a small TV set. Nothing out of order in the spotlessly clean room except for the corpse, who was sprawled across a stainless steel food cart in the window, eerily similar to Martin Rogers. Except that this person was nothing like Martin Rogers to look at. He was big, overweight, olive skinned, and balding. Lying there in his grubby white T shirt and white apron, he looked like a beached whale. His head was turned away from them, toward the open window, but one puddle of blood had soaked the T-shirt, while a second had collected on the floor.

There were five other people in the room, three men and one woman, in white coats, who were busily engaged with fluoroscopes, tweezers, and plastic bags, and one man in a raincoat. They looked up as Bragg barged in.

"What's this then, some kind of delegation?" The man in the raincoat came toward them. He was middle aged, with a receding hairline and the beginnings of a paunch.

"Are you Mostyn?" Bragg asked.

"Yes, and who the hell are you?"

"Bragg. Major Crimes Unit from HQ. Obviously they didn't tell you we were coming."

"Obviously they didn't." Mostyn eyed him belligerently.

"Well, no matter. We're here now, and we'll be taking over."

"Is that a fact?" Mostyn asked.

"Weren't you at the meeting the other day? They've established a Major Crimes Division to be deployed in cases like this."

"Yes, so I heard," Mostyn said. "I couldn't make the meeting personally. We had a nasty case of an old woman being beaten up and her handbag stolen. I thought that took precedence over listening to some windbag."

"Well, we've been deployed, and we're here." Bragg said bluntly. For a second the two men faced each other like two dogs, fur bristling. Then Mostyn said, "You'd better get on with it then."

"So let's hear how far you've got," Bragg said. "The call came in when?"

"Three o'clock this morning. The wife noticed that her husband hadn't come to bed. She got up and found him lying here, dead."

"Three o'clock this morning, and we've only just been notified?"

Mostyn shrugged. "Nothing to do with me, boyo. I wasn't told to notify anybody. And I'm not obliged to call for backup unless I need it. They called me, and I got here just after four. Then the doctor came and certified time and cause of death."

"And the time of death was?" Bragg asked. His manner was only just shy of insolent.

"Before midnight."

"Midnight, eh?" Bragg glanced back at Wingate, Evans, and Pritchard, who were standing in the doorway. "Someone must have heard a shot around midnight. Have you ascertained who heard it?"

"It was shots actually." The forensic tech looked up from where he was crouched on the floor. "Three shots fired. One missed altogether and stuck in the wall over there. The victim took one to the chest and one to the forehead."

"So the shooter wasn't quite as tidy as the last one," Bragg said.

"Last one?" Mostyn looked around at the other men.

"This is the second time in three days that a man has been shot dead at an open window, using what seems to be the same weapon."

"Probably was the same weapon, sir." One of the techs looked up from the floor. "The bullets are identical anyway."

"Holy shit," Mostyn commented. "Nobody told me that. Who was the other one?"

"A professor at Bangor University. Big house in Bangor."

"That's odd." Mostyn scratched his head. "What can he have to do with this man?"

"I don't know. What can you tell us about Alessi?"

"Nothing much. This place has been operating since I came on the force here, and that was fifteen yeas ago. Of course, this isn't the best of neighborhoods. We get break-ins, kids selling dope, slashed tires. The kind of things you find in any urban neighborhood with a high unemployment rate. And Mr. Alessi was known to us—the occasional drunk and disorderly, disturbing the peace. Let's just say he was a loud and belligerent drunk, but no real harm in him."

"So no Mafia connections, that kind of thing?"

"I suppose he might have been paying protection money. I know some shops around here have got themselves involved in that kind of thing."

"And he might have got behind with his payments?" Bragg suggested.

"Possible."

"Anybody I should go to talk to about that?"

"Try the local Catholic church," Mostyn said dryly. "They all go to confession, don't they?"

"So there's not a real underworld boss on your turf that you'd know about?"

Mostyn's look was scornful. "This is Llandudno, mate. Nice little seaside resort. We've got our petty crime, the same as anybody, but as for suggesting that the Cosa Nostra is alive and flourishing up here, then that's just bloody nonsense."

"All right. Keep your hair on," Bragg said. "You know as well as I do that sometimes these petty criminals start getting ideas above their station. One of them sees himself as a kingpin, gets a few blokes into a gang, and you've got a full-blown protection racket going."

"Yeah, true enough." Mostyn nodded. "I've seen it. But I think we'd have heard if anything organized was going on around here. In my experience it's only been the ethnic restaurants, Chinese, Vietnamese, targeted by their own people."

"Have you asked the widow?"

"Frankly I couldn't get much out of her. She'd taken a sleeping pill, see. And she was still groggy when we questioned her. Maybe she's woken up by now."

"Right." Bragg rubbed his hands together. "Let's get started, boys." He turned back to the others, still waiting in the doorway. "Mostyn, thanks for your spade work. We'll keep you posted. And you can do something for me."

"Oh yes?"

"You know the criminal element that operates around here. Have a word and see whether Alessi was paying protection money to anyone."

"All right." Mostyn gave a grudging nod. "I can do that, I suppose." He looked around the room at the technicians. "Thanks for your help, boys." And then he pushed past Evans and Pritchard without waiting for them to step aside.

"There go some toes seriously stepped upon," one of the techs muttered.

"What else am I supposed to do?" Bragg asked. "We've been appointed by the Chief Constable and sent out on this case. If he'd been at the meeting, he'd have bloody well known that."

"Oh, I think he knew it all right," Wingate said. "He just wasn't willing to hand over his turf. I expect you'd have felt the same, sir."

"I probably would have." Bragg agreed. "Right. Let's get to work, boys. We're wasting valuable time. The widow first, I think. Come on then."

He led the way out of the kitchen.

Chapter 15

"You want all four of us to be there when you talk to the widow?" Wingate asked, giving Evan a significant glance. Evan suspected that he was used to more autonomy too and was chafing at the bit having to follow Bragg around all day.

"Have you got something better to do, Wingate?" Bragg asked. "Got an appointment to have your nails manicured?"

Evan thought that Wingate remained remarkably calm, considering. "It's just that four of us can't find out anymore than one of us can, and time is of the essence."

"And you'd be doing what?"

"There's a crowd outside. They won't hang around all day. I thought someone should question them to see if anyone noticed anything last night or to find out what the neighborhood buzz is about Alessi. These rumors often have a lot of truth in them, you know."

For a while Bragg studied Jeremy Wingate's elegant profile, then he said, "All right then. Get on with it. I want Evans with me when I talk to the widow. You can take Pritchard."

"Thank you, sir," Wingate said. "Come on, Jim. Let's get cracking."

Evan watched as they stepped back out into the sunlight, then he followed Bragg up the stairs. He was glad that Wingate had voiced his own frustration. Bragg turned back to him. "What he doesn't seem to understand is that it's good to have more than one person in the room. While I'm talking you can notice things—what the room looks like, how she reacts to questions. I've always found it's very useful to have extra men hanging round, apparently doing nothing."

So now Bragg was trying to make him into an ally—two against two. Evan stomped behind him up the stairs.

The door at the top of the stairs was not locked and led to a small, square hallway. Ahead of them was a living room. Evan poked his head in and looked around. Shabby, old fashioned. Carpet that had seen better days. A hand-crocheted afghan thrown across the back of the sofa. A lurid print of an Italian street scene on the wall. A new big-screen TV in one corner. There had been a TV set in the kitchen, too. It was clear where Luigi's priorities lay.

"In here, Evans," Bragg barked a summons. Evan followed him into the adjoining room, which was a front bedroom. The curtains were closed. Only a fringed pink lamp beside the bed was on, illuminating the figure in the bed, but plunging the rest of the room into deep shadow. A woman was lying propped up on pillows, wearing a purple satin robe. She was rounded but not fat, with bleached blonde hair, already showing traces of dark at the roots. She must have been quite a looker in her younger days, Evan thought, but now she'd started to sag. And there were plenty of worry lines too.

"Mrs. Alessi?" Bragg said softly. "May we come in?"

"Oh yes. Of course." She pulled up the covers instinctively as they came in.

"Sorry to trouble you, Mrs. Alessi," Bragg said. "We're police officers from the Major Crimes Unit. I'm Detective Inspector Bragg and this is Detective Constable Evans. We'd like to ask you a few questions if you're up to it."

"Yes, I think I'm all right now," she said. It was hard to pinpoint her by her accent. "I was so zonked out earlier. I've no idea what I said to that other officer. Then I went right back to sleep. Can you believe it? Those bloody pills do that to me."

"How often do you take them?" Bragg asked. He looked around for a chair and found none. "Evans, be a good lad and bring me something to sit on."

"Yes, sir." Evan went through to the unit's tiny kitchen and brought back a lime green plastic-and-chrome kitchen chair. Bragg pulled it up close to the bed and sat.

"There, that's more comfy. Now you were saying about your sleeping pills."

"I've been taking them every night recently. The doctor prescribed them because I was having such trouble sleeping. I haven't been well lately."

"Really, what's been wrong?"

"My nerves," she said. "Luigi said it was the change. I'm getting to that age, you know. He may be right. Doctors don't really have time for you these days, do they? They just hand out prescriptions and want you out of there."

"So he prescribed sleeping pills, did he? How long ago?"

"I've been taking them for about a month," she said.

"And they knock you out until eleven in the morning? That can't be good for you."

"Well, you see I don't take it until I have a cup of cocoa around nine. Then I fall asleep around eleven and usually I wake about nine the next morning. Luigi doesn't like to wake up too early, seeing as he's never done cleaning up downstairs until at least midnight, and then he has to watch some telly to wind down."

"So tell me about last night," Bragg said.

"I took my pill as usual around nine," she said. "I fell asleep soon afterward because there was nothing worth watching on the telly. Then I woke up to go to the loo. I often have to go in the middle of the night. When I got back from the bathroom, I looked at the clock and it was almost three, and Luigi wasn't in bed. He falls asleep watching TV in the living room sometimes, so I went in but he wasn't there. So I went downstairs and the light was off in the kitchen. I switched it on . . . and . . . and he was lying there. I went over to him and saw the blood. Blood all around him. Blood on the floor. My head was still so groggy that I couldn't think straight, but I did manage to call the police."

"What did you think when you saw him lying there with all that blood?" Bragg asked.

"What did I think?" her voice rose dangerously. "That he was dead, of course."

"Did you think he might have killed himself?"

She looked incredulous and then laughed. "Luigi? Kill himself? That man had the biggest ego in Wales. He'd never kill himself. Kill somebody else, yes. He could do that all right."

"He had a violent temper then?" Bragg asked.

"When he'd been drinking."

"Did he ever hit you?"

She paused for a moment. "Yes, once or twice. But that was a long time ago. He's been off the booze lately and much better."

"So he hadn't quarreled with anybody recently? Can you think of anyone who might have had a score to settle with him?"

"Not that I know of," she said. "Most people liked my Luigi. He was a friendly sort. He'd go over to the pub and have a few laughs. It was only when he'd drunk too much and somebody got him riled up that he'd take a swing at them. But they were probably as drunk as he was, and they'd swing right back. That's nothing like shooting someone to death, is it?"

"No, it's not. Your husband wasn't in any sort of trouble, was he, Mrs. Alessi? He was Italian, after all. The word Mafia always springs to mind when you think of Italians."

Evan shot a glance at Bragg. It was just the kind of stupid remark he had come to expect from his new boss. Mrs. Alessi obviously agreed with him because she laughed.

"Mafia? That's the kind of thing you see on the telly, not in real life."

"So you don't know whether he might have been paying protection money on his business?"

"Protection money?" She laughed again. "What's there to protect? This dump? To tell you the truth, we'd both have been glad if somebody burned it down. Then we could have collected the insurance and got out of here. Luigi was talking about retiring. The long hours were getting to both of us. He hardly ever took a day off."

"Did you work in the café too?"

"Not normally. When someone called in sick, I helped out."

"So are you employed somewhere else, Mrs. Alessi?"

"Not recently. I used to be a bookkeeper, years ago, but my health hasn't been too good for some time and it got—difficult."

"Right, let's go back to the beginning," Bragg said. "Are you getting this down, Evans?"

Evan whipped out a notebook. "Right."

"You were born where?"

"Not too far from here. In Rhyl actually."

"You're Welsh then?" Evan asked. Bragg turned to look at him.

"Oh yes. But I don't speak the language. Neither do my parents. The family originally came from around Birmingham, back in the days of the slate mines."

"How did you meet Luigi?" Bragg asked.

"I met him at a dance at the Rhyl pavilion. He'd just come here then, and he didn't speak much English, but he was very good looking and all the girls were fighting over him. I wasn't a bad looker myself. We made a good couple."

"What was he doing in those days?"

"He was working in a hotel, but he had plans to open his own place. Big ideas in those days, of course. A fancy Italian restaurant, white tablecloths, the lot. Always did have big ideas, my husband."

"So what happened to the big ideas?"

"What always happens," she said bitterly. "I got pregnant. We had to get married in a hurry. My folks gave us some money as a wedding present, and we took over this place. Been here ever since."

"You have children then?"

"One child. A daughter. Paulina. She's eighteen now."

"Away at college?"

"She moved out when she was sixteen," Mrs. Alessi said. "She and Luigi didn't get along. She couldn't take his drinking. She went to live with her aunt in Manchester."

"Do you see her often?"

"Not really. We don't get along either. She blames me as much as Luigi for not stopping him."

"Stopping him what?" Bragg asked sharply.

"Drinking."

"So did he ever—attack her?" Bragg asked.

"Of course he didn't. He idolizes that girl. It broke his heart when she moved away."

"We'll need an address to contact her."

"I already gave it to the policeman who was here earlier. She'd want to know about her dad."

"If you can give it to my constable again, it will save time," Bragg said. "And we'll want the names and addresses of your employees here."

"If you wait a few minutes, they'll be arriving for work," she said. "They won't have heard the news yet."

"Right. Evans, go down and warn the constable on guard that any employees are to be sent straight up to me."

Evan went down the stairs and stood outside for a moment, looking at the kitchen window with that arm still hanging out of it. It would have been easy enough to stand in the alley without being seen, get a good angle at the window, watch Luigi moving around inside, and then call him over. And the moment he looked out to see who was calling him—bam. Only this time it was bam, bam, bam. Not such a good shot on this occasion.

Evan made his way around to the front of the building. He had just finished delivering his message to the constable standing duty when Wingate emerged from the hairdresser's shop.

"He's let you out alone, not on a leash?" Wingate said.

"Only to pass on a message to the officer standing guard. Then I've got to go back and stand to attention with my little notepad."

"Bloody twit," Wingate muttered. "Anything come up yet? She hasn't confessed to shooting him, has she?"

"Why do you ask that?"

"Because the Asian family next door say they have some bloody good shouting matches. He's always yelling, they say. Not the best of pals, Luigi and the Asian bloke at the curry place. He said Luigi always had his television blasting away late at night and then complained if they ever played their music. He called Luigi an uncivilized man, a bully and a drunkard who liked to throw his weight around. Of course, being Muslims, they don't drink."

"They're Muslims?" Evan said. "I thought they were Indians."

"They are. Muslims from North India."

"Oh, I see. Did they hear the shots last night?"

"They said Luigi's television was going full blast as usual, and he always keeps that window open because it gets so hot in the kitchen, so if they'd heard anything they would have thought it came from the television."

"But they didn't notice the shots particularly?"

"They were in bed, and the bedroom is at the front."

"Too bad," Evan said. "What did the hairdresser say?"

"She thinks Luigi was charming. An attentive gentleman. But then she doesn't live above the shop. She goes home at five, and she's never seen him drunk."

"So who lives above the shop?"

"Nobody at the moment. It's vacant."

"Someone along this row must have heard something. Or in one of the houses behind."

"They're not likely to have seen anything though," Wingate said. "I've checked the alley. There's no light. They wouldn't have seen much even if they'd looked out of a window at the right time."

The last part of this sentence was drowned out by the toot of a diesel horn and the rumble of another train.

"And if the killer timed it correctly," Evan said as the train passed, "the telly and the train between them would mask most sounds."

"You're right. It wasn't as big a risk as I originally thought. I'm going to see what Pritchard's turned up. I left him to chat to the lads across the street. He's more their age. He's speaks their language, and I don't mean Welsh."

Evan grinned as he headed back to Bragg. He glanced up thoughtfully at the Taj Mahal Take-out. Funny how he hadn't been aware of a Muslim community in Wales and now everywhere he went there seemed to be Muslims involved. He climbed the stairs back to Mrs. Alessi's room.

She was sitting up in bed now, looking distressed and fully awake. Evan thought that ten minutes alone with DI Bragg would have that effect on most people.

"I really don't know what else I can tell you," she said. "He was an ordinary man. He had his ups and his downs; but as for suggesting that he was mixed up with the underworld just because he was Italian, that's just plain silly."

"Someone wanted him dead and carried it out efficiently, Mrs. Alessi," Bragg said. "Very different from getting into a bar brawl."

"I can't really comprehend it." She ran her fingers nervously through her mop of blonde hair. "It doesn't seem real. Like watching a movie. Someone else's life. I expect it will sink in soon enough."

"I'll arrange for a female police officer to be with you, if you like. You shouldn't be alone at a time like this. Have you got a relative or friend living nearby you could call?"

"My parents moved away," she said. "They live on the Isle of Wight now. Nice little bungalow. But I should call my daughter. She may come down to be with me." There was a wistful look in her eyes.

"That's right. Call your daughter. And in the meantime we'll have someone here with you to make you a cup of tea or whatever you need."

"You're very kind," she said. "You will find who did this, won't you?"

"We'll do our best, Mrs. Alessi. If you can tell us everything you know—names of his friends and family. What he did in his spare time."

"Spare time?" She laughed. "When did he ever have spare time. He had Sundays off, and that was it. Most of the time he was so bushed that he'd watch telly and sleep."

"So he had no close friends nearby?"

"Blokes he met at the pub, I suppose. I don't know their names. I never went with him."

She broke off as there were heavy footsteps on the stairs.

"The employees have shown up, Inspector," Pritchard said. "Where do you want me to put them?"

"Take them through to the café, get their names and addresses, and I'll be with them in a minute," Bragg said. "Anything you can tell me about the employees, Mrs. Alessi? Got on well with your husband, did they?"

"Pretty much. The waitress, Mona, has been with us for years. The two boys who help in the kitchen haven't been with us long. Tommy's been here about a year, and the other one, Sean, only a month or so. There's a lot of turnover in the restaurant business. Usually they're looking for something better, or they're students supplementing their income."

"And these two?"

"Yeah, they're both students, I believe. Nice boys, from what I can see. No problems with them, other than the usual. Not always being reliable; not turning up when they have to study for an exam or drank too much the night before."

"Students at the university in Bangor, are they?"

"I believe Sean is. Tommy's just at the local community college."

Bragg looked at Evan. "Right. Let's go and chat with the young men, shall we? I wonder if Sean is studying history." He patted the eiderdown over Mrs. Alessi's legs. "We'll let you rest for a while, Mrs. Alessi. And if you can think of anything else that might be important, you'll know where to find us. There's a constable stationed outside, and the forensic team will be out of your hair soon, I expect."

"And my husband's body?"

"Will be taken to the morgue any moment now."

"That's good because I don't want to see—I couldn't go through. . . ." She shuddered.

"Get some rest," Bragg said. "Evans, why don't you make Mrs. Alessi a cup of tea?"

"I can make my own tea," she said. "I'm not quite an invalid, you know. I'd rather have something to do. I'm not used to being waited on. And I want to call my daughter in private."

"Right. Come on, Evans." Bragg stomped down the stairs.

"You didn't mention the other crime to her," Evan said.

"No. That will come later. My philosophy is to question them in small doses. Make them think they're off the hook, then come back with more."

"You don't suspect her, do you?"

"Not when she was snoring her head off, I suppose," Bragg agreed. "But in my experience people often know more than they want to tell you. Silly little things like owing money or feuding with neighbors. They can all be important."

"Are you going to requisition her phone records?" Evan asked.

"Not a bad idea."

"And the Rogers's too. If we found the same number turning up on both. . . ."

Bragg laughed. "I can't see Mrs. Rogers calling Mrs. Alessi to chat, can you? But it's worth a try. Anything's worth a try at this point."

Bragg and Evan found the three employees were sitting, wide eyed and ashen faced, on the vinyl benches of the café. Mona, the waitress who had been with them since the café opened, was decidedly weepy. "He was such a nice man," she repeated over and over.

All three of them had left well before midnight. They all claimed to get along well with Luigi and couldn't offer any suggestions as to who might have wanted to kill him.

"You do get bad types hanging around here at night sometimes," Mona ventured. "Homeless people, druggies. We're too close to the railway station. You'll probably find it turns out to be some crazed druggie."

"What do you boys think?" Bragg asked.

The boys stared at him and shrugged.

"Don't know what to think," Tommy muttered. "It don't seem real."

"Did you ever see any suspicious types hanging around here?" Bragg asked. "People who might have underworld connections?"

"Crooks, you mean?" Tommy asked.

"I wouldn't know what a crook looked like if I saw one." Sean had a choirboy's face.

"I was wondering if you ever saw your boss meeting with someone who upset him or got him rattled," Bragg went on.

The two boys shook their heads again.

Bragg looked up at Evan. "I think that's all for now, don't you, Evans? We've got their names and addresses in case we want to ask them more questions."

"So I suppose the place won't be opening again for a while?"

Tommy asked. "Now I'll have to find another job with the right sort of hours."

"I was thinking of moving in with friends closer to the uni anyway," Sean said.

"What subject are you reading, Sean?" Evan asked.

Sean blushed. "Theology."

Chapter 16

"I don't know about you blokes, but I could use some coffee," Bragg muttered, as they met in the alleyway outside after interviewing the three employees. "And I don't mean around here. I mean some real coffee."

"Did somebody say coffee?" one of the techs poked his head out of the window. "You wouldn't like to bring us back a cup when you come, would you? I'd murder for a coffee right now."

"Bad choice of words, Tim, given the circumstances," the female tech said. "But I could certainly use one too. We've been here since seven."

"What do you think I am, the bloody maid?" Bragg snapped.

"No sweat to me, mate," Tim said. "If someone brings us back a coffee, then we keep on working. If not, we take a break to get some, and you'll have to wait for our findings."

"Bolshie lot," Bragg said, but he was smiling. "I suppose we can bring back coffees. Evans, I'll leave you in charge of that."

"I hope the responsibility doesn't go to his head," Pritchard muttered, getting a laugh.

"When's this poor bloke going to be moved then?" Bragg asked, pointing at the arm hanging over the windowsill.

"The morgue wagon is on its way now," the female technician said. "And we're almost done in here."

"Like to share what you've found?"

"Only the obvious. He was shot through the window, from about six feet away. The alleyway was dark, the kitchen was light. He'd have been an easy target. As for the killer coming into the building—there are unidentified fingerprints all over the place, but we should know more about them when we've fingerprinted the restaurant staff, which we're going to do next. It doesn't appear to be any kind of break-in. There's money in the till. The kitchen's spotless, as you can see. Nothing disturbed. So we have to conclude that the point was to shoot Alessi."

"Any other shootings in this area that you know of?" Bragg asked.

The two techs looked at each other and shook their heads. "Not that I can remember," Tim said. "To tell you the truth, we don't often get a chance to handle a murder scene, so it's rather exciting."

"Not for him." Bragg tapped the dangling arm. "Right. Milk and sugar for everyone? Take orders, Evans."

Fifteen minutes later they were sitting in the Happy Bean, at the more upscale end of the shopping precinct, between the Gap and Benetton. It was frequented mainly by trendy young people, yuppy mums with toddlers in designer pushchairs, and one elderly couple, looking decidedly uncomfortable with the loud music.

"It might be a good time see what we've got so far," Bragg said. "The widow might have a motive. She admitted he had hit her before now, but supposedly that was when he was drinking and he'd given it up."

"And she does have a good alibi," Evan added. "She's on medication. Strong sleeping pills that knock her out for the night."

"And she definitely took one last night?" Wingate asked.

"Oh yes. Mostyn said he couldn't get much out of her, and I'd say she was still a bit groggy when we first talked to her, wouldn't you, Evans?"

"She wasn't the sharpest," Evan said. "Of course, shock can do that to some people too."

"So how did she conveniently wake up to find him and call the cops if she was lying there doped on pills?" Wingate asked.

"She said she always has to visit the bathroom in the middle of the night. Even though she was half asleep, she noticed he hadn't come to bed and went looking for him."

"So why was she taking sleeping pills?"

"She hasn't been well lately. Something to do with nerves. We'll need to see her doctor about that. Make a note, Evans."

"And did she have any ideas about who might have killed him?" Pritchard asked, seeing Evan frown as he took out his notebook.

"None at all, Bragg replied. Laughed off the idea of any Mafia connections. Laughed at paying protection money. Said they'd both be grateful if the place burned down."

"We'll need to get background information on him—who he knew, what he did in his spare time," Wingate said.

"Mrs. Alessi claims they never had any spare time. He was working until midnight all week and then slept in his armchair watching the telly all Sunday."

"Doesn't sound like much of a life," Wingate muttered.

"What did you find out from the crowd outside, you two?" Bragg asked.

"We couldn't come up with anybody who had heard the shots," Wingate said. "The lads Pritchard spoke to had been at a disco they hold on Friday nights at the pub, and the music is always very loud."

"So if music was spilling out, and a train was going past, we've got a lot of noise competing with the shots," Bragg said.

"All the same it's odd that nobody heard them," Evan said.

"We haven't tried the houses behind yet. That's something we should tackle next. Wingate, why don't you do that? And Pritchard, I've got a special assignment for you. I want you to hang out in the pub this evening and see what you can find out about Alessi. Did he have friends among the regulars at the pub? We know he got into the occasional punchup. Anyone with a grudge? Any particular enemy? Only don't make it too obvious that you're a copper, got it?"

"Right," Pritchard said. "My kind of assignment at last. Spend all evening in a pub. I like it."

"And remember you're on duty. One pint if you must, to look authentic, but that's it."

"That will teach you," Evan joked. "Help you to learn moderation in all things."

"And I've got a job for you tomorrow, Evans," Bragg said. "I'm sending you to church."

Evan grinned at the other men's laughter. "Hey, I've been a good chapel-going man most of my life. Now you want me to switch to church, is it?"

"The local Catholic church," Bragg said. "I don't know what time they have their mass, but take a look and see if there are any other Italians there, and find out if Luigi was a regular attendee."

"Just one thing, sir," Evan said. "We're rushing around, trying to find out if Luigi had quarreled with anyone, but we're overlooking the main fact—he was shot with an identical bullet to the one that killed Martin Rogers. So we have to assume that the same gun fired both those bullets. And we have to assume that the same person was the killer of both men—don't we?"

"I suppose we do." Bragg nodded. "But we still need to keep digging into the lives of both men until we find what the link is, what they have in common."

"That's not going to be easy, is it?" Wingate said. "I mean, look at the contrast in the two houses, and the different sort of lives they led. Where could they possibly have met? Who could possibly have a score to settle with both of them?"

"Maybe both wives hired the same killer to dispose of their husbands," Evan suggested. He had meant it half jokingly, but he saw the others all look up from their cups of coffee.

"You're not trying to say that Mrs. Alessi and Mrs. Rogers planned to hire a hit man together when they were doing the church flowers or having their hair done at the same beauty parlor, are you?" Bragg demanded.

"No, I suppose not," Evan admitted. "I can't think of anything that they'd have in common."

"So you're suggesting coincidentally, then?" Bragg grinned, clearly enjoying baiting Evans. "Two unrelated killings in two days, or do you think he makes his rounds of North Wales once a year and does two for the price of one?"

"Besides, I'm no gun expert, but what we know of the weapon doesn't go along with a hired killer," Wingate said. "An old war souvenir brought back from Japan? The ballistics tech mentioned that those bullets cost a couple of pounds each. Why waste that kind of money? And a hired killer would have an efficient handgun, probably with a silencer."

"Nobody heard the gunshot either time," Pritchard pointed out. "Can a gun like that be equipped with a silencer?"

"It's a weapon, Pritchard. A gun is what you use to shoot grouse on the moors. Do get your terminology right." Bragg drained the last of his coffee. "And in answer to your question, we'll ask the ballistics bloke. Ready to go? We'll have that bolshie lot panting for their coffees."

Evan picked up the tray of coffees and followed the others to the door.

By the end of the afternoon they had interviewed the families who lived in the houses behind the alley. Two couples remembered being woken by something around midnight, but couldn't say whether it was a gunshot or not. One woman did look out of the back bedroom window but said nothing moved in the alleyway that she could see. And there was one old dear who told them it had to be terrorists. "They're everywhere, these days, so they tell us," she said. "I'm sure I saw a dark man in white robes last night. I see them all the time. They're everywhere, you know."

"Batty, and watches too much TV news," Bragg muttered, as they left her.

"I have to confess, I'm stumped." Bragg looked around the empty kitchen, now with the body removed and cleared of blood. "Who the hell would want to shoot a university professor and then an Italian pizzeria owner? Something tells me it has to be a gangland killing—efficient, opportunistic, through a window. I can see that the Italian might have crossed paths with a criminal element but not Professor Rogers. It's like nothing I've ever come across before. I certainly don't want to admit failure on our first case, but I'm not sure where we go from here."

Evan looked at him with new understanding. Beneath the brash exterior obviously lurked a fragile ego.

"In every case I've worked on so far," Evan said cautiously, "the key has been in finding the connection."

"Thank you, Sherlock Holmes," Bragg said dryly. "What the hell do you think we're trying to do?"

Evan's new-felt sympathy and understanding vanished as quickly as they had come. "I just meant that we have to keep on digging. Find out who Alessi was fighting with when he was arraigned for disturbing the peace. Talk to Professor Rogers's colleagues some more. I get the feeling they have more to tell us if we give them time and opportunity."

"I agree with Evans," Wingate said. "There were definitely undercurrents going on there. And there was that student we were told about—the one who felt cheated out of a first. Who knows, maybe he came back here to settle scores."

"With a pizza parlor too?"

"Maybe he was employed here and Luigi gave him a hard time, or even that he used to buy his pizzas here and was shortchanged." Wingate shrugged. "I don't know. It sounds outlandish, but when someone goes off the deep end, they become trigger happy, don't they?"

"Right. So tomorrow we visit the faculty members at home. We attempt to ascertain the whereabouts of that student Simon whatsit and see if he really is abroad. Pritchard can tell us what he picked up at the pub—and it better be nothing in skirts, Pritchard. And Evans can do some praying for us all when he goes to church."

"What about right now, sir?" Pritchard asked.

"Back to HQ to take a look at the records. See what's on Luigi's rap sheet and who he and his wife talked to on the phone. I don't think we can do anymore interviewing today, do you? People don't take kindly to having their Saturday evening disturbed. And I expect you blokes like the occasional Saturday evening at home as well."

With that they were dismissed.

Chapter 17

The road that wound through the village of Llanfair was usually deserted, apart from a woman on her way to the shops, a mother pushing a pram, or a solitary vehicle winding its way up the pass. It was surprisingly full of pedestrians as Evan came down from the cottage to his car on Sunday morning. He wondered for a moment what was going on until a distant church bell reminded him what day it was. This was still a decent, God-fearing community, and everyone was off to the service at Capel Bethel or Capel Beulah, depending on how big a dose of hellfire they wanted. Capel Bethel's minister, Reverend Parry Davies, went in for a more humanistic approach, while Reverend Powell-Jones over at Capel Beulah was still a firm believer in the wages of sin being death and of hellfire waiting for most of his congregation. Since his sermons tended to go on for over an hour as well, repeated in both Welsh and English, his congregation was noticeably smaller.

Evan had just opened his car door when he heard his name called and saw Mrs. Williams, dressed in her Sunday best, black coat and hat, bearing down on him.

"And where are you off to now, Mr. Evans?" she asked.

"To work, I'm afraid," he said. "I'm in the middle of a murder case."

"Criminal just, it is, making you work on the Sabbath," she said. "You should speak to your superiors about it."

"It's the murderers I should speak to," Evan said, smiling, "and ask them to plan better when they're going to kill somebody."

"It's no laughing matter, missing chapel." Mrs. Williams gave him a severe look.

"Actually, I'm on my way to church," Evan said. "A Catholic church."

"Catholic?" Mrs. Williams's hand went to her heart. "That's even worse than not going at all. Praying to idols, that's what it is. What on earth would you be doing that for?"

"Orders, Mrs. W. I've got to spy on some Catholics."

"Oh well, that's all right then." She nodded. "I thought for one awful minute you were thinking of converting. Ever since you had the wedding ceremony in one of those papist kind of churches, and I haven't seen you or Mrs. Evans at chapel recently, I've been worried about you."

"Don't worry about us; we're just fine," Evan said. "And you better get a move on if you don't want to be the last one in."

"That would never do, would it?" she exclaimed, and waddled with great speed up the street to overtake Mair Hopkins.

Evan got into the car and smiled to himself as he drove down the pass. How simple life was around here. People worked all week, went to chapel on Sunday, had an occasional drink in the Red Dragon, and reared their families in peace. Usually he enjoyed his job and looked forward to driving down the pass to work every day. These last few days his job had felt like a burden. He had to honestly admit that he did not enjoy working with DI Bragg. It wasn't just that he was treated as a brainless junior. It was that constant state of tension—Bragg versus the world. He sensed that Bragg was the kind of man destined to put the backs up of all he encountered, and he wondered why, out of all the officers in the North Wales Police force, Bragg had been chosen for this particular assignment. After several years in the mostly pleasant, stress-free company of DI Watkins and WDC Glynis Davis, he found this tension hard to take.

The problem was that the tension was now spilling over into his private life.

"I thought I might take a hike this morning," Bronwen had said, as she poured coffee. "It's so nice and bright now, but they are forecasting another storm for later. I haven't been up the Glydrs for ages."

"I don't want you hiking alone," Evan had said.

Bronwen looked up, surprised. "Oh, you're dictating how I live my life now, are you?"

"There are too many strange people around these days, and it's not as if you'll encounter a lot of other hikers at this time of year. And what if the storm comes in early?"

"So what am I expected to do—sit home with my knitting?" Bronwen demanded, her face pink with anger. "You're never free to come with me, and I enjoy hiking. It gets out the frustration after the work week."

"I know, but . . ." Evan began.

"Then stop fussing over me. I've taken care of myself for most of my life. I hiked alone all the time before I met you, and I intend to continue doing so."

Evan had stomped down the hill feeling anger and frustration of his own. He wasn't being unreasonable. He knew better than anyone that there were crackpots who wandered the hills, and he didn't feel comfortable with Bronwen out on her own. But in his heart he also knew that he'd come across as a dominating husband, and that had put Bronwen's hackles up. He'd have to make it up to her. If he could get home early enough tonight, he'd take her out for a meal.

Evan had rarely been inside a Catholic church, apart from a school trip to Paris, when they had been taken around Notre Dame. And he had never attended a service there. Used to the simplicity and lack of adornment of the chapel, he felt most uncomfortable amid the statues and ritual. It seemed they were constantly standing, sitting, kneeling, and chanting in a way that was impossible to follow, and he was glad he'd taken up position behind a pillar where some particularly bad-tempered saint was scowling down at him. The hymns were unfamiliar and sung without the zest of the usual Welsh congregation. There was incense too, that curled around the pillars and made him want to sneeze.

The church was by no means full. The majority of the congregation was over the age of fifty, but there was a sprinkling of young families. As soon as mass was over, Evan made for the priest, now standing at the front door to shake hands.

It appeared that there was only one Italian family who were regular mass goers, the Salvatores, and they were in their seventies. The priest had only been assigned to this parish for the past two years, and the name Luigi Alessi didn't ring a bell. Not a regular churchgoer then. One item they could cross off their lists.

Reluctantly Evan drove on to police headquarters to meet with the rest of the team. Pritchard hadn't much to report from the night before. Most of the customers at the pub knew Luigi. They could confirm that he was inclined to talk big and get easily riled when he'd had a few, but the general feeling was that there was no real malice in him. Nobody with whom he sparred on a regular basis, anyway. Another item to cross off the list.

"I've got a list of recent phone calls here." DI Bragg waved sheets of paper. "Nothing that stands out as suspicious. Mrs. Alessi called her doctor quite a lot. Mrs. Rogers, on the other hand, hardly made any phone calls at all."

"No numbers in common then?" Evan asked.

"No, they didn't both call the same hired killer, Evans. So you can put that theory out of your mind." Inspector Bragg smirked.

"So where do we go from here?" Wingate asked, with obvious frustration in his voice.

"You have suggestions for things we're not doing and should be, Wingate?" Bragg asked.

"Well, no sir. Finding the link. That's what we've got to do."

"And how do you propose to find it?"

Wingate frowned. "Well, I thought one of us should follow up on Simon Pennington, the student."

"Can I assign that to you, then, since you're so keen?" Bragg said. "I take it you know how to contact Interpol and British embassies and all that kind of stuff you're going to need to find out where in the world he is?"

"I think I could handle it, sir," Wingate answered stonily.

"Then you go for it, son." Bragg looked at Pritchard and Evans. "Any other bright ideas? Any volunteers?"

"I wouldn't mind tackling Dr. Brock again," Evan said.

"Brock?"

"The one they call Badger. He was the one who wasn't surprised that Martin Rogers had been killed. In fact he seemed delighted. Dr. Humphries said he enjoyed baiting Professor Rogers. It might be interesting to get more of his take on things."

"Do that, if you think it's worth doing," Bragg said, with a resigned shrug. "Frankly I have a gut feeling that this has nothing to do with the university. Okay, a faculty member could have shot Rogers, but what connection could any of them have with a pizzeria ten miles away? None of them lives in Llandudno, do they?"

"No, they all live within reach of the university," Evan said. "But something's got to come out eventually. The killer had the habits of the Rogers's household down pat. Exactly when Mrs. Rogers took the dog for the walk. The fact that Martin Rogers sat at the window to have breakfast."

"Ditto for the Alessi murder," Wingate added. "Although it wouldn't be hard to establish that he cleaned the kitchen alone late at night with the TV on loudly. Any one of the neighbors could have told him that."

"I'm going to stay here and take a look at old arrest records," Bragg said. "I want to see where Alessi's name comes up and in what connection. As you say, we have to stumble upon something eventually."

"Bragg is about to throw in the towel," Wingate muttered to Evan as they walked down the hall together. "I get the feeling he's never had to handle a complicated case before. He likes the sort of murder where they catch the bloke red-handed with a smoking gun, and he hands over the weapon saying, 'I shot the bitch. She had it coming to her.'"

Evan chuckled. "It's true that most of us don't come up against a really complicated crime often. Let's hope that you and I can get somewhere on our own. He might eventually come to trust us with a little freedom."

"Dream on, sonny." Wingate chuckled as they reached the exit doors.

Chapter 18

Badger Brock wasn't at home. This wasn't too surprising given that it was a fine Sunday morning, but he lived alone in a modern block of flats and Evan had no way of knowing where to find him. On impulse he drove out to the only place he knew where archeological digging was going on. It was the site of a Roman camp on the other side of Caernarfon, and he was rewarded by spotting a solitary figure, long, dark hair blowing out wildly in the wind, picking his way through the puddles. Evan parked, climbed over the barrier, and went to join him.

"Hey, you're not allowed in here. Didn't you read the signs?" Brock shouted as Evan approached, then recognized who it was. "Oh it's you. How did you know I was here?"

"I'm a detective," Evan said. "It's my job to find what I need to know. And right now I need to talk to you about Martin Rogers."

"I thought I'd told you everything I knew the other day." Brock sounded annoyed. He picked up a piece of plastic sheeting. "The storm the other day blew off the tarpaulin. The students couldn't have secured it well enough. Now God knows what the rainwater's washed away."

Evan looked down at the square pit, with a couple of inches of water sitting at the bottom.

"So this was a Roman camp?" he asked.

"Absolutely. They used this as a staging area for the final assault on Anglesey."

"I never knew any of this existed when I was a kid," Evan said, squatting to examine the pit, "or I'd have been over here trying to help."

"Keen on archeology are you then?" Brock asked.

"I suppose I am. I've never had the chance to pursue it but I can see myself digging away and being excited at finding a bronze coin or a broken beaker."

Brock nodded. "Yes, it is heady stuff. Most of the time it's boring, routine work, of course. Day after day of sifting through soil, finding maybe a small fragment of pottery, and then one day, bingo—you find something so wonderful that it keeps you going for years. I found a Celtic torque in Ireland once, you know. Fabulous."

His face was alight with joy as he spoke.

"You were not surprised that someone had killed Professor Rogers," Evan said, straightening up again. "You seemed more amused than anything."

Brock flushed. "That's just my way," he said. "When I'm uncomfortable, I joke about it. Actually I was shocked."

"But still not surprised," Evan insisted. "Do you have someone particularly in mind who might have done it?"

"Good Lord, no. No one at all. I mean, Rogers could be a bit of a bastard. He was autocratic. He liked to act like admiral of his own ship. His way or no way at all. He knew little about archeology, and yet he would tell Skinner and me how to do our work and run our classes."

"There are rumors . . ." Evan said slowly, "that he was trying to get rid of you."

"What are you insinuating?" Brock demanded. "That I killed him to keep my job?"

"It's one of the best motives we've come up with so far."

"Then think again, mate," Brock said angrily. "I'm a pacifist. I don't believe in wars. I don't believe in killing. I've attended antiwar rallies. And you should check on your facts—I gather Rogers was killed at eight o'clock in the morning. At that hour I was kneeling in the mud here with half a dozen students to vouch for me."

"I'm sorry," Evan said, "but we have to rule people out to get at the truth. In your case, you've a bloody good alibi, unless you bribed all your students to lie for you." He smiled. "That was just a joke, by the way."

"My students probably would lie for me," Brock said. "They think I'm the greatest. I'm not stuffy like the other professors, you see. I'm quite happy to have a pint with them after we've finished at the dig."

"Not like Professor Rogers, one gathers," Evan said. "The students didn't like him?"

"He's had some nasty blowups with the Student Union, I know that. He was on the site council, so he had the power to veto any activities he didn't like. And he was pretty narrow in his views. No gay/lesbian activities. Nothing religious or inflammatory or controversial. He vetoed a speech by an extremist Muslim cleric last year. That caused a fuss with our Muslim students. Big demonstration. Oh, and he vetoed a piece of artwork he found obscene. He was a bit of a prude. I thought the sculpture was good, personally. And you needed a good imagination to spot that it was a couple having sex."

"How long ago was that?"

"Also last year. This year's been tranquil so far. Of course, students are still finding their feet this first month of classes. There are more freshmen mixers than radical speeches."

"The rest of your History Department," Evan said. "Is there anything you could tell me about them?"

Brock laughed. "There's a lot I could tell you, but none of it would have any relevance to shooting Professor Rogers."

"Gwyneth Humphries, for example?" Evan asked. "She was sweet on Rogers?"

"Clever of you to notice that. Yes, she certainly had a love/hate relationship with him. She had been known to come on strong to him, especially after a couple of glasses of wine."

"And did he respond?"

"Good Lord, no. Like I said, Martin Rogers was a prude. And Mrs. Rogers was always there, hovering in the background."

"So you can't see Gwyneth Humphries being driven mad with desire?"

Brock paused, then laughed. "No, I can't," he said. "And as for shooting somebody—she's so ham-fisted that she'd probably shoot herself in the foot first."

Evan looked around. The breeze off the Irish Sea had picked up. It wouldn't be long before those clouds on the horizon came rushing in. "I'd better leave you to put your tarpaulin back in place," Evan said. "We're due for more rain later."

"When are we not due for more rain?" Brock said. "I've lived in Wales for ten years now, and it rains with monotonous regularity."

"Where did you come from before?" Evan asked.

"Patagonia. I was born in the Welsh community there."

"Good God, were you? I've always wanted to meet someone who'd lived there. Is it true they still speak Welsh?"

"Absolutely," Brock said, switching to that language. "As you can see, I speak the language quite well."

"So we could have had this whole conversation in Welsh rather than English." Evan shook his head. "Well, sometime, when things are not so hectic, I'd really enjoy hearing about your life in Patagonia. It's always fascinated me."

"Right. You know where to find me." Brock picked up the large piece of black plastic, and Evan helped him drag it into place. "Thanks. *Diolch yn fawr,*" he repeated it in Welsh.

Evan could see why the students liked Badger Brock. Interesting what he had said about Martin Rogers and his blowups with the Student Union. If that demonstration over the Muslim cleric had happened this year, Evan could guarantee that Rashid would have been at the forefront of it. Evan wondered if those mates Rashid had found were equally militant.

He drove on toward Bangor, looking wistful as he passed the Caernarfon Police Station, deserted on a calm Sunday. Would he ever be sent back there again, he wondered. He stopped to pick up a hamburger at a McDonald's, which was one of the few businesses that opened on Sundays, and continued on to Dr. Humphries's house.

• • •

She was at home and reacted with surprise as she opened the door to him. She was not wearing scarves today, but what appeared to be a Middle Eastern caftan. Her hair was down around her shoulders, making Evan wonder if this was her dressing gown and she hadn't been up long. She appeared flustered when she saw who was standing outside her door, but she invited him in.

"I didn't expect to see you again," she said. "Has new evidence come to light?"

"Something has come up, actually," Evan said, "and I thought that you probably knew Martin Rogers better than anybody so you might be able to shed some light for me."

"I'll be happy to do what I can." She led him through to a cluttered sitting room. It wasn't messy, just overfull of things, ranging from piles of books and magazines to stuffed teddy bears and photos of Gwyneth around the world.

"You like to travel?" Evan said, taking a seat where directed in a chintz armchair.

"Oh yes, it's my passion," she said. "Every vacation I'm off somewhere. Italy mainly, but I've covered most historic sites in my life."

"I don't think Professor Rogers shared your passion," Evan said. "There are no photographs of pyramids or leaning towers in his house, and his wife said she hadn't seen her sister in Provence in years."

"No, Martin was a stick-in-the-mud," she said. "His books were his travel. He liked his life to be orderly. He liked his food plain. He was not a good candidate for adventures abroad."

"His wife, was she similarly minded?"

"Who knows what Missy might have wanted had she not married Martin," Gwyneth said. "She deferred to him in everything. They ate what Martin wanted, when Martin wanted. I think she worked so hard at making his life perfect that she forgot she was entitled to a life of her own."

"This may seem a rather delicate subject," Evan said carefully, "but was it possible that Professor Rogers had a mistress?"

She stared at him, openmouthed, then she laughed. "Highly unlikely, I should think. When Missy was away, a few weeks ago, he was like little boy lost. He invited himself to my place to eat because he didn't know how to fend for himself. Very much the hangdog without her."

"So Mrs. Rogers went away," Evan said. "She didn't mention that."

"She was probably embarrassed," Gwyneth said. "She went into hospital for a few days. Some feminine complaint that one doesn't talk about."

"Oh, I see. Nothing serious though?"

"Oh no, I don't think so. She was gone a few days and Martin never mentioned it again, so I presume whatever it was went okay." She smoothed back her hair. "Look, I was about to have a glass of sherry, would you like one?"

"I'm on duty, unfortunately, but please don't let me stop you," Evan said. "We should all make the most of our time off. I get so little these days that I've almost forgotten what it's like."

"I know the feeling." She poured a generous amount from a crystal decanter. "See that pile of papers. They have to be marked by tomorrow. I'll probably be up half the night." She resumed her seat, took a long sip, and then looked up suddenly. "So what was this new evidence you've come to see me about?"

Evan phrased it carefully in his own mind. "Did Professor Rogers ever mention any connection to a pizza parlor in Llandudno? Did the name Alessi ever come up? Luigi Alessi?"

"A pizza parlor? Martin loathed pizza. He wouldn't be caught dead near a pizza parlor. When we were working late at a staff meeting and someone suggested sending out for pizza, Martin said over his dead body." She put her hand up to her mouth. "Oh dear. That's not funny anymore, is it?"

"I don't think that anyone killed him because he refused to eat pizza," Evan said.

Gwyneth sighed. "I've been thinking and thinking about who might have done it, and frankly I've drawn a complete blank. I'm sure it had nothing to do with the university—and yet the university was Martin's life. He lived and breathed his work. I hate to admit it, but he was a very good historian and quite a good department head as well."

"So who will take over the department now?" Evan asked.

She flushed bright red. "I hadn't really considered it. I suppose I will, for now. Until they hire someone permanently, that is."

But she had considered it, Evan thought. She had considered it from the moment she heard about Martin Rogers's death.

At the end of another long and fruitless day, Evan finally headed for home. The predicted rain had begun and came at his windscreen in great squalls, almost too much for the wipers to handle. The clouds had come down almost to road level as he passed the lake beyond Llanberis, and the tiers of slate cliffs loomed out of the mist like castle battlements. A whole day's work, and they were no further ahead. Simon Pennington had been located, with relative ease, in Florence, where he had been staying for over a week. The arrest record on Luigi Alessi had shown no activity for several years. Before that only a couple of citations for disturbing the peace, and one on which the police were called out to a domestic dispute. But it seemed Mrs. Alessi was telling the truth that he had cut back on his drinking, and consequently, his bad behavior had improved.

Evan parked the car and slithered up the track to the cottage, which had been completely swallowed into the cloud.

"Bron?" he called, and was immeasurably relieved when she appeared from the kitchen.

"Oh good, you're home," she said. "What nasty weather to be out in. I was worried about you." He came toward her, but she backed away. "I'm not going to hug you until you change your clothes. You're all wet."

"I was thinking of taking you out to dinner," Evan said, "but I suppose I've left it too late and you've started something?"

"It's lamb chops and they could keep," she said, "but in truth it looks and sounds so horrible out there that I think I'd rather stay warm and dry and eat at home."

"We'll go out as soon as I have a day off, I promise," Evan said, hanging his raincoat on the hook by the front door. "Did you get your hike in today before it rained?"

"I did, but I didn't really enjoy it, thanks to you," she said stiffly. "You were acting like such a nervous Nellie that it rubbed off on me. When I was up on the mountainside, miles from anyone, I started to feel uneasy. I remembered that girl who disappeared last summer. So I found myself almost running to get down again. That's just not like me, Evan."

"No, it's not like you, but I can't help wanting to protect you, can I? It's a husband's job."

"Husband's job." Bronwen ruffled his hair. "You are so old-fashioned."

"And it's a wife's job to grill the lamb chops," Evan said, "while the husband finds out if there's still some red wine left in that bottle we opened."

He had just picked up the bottle when there was a thunderous knocking on their front door.

"Who on earth would come up here in this weather?" Bronwen appeared, white faced, from the kitchen as Evan went to the door. "Be careful. Don't open it."

Evan opened the door. "Mr. Khan," he said in surprise. "What's wrong?"

"You know bloody well what's wrong." The Pakistani pushed past him into the living room. Rain had plastered his hair to his face and ran down his raincoat onto the doormat. "Answer me this: What have you done with my daughter?"

Chapter 19

"Your daughter?" Bronwen had come to join Evan in the doorway. "Something's happened to Jamila?"

Mr. Khan came toward her, waving a finger menacingly. "Don't play the innocent with me, missy. You know very well that you put her up to this."

"I'm afraid we're completely in the dark, Mr. Khan," Evan said. "Won't you take off your coat and sit down?"

"I'm not sitting with the people who have turned my daughter against me," Khan said. "She would never have done this if it hadn't been for you."

"Done what?" Bronwen asked. "We haven't seen Jamila all weekend, and we have no idea what she has or hasn't done."

"Run away, of course." Mr. Khan almost spat out the words. "She's gone. Missing. I drove her mother down to the Home Improvement Center to see about rugs for the floor, and when we got back there was no sign of Jamila. We thought she might have disobeyed us and gone to a friend's house. Then it got dark and we started worrying. She would never be out after dark without calling her mummy and daddy first."

"Have you called the police?" Evan asked.

"Aren't you supposed to be a policeman?" Khan demanded, "and yet you are the one behind this. How can I hope for any help from the police when they will all side with you?"

"Please stop shouting, Mr. Khan," Bronwen said. "We're very fond of Jamila. We're as worried as you are. Now what do you think has happened to her?"

"She's run away, of course, because she found out we had plans to arrange a marriage for her."

"If that's true, I can't say I blame her," Bronwen said. "I tried to talk to you the other night, but you weren't prepared to listen to reason."

"It's none of your bloody business what I do with my daughter," Khan said. "This is what is wrong with Western culture, Western women. They get too many ideas. They interfere. They don't believe the husband and father knows best. And now you've got Jamila thinking that way too. She was an obedient little girl before we came here."

"Jamila has been thinking for herself for a long time," Bronwen said. "She was just afraid to express her views to you and her brother. But believe me, the one thing in the world she doesn't want is to marry someone she doesn't know and go and live far away in Pakistan. If you love your daughter at all, you'll listen to what she wants."

"She's a child. A female child. How can she possibly know what is best for her?"

"Now you're sounding like your son," Bronwen said. "This is Wales, where every person has the right to decide for him or herself."

"So you helped her hide from us."

"No, I didn't," Bronwen said. "Although if she'd come to me and asked for my help, I'd probably have given it to her."

"But you must have suggested where she could go. She doesn't know many people yet in this area."

"Have you asked her school friends?" Evan said. "She said she'd already met some nice girls at school."

"I've no idea who they are," he snapped. "Jamila never confided in me."

"But your son followed her to a friend's house once. She told us that he made a scene and dragged her home."

"From a wild party with boys, yes indeed. Rashid cares about his sister. He cares about family. He is trying to live the life of a good Muslim."

"According to Jamila, it wasn't a wild party. They were sitting around talking, getting to know each other the way teenagers do. And your son overreacted, as he did with me the other night."

"Rashid is a young man. Young men sometimes feel a fire burning in their hearts. This is a good thing."

"Just as long as it doesn't consume them," Bronwen said. "So have you checked with the friend's house where Rashid found his sister that time?"

"I haven't, but Rashid did. The girl had not seen Jamila, so she says. Of course she could be lying. One of them could be harboring Jamila."

"What time did she leave today?" Evan asked.

"I don't know. My wife and I went out around eleven."

"And your son?"

"He left soon after. He has found a place to live near the university. He was moving his belongings today. When we arrived back about three, Jamila had gone."

"I know how worried you must feel, Mr. Khan," Evan said, "but I can assure you that neither Bronwen nor I had anything to do with your daughter's disappearance. I was out on a case until ten minutes ago, and Bronwen was hiking in the hills. I'll be happy to call the police for you and instigate a search."

"I just want her back," the older man said in a broken voice. "I just want my daughter home safe." He looked as if he might cry at any second.

Evan put a hand on his shoulder. "Go back to your wife. I'll have the police up here right away. And you'd better take a walking stick to get you down the mountain safely," he added, handing him one from the coat rack.

"Thank you." Mr. Khan was like a deflated balloon. He went away meekly.

Bronwen waited until the door closed and then turned on Evan. "What on earth did you do that for? Call the police for him? Whose side are you on?"

"He is her father, Bronwen."

"Yes, and he's about to ship her abroad and sell her as a slave. Some father."

"She's not legally old enough to be off on her own, and they do have a right to know where she is. What if something has happened to her? When they find her, then we can get social services involved, if that's what Jamila wants."

"She clearly doesn't want to be with her family any longer," Bronwen said. "And who can blame her. With that fanatic of a brother poisoning their minds—" she stopped and put a hand to her mouth. "Oh God, Evan. I've just had the most terrible thought. The brother was alone with her today. And you know what they do in places like Pakistan when a woman disobeys the men in the family? Sometimes they kill her."

"You think Rashid might have killed Jamila? That's absurd, Bron."

"She stood up to him, didn't she? She would have told him that she wasn't going to marry someone in Pakistan. And he's a violent person, Evan. He could easily have lost control and beaten her to death—or equally taken her down to his Muslim friends. If they are as extreme as he, they could have helped in the killing."

"This is all wild supposition, Bronwen," Evan said uneasily. "After all, Rashid was born in the UK. He's been to British schools. He's attending a British university."

"And a fat lot has rubbed off on him," Bronwen snapped. "He's a fanatic, Evan. He's made up his mind and he twists everything to conform with his own narrow views. I think it's highly likely that he could have killed his sister."

"We'll just have to wait and see, won't we?" Evan said. "We can't mention this possibility to the police yet. They'll think we're being racist. If they haven't found her after a day or so, then we'll start to worry."

"I want you to be down there when they question the family,"

Bronwen said. "You're good at observing people. Watch Rashid when they question him. See if you think he had any part in her disappearance."

"All right," Evan said. "I'm making the call now. That probably gives me fifteen minutes to eat supper before they get to the Khan's place. Do you think you could get cracking with those lamb chops?"

Evan put through the call to dispatch, and then he phoned Inspector Watkins at his home.

"I might have known it was you," Watkins said. "Nobody else would dare to disturb me on a Sunday evening, when I've just sat down in front of the telly with a pint of Watneys. I thought we'd finally got rid of you. Don't tell me you've just phoned up to chat?"

"Sorry. I wouldn't have called except it's very urgent," Evan said. "I'd look into it myself, but I'm working on another case, and Bronwen is scared all the facts might not come out. We've just reported a missing minor. Young girl in our village hasn't come home tonight. The parents are frantic."

"How old?"

"Fifteen."

"Well, then. I expect she's just gone off to the pictures with friends and forgot to tell them. You know what teenagers are like—when they're having fun everything else goes out of their heads. Our Tiffany is only eleven, but she's already getting like that. When we tell her what time she has to be home, she just rolls her eyes."

"But this is different," Evan said. "This is a Pakistani family. They've just moved in, and the girl's become friendly with Bronwen. She came to us very upset because she'd found out her family was plotting to take her back to Pakistan to marry her off to some old man she'd never met. So Bronwen went to try and talk to the family. They refused to listen and pretty much drove her out of their house. Now the girl hasn't come home, and they're blaming us."

Watkins sucked in air through his teeth. "So you're saying she'd have a good reason to want to run away?"

"Absolutely. And there's another twist—there is a fanatical brother. Very religious, very extreme. Bronwen's scared that he might have killed her because she disobeyed the men in her family. Either that or he's taken her off somewhere, and he's planning to ship her back to Pakistan right away."

"I see. So what do you want me to do?"

"I was hoping that maybe you'd oversee it yourself and treat it as more than the usual runaway teenager kind of case."

"I'll see what I can do," Watkins said. "What's the address? Have we got squad cars headed up there right now?"

"Yes, they're on their way."

"Then I suppose I'd better join them. Bloody nuisance you are. And I suppose you want to be present too?"

"If I may tonight."

"See you there in half an hour," Watkins said and hung up.

"I'll put Glynis onto it in the morning if the girl hasn't shown up by then," Watkins said, as they walked back to his car together. The interview had not gone well, with Rashid hurling abuse and the two parents alternately accusing and pleading. "Glynis can go to the girl's school and get info out of the classmates more easily than I can. I don't blame the poor kid for running away. He's something else, that Rashid, isn't he?"

"I'm inclined to take Bronwen's suggestion seriously, and I think you should too," Evan said. "I really believe that he is the type who might kill his sister for disobeying him. What makes someone turn extreme like this? He went to a perfectly normal comprehensive school."

Watkins turned up his collar against the driving rain. "Who can say what makes some people into religious fanatics? In his case he probably felt attracted to the Muslim religion because it gives him the superiority he craves and a sense of belonging. It must be hard to live in a country where you are an obvious outsider."

"Turning into quite a psychologist in your old age, I notice," Evan said.

"And no lip from you, boyo," Watkins said. "Just because you're on some elite task force, don't let it go to your head."

"Elite task force." Evan grunted. "You've worked with Bragg before, have you? He's an idiot with no social skills. We have two murders at the moment, and we're getting nowhere."

"I warned you, didn't I? Rumor has it that Bragg couldn't get along with his boss at Central Division, so strings were pulled to have him assigned to this new Major Crimes Unit."

"Is that why I'm there too?" Evan asked. He had meant it to be flippant.

"Possible."

Evan looked at him in surprise. "Thanks a lot."

"Not me, boyo. DCI Hughes. You've made him look like a bit of an idiot before now. Not deliberately, of course, but you know what his ego is like. Anyway, it will be good for your career. And you won't have to spend your days worrying about trivial things like who is selling pot at the Wednesday market."

"About Jamila," Evan said. "Can you put out an APB to the airports to stop her from being taken abroad against her will? I'm sure it's a gray area as far as the law is concerned to stop parents from taking their own child out of the country, but in this case it's so clearly against her welfare, isn't it? And maybe ask the Leeds police to search the area where the Khans used to live, just in case Rashid has taken her back there to the custody of a family friend?"

"Telling me my job again, I see."

"No sir, just making suggestions," Evan said.

Watkins clapped him on the shoulder. "I'll do everything I can. And if she hasn't shown up in a couple of days, then we'll start considering the more serious possibilities and send out the search teams. Does the son have transportation?"

"The family has a van and a car. I presume they'd have taken the van shopping yesterday so the car would have been sitting there for Rashid to use."

"So the search might extend beyond the immediate area then," Watkins said.

"Although I can't see Jamila willingly getting into a car with him."

"If she was alive, you mean."

"Don't let's even think it. It's too horrible. Bronwen's really upset. She's very fond of this girl."

"You sound pretty upset yourself," Watkins said.

"Well, I suppose I am. Nice, bright young girl and now this."

"We'll do what we can," Watkins said. "Ten to one she's hiding out at a friend's house, and it will all turn out okay."

"I hope so." Evan left the inspector getting into his car and walked slowly back up the hill.

Chapter 20

"Evan, do you think I could take your car today?" Bronwen asked, as she poured coffee on Monday morning.

"That would mean you'd have to drive me all the way to Colwyn Bay, and I've no idea what time I'll finish up so I'd have to call you to come and get me."

"I know," she said, "but I really wanted a chance to go to Jamila's school and talk to her friends for myself. I could do that on my lunch hour if I had a car."

"You're taking over from the police now, are you?"

"I just thought that maybe I'd look less threatening to teenage girls. When they find out that I'm Jamila's friend, they may tell me something they'd promised to keep secret from the police."

"That's true enough," Evan said. "It's at times like this that two cars would be useful, wouldn't they?"

"Won't they let you check out a police car at headquarters? You surely don't have to use your own car when you're out on a case."

"Not officially," Evan said. "But if I'm in a squad car, it's usually with DI Bragg these days. And if I wanted to slip away and do a little investigating on my own, I'd need transportation."

Bronwen sighed. "Well, then you'd better take the car after all. I can't hold you up on your job. Maybe one of the other teachers would lend me her car during the lunch break. That's the one good thing about this new school so far—I don't have to be in charge of the children during the breaks. I can actually eat my lunch in the quiet of the staff dining room."

Evan thought about this as he made his way down the steep slope to the village. If eating lunch without having to supervise children was the one good thing about her new school, then Bronwen wasn't enjoying herself much. She had hardly complained, but then Evan had been so wrapped up with his own new assignment that he hadn't given her much chance to complain. Getting so upset over the Khans wasn't like her. It had to be her own frustrations coming out. Evan resolved to let her talk about it when they finally had time for a meal together. He felt guilty about taking the car now, but it really would be too awkward to find himself without transportation if he suddenly needed it. He reminded himself that Jamila's case was now in the hands of other officers. He also knew that he would find it hard to stay uninvolved until she was found again.

The village street was just springing to life. Evans-the-Milk's electric milk float hummed pleasantly as he made his way up the street, delivering the morning pints to doorsteps. The sound of children's voices came from the bus stop where they waited for the school bus to take them down to the valley. Some of the older women were already out sweeping and washing their front steps, as women in the village had done since the dawn of time. The younger ones hadn't picked up this habit, much to the dismay of Mrs. Williams and Mair Hopkins. If a house didn't have a spotless front step and polished brass door knocker, what hope was there for tidiness inside?

Evan was about to get into his car when he changed his mind. He knew that Inspector Watkins would have his own people on the job, but Evan couldn't just drive away. He went up to the children at the bus stop.

"Hello, kids," he said, smiling at them. "How's the new school then?"

"Horrible," one boy said. "Not as nice as Miss Price. The teachers are mean."

"It's all right," a little girl said. "They have a lovely art room and a beautiful library full of books. There's more to do."

"More work, you mean," the boy growled.

"Tell me, kids," Evan went on. "You know the new family at the grocer's shop?"

"The Paki's, you mean?"

"Pakistani, Alud," Evan said firmly. "We don't call people nicknames. Did any of you happen to see their daughter yesterday? You know her? About fifteen years old with a long plait down her back?"

They looked at each other, then shook their heads. Nobody had seen her.

Evan then went up the street, stopping the women on their front steps, the younger women and men leaving for work and asking them if they had seen Jamila. They all vaguely knew who Jamila was, but nobody could remember seeing her the day before. Some of them had been to chapel in the morning. After that they'd either been indoors watching football on the telly or out doing the big weekly shop.

Evan wandered on aimlessly, looking up above the village to the top of the pass where the giant Swiss chalet outline of the swank Everest Inn dominated the skyline. He supposed he could ask up there. He could even check out the various hiking trails up Mount Snowdon. If Rashid had taken Jamila somewhere, he'd have had so many choices. There were mountains and deep lakes and pine forests and even mine shafts in the area. Too many places to hide a body if that was what he had in mind. But he'd have to have carried her somewhere, and Jamila would have put up a good fight, Evan was sure. She wouldn't have left the house willingly with Rashid. That was his only hope. And if Rashid had killed her first, someone must have seen him loading her body into his car. The villagers of Llanfair didn't usually miss much.

Evan paused as he reached the two chapels at the top of the village. As usual there was a biblical text on each of their billboards. Although he was now in a hurry, Evan couldn't help glancing at Capel Bethel. The text read: "Honor thy father and mother, that thy days may be long in the land of the living." Expectantly he turned to Capel Beulah and was not disappointed. Their quotation was, "For I have come to set a man against his father and a daughter against her mother. Matthew 10, 35." Thus did the ministers of Capel Bethel and Capel Beulah wage polite and Christian warfare. Only this time Evan didn't smile. He knew they couldn't know about Jamila, but the text was too close to home.

Evan got into his car and drove away. When he came to the junction at the bottom of the pass, with the A55 going to Caernarfon in one direction and toward Colwyn Bay, Chester, and England in the other, Evan changed his mind at the last second and put his foot down, heading toward Caernarfon. He parked in the police station lot and sprinted toward the building.

"Any news yet on the missing girl?" he asked the duty sergeant.

"What missing girl is this? First I've heard of it," the sergeant replied.

"I reported her missing last night. We had men up at their place in Llanfair. Jamila Khan."

"Sounds like a good Welsh name," the sergeant commented. "I've not heard anything about it."

"Is DI Watkins in yet? Or DC Davies?"

"I've not seen either of them. They may be out on a case."

Of course, Evan thought. They'd probably be at Jamila's school, interviewing the students about her, seeing if she was going to show up there this morning. And he felt annoyed that he had to report to headquarters and not be able to join them. All the way down the A55 he was plagued with doubt. Why hadn't the duty sergeant heard anything about the missing girl? Were they going to consider this like they would any other runaway teen—in which case Jamila wouldn't be considered a runaway for at least twenty-four hours. Evan had a sinking feeling that even though it was Watkins and Glynis, they might not do enough, and it occurred to him to ask Bragg for permission to help look for Jamila.

That morning Mrs. Williams tucked her basket over her arm and made her way up the street to the shops. It was true that the new grocer's prices couldn't compete with Tesco's or Safeway's, but by the time you added in the cost of a busfare and the added annoyance of waiting for buses, she was definitely prepared to spend a few pennies more at the local store. She had felt rather strange about dealing with such different people, but both Mr. and Mrs. Khan seemed polite and helpful.

So she was annoyed to find the CLOSED sign hanging in the window at ten minutes past nine. Shopkeepers weren't supposed to oversleep. She went up to the door and tapped on it. By this time she had been joined by several other women.

"Well, that's not much good," Elsie Davies muttered. "Open for a couple of weeks and then closed again."

"Perhaps it's some kind of religious holiday," Mair Hopkins suggested.

"If they are going to close on all sorts of strange religious holidays, I'm taking my custom elsewhere," Elsie Davies said.

"I thought maybe they just overslept," Mrs. Williams said.

"Bang on the door again."

She stepped forward and banged, more forcefully this time. There was no sign of life, either in the shop or the flat above.

"That's the trouble with foreigners. They're just not reliable," Elsie Davies said, "and me needing eggs to make a Yorkshire pudding tonight. Now I'll have to take the bus down the hill after all."

One by one they trickled back to their homes.

The Monday morning traffic was bad between Caernarfon and Colwyn Bay. The A55 was choked, with lorries from the Irish ferries added to the local delivery vans. Evan had to sprint across the car park and up the stairs at headqarters. Even so he came into the room to find he was the last one to arrive.

"We've got the ballistics report," Bragg was saying, as Evan opened the door. "Oh, you've chosen to grace us with your presence, have you, Evans?"

"Sorry, sir. The traffic was terrible." Evan pulled up a chair beside Pritchard. "It's a long drive, you know."

"Then plan accordingly. Leave at the crack of dawn if you have to. It's all right today; you haven't missed anything." He waved the piece of paper again. "The ballistics report. Three bullets were fired from the same weapon as in the Rogers's case. No obvious fingerprints that we can't identify in that kitchen. Restaurant staff all check out okay. So somebody please tell me where the hell we go from here?"

"It seems to me that the only link we've got between the two homicides at the moment is the gun," Evan said. "Two men killed with the same weapon. That's important."

"We know it's bloody important, Evans," Bragg snapped.

"Hold on a second," Evan continued. "You say the weapon was probably Japanese from WWII. There must be collectors who deal with such things. Maybe this is a rarity, and the person would have had to buy specialized bullets only from a certain dealer. Maybe he's had it serviced recently to make sure it still fires."

"That's not a bad thought, Evans," Bragg agreed. "Can I put you onto that? How are you with computers?"

"Slow, and not very comfortable," Evan said. "We had one officer who was a computer whiz, and we let her handle all the complicated stuff."

"Glynis Davies, you mean?" Pritchard said. "Yes, we've heard about her. Not a bad looker either. Is she seeing someone at the moment?"

"Pritchard, I'm not running a dating service here," Bragg snapped. "Whether Detective Constable Davies is or is not a whiz with computers has no relevance. Nor whether she's dating someone. We've got two homicides, two men shot with the same gun, and no leads at all. We're going to look like bloody fools when I have to make a report to the powers that be."

"Sorry, sir," Pritchard said. "We're all doing our best, you know. We want this new unit to succeed as much as you do. We're all putting up with ragging from our old units about being selected for this detail. We'd never hear the last of it if we had to call for backup."

"He's right," Wingate said. 'It's not a comfortable position to be in."

"Tell me about it," Bragg said. "If I had a pound for the number of times somebody asked why they had selected me of all people, I'd be able to retire tomorrow."

"Then we have to prove them wrong," Wingate said.

“Right.” Bragg sat up, suddenly alert. “Evans, you’re doing the gun search.”

“Don’t you mean weapon, sir?” Pritchard asked sweetly.

“Pritchard, you’re asking to be kicked off this team,” Bragg said, “but maybe that’s what you’re angling for. Maybe I’m just not working you hard enough. I want everything you can come up with on protection rackets within a ten-mile radius of that pizza parlor. Wingate, I want reports on any crime involving a weapon on the north coast within the past five years. If someone’s owned that gun since World War II, then it’s quite possible they’ve used it before.”

“Right, sir.” All three men rose to their feet. Bragg stayed sitting at the table until they had gone out.

“Grasping at straws, I’d say,” Pritchard muttered. “Anything to keep us busy.”

“It’s not as if we have better ideas,” Wingate said. “And frankly I’d rather be busy on my own than sitting at a table with him.”

Evan went off in search of the computer room, hoping he might run into a kind and able young girl who would whisk him through Internet searches. He didn’t. There were two other officers staring at computer screens when he entered, both fully engrossed in their own tasks. Evan chose a machine and prayed that he wouldn’t crash the whole system. After an hour he was feeling discouraged. The pistol had turned out to be more common than they thought. Almost every dealer could get his hands on one. Most of them were merely curios these days and had been disabled. Not too many people actually fired them, Evan was told. The bullets were just too expensive.

Evan jotted down names of dealers who had sold bullets for that particular pistol recently. One to a member of a gun club in greater London. One to a collector in Newport, South Wales. Both men licensed. And Newport was close enough to be promising. Evan was about to follow up when Wingate’s head came around the computer room door.

“Bragg wants you on the double,” he hissed.

“What now? Has he actually turned up something?” Evan hastened to his feet.

“More than that,” Wingate said. “There’s been another murder.”

Chapter 21

Bragg was waiting impatiently, standing beside the table in the office where they had previously met.

"Right, lads. In the car," he barked. "I'll explain as we drive."

They followed him down the stairs at a great rate and out into a waiting squad car.

"Another homicide, sir?" Wingate asked. "Similar modus operandi?"

"Do we always have to have your public school education thrust down our throats, Wingate?" Bragg said wearily. "As to whether the crime had the same trademarks, I can't tell you yet. For once the call has just come in, and we were on the spot. A young woman called Megan Owens. Lives on one of those new housing estates outside Rhyl. She arrived home from doing the shopping to find her husband lying in a pool of blood. We've got the doctor and forensics both on their way, and hopefully we'll get there first this time. Put your foot down, Evans."

Evan obeyed, feeling the rush of excitement that was always present when he was on his way to a crime. Rhyl was one of the string of seaside towns that straggled the North Wales coastline. It had long been popular with budget holidaymakers, filling the entertainment needs of the workers in Manchester and Liverpool with arcades, dodgems, splash pools, and dances at the Rhyl pavilion. It lacked the faded charm of the Llandudno esplanade or the historical majesty of Conwy and Caernarfon. On this cloudy autumn morning the effect was just plain dreary, as Evan drove past factories, warehouses, and plenty of newly built housing developments. It was on the grandly named Prince of Wales Crescent in one of these new housing estates that the Owens lived. A modest, two-story semidetached home, flat fronted, made of yellow brick and wood facing, just like the one next to it and the rest of the street.

A squad car from the local police station was already outside, and the crime scene had already been secured. The fresh-faced female constable standing guard looked green around the gills. She'd probably had a peek at what lay inside, Evan thought.

"Is anyone with the widow?" Bragg asked.

"Yes, Sergeant Hopkins," she said. Then timidly, "Excuse me, sir, but who are you?"

"DI Bragg. The senior officer assigned to this case," he said. "Do you need to check my warrant card?"

"Oh no, sir. I saw you arrive in a police car," she said.

"Make sure you keep everyone well away. We don't want any gawkers. And don't let any reporters anywhere near the house. Tell them there will be a statement later," Bragg said. "Come on, you lot. Let's go and see what we've got here."

They walked up the front path beside a sad-looking lawn. Gardening was clearly not the hobby of the occupants here. Bragg pushed the front door open and went in. The kitchen door ahead of them was open and they spotted the back of a man in blue uniform. He turned when he heard them.

"Are you the blokes in charge? I'm glad you've got here. It's been giving me thc creeps being in the house with him."

"DI Bragg," the detective introduced himself. "Let's take a look at what we've got."

"From what it appears, sir," the sergeant began, "I'd guess that somebody shot him through the open window."

"You haven't moved him or touched anything, have you?" Bragg barked.

"Oh no, sir. He was so clearly dead when I got here. I don't know whether his wife tried to move him. I was just using my powers of observation."

"Quite correctly, as it turns out," Bragg said. "Now be a good lad and wait for the doctor and forensics to get here while we have a look. There's not enough room to swing a cat in here."

He went through into a tiny box of a kitchen. It was neatly designed with built-in cabinets down one wall, cooker and sink along another. Squeezed in by the window was the smallest of dinette tables with two chairs. It was across this table that the body was sprawled. Evan could see that he was wearing a dark green T-shirt and jeans. He was still half sitting on one of the chairs, which had obviously stopped him from sliding down to the floor. Blood had spattered everywhere, spattering those new white cabinets and even the ceiling above.

"I'd say this one was shot at closer range, wouldn't you?" Bragg remarked, stepping nearer gingerly. "Literally blew his brains out."

"Maybe you should wait for the tech boys to get here, sir," Wingate suggested. "You could be disturbing the blood-spatter patterns."

"I know what I'm doing, Wingate," Bragg said, but he retreated to the hallway.

"The back window's still open this time," he said. "Let's go and take a look outside. Not the back door, Pritchard," he bawled, army fashion. "We don't want to disturb any evidence, do we? We'll approach from the front."

They went back through the front door, around to the right side of the house. On this side there was a narrow concrete driveway, leading to one of those free-standing prefab garages. A Ford Festiva was parked in front of the garage. A side gate, between the house and garage, led through to the back garden. The gate was open and Bragg led them through this way. It opened onto a narrow concrete area with the house on one side of it and the garage on the other. Some straggly bushes had been planted in front of the garage, in an attempt to disguise what was a very ugly building.

It appeared that Megan Owens had carried her groceries through this way from the car directly into the kitchen. This was confirmed as they saw several shopping bags lying on the step outside the kitchen door. She had put down her bags to open the back door, then seen what lay inside and forgotten about them. Bragg stepped around them.

"Another easy target," he said. "You could stand between the bushes and the garage and not be seen, then step out and take a clear shot through that window."

Evan looked around the back garden. It was quite long and narrow, with nothing more than some more straggly bushes, a patch of lawn, and a clothesline. It backed onto a similar garden belonging to the house behind. The gunman would have been well hidden, standing between house and garage. Evan wasn't even sure if anyone would have seen anything from an adjacent upstairs window.

"Do you want me to go and see if anyone is home in the houses on either side?" Evan asked. "They might have had the only view of the shooting. The gunman would have been pretty well hidden between the house and garage, wouldn't he?"

"Let's talk to the widow first and see what she's got to say," Bragg said. "Come on. Back inside before we mess up any footprints."

Like a row of ducklings, Evan thought again. As they came around to the front of the house the police doctor was just getting out of his car.

"This is getting to be a habit," he said dryly. "Nasty business. We're dealing with a wacko—a really sick mind, if you ask me."

"Take the doctor through to the kitchen and stay with him, Wingate," Bragg said. "Pritchard, you go and see if the neighbors are home and whether they heard or saw anything. Evans, come with me. I take it the wife's upstairs in her bedroom?"

This was directed at the sergeant, who still hung about awkwardly in the hallway.

"Yes, sir. I would have stayed with her, but she didn't want me there."

"Didn't want you there? Good God, man, it's not what they want. What if she tries to commit suicide from grief and shock?"

"Sorry, sir. I just thought . . ." the sergeant began but Bragg had already pushed past him, taking the stairs two at a time.

The bedroom was just big enough to fit in a double bed and a chest of drawers. Luckily there was a built-in wardrobe down one wall; there would have been no space for a freestanding one. The bedroom furniture was white and looked like the Scandinavian type you assemble yourself, but an attempt had been made to make the room pretty with a lilac duvet cover and flowery curtains. Megan Owens had been sitting on the edge of the bed and jumped up as she heard them. Evan got a shock when he saw how extremely young she was. Hardly more than a teenager. She was wearing jeans and a Gap sweatshirt. Her face was free of makeup, and she could still easily ride for half fare on the busses if she'd wanted to. A pretty little thing too—small elfin face and dark hair pulled back into a ponytail. She was ashen white, and she clearly had been crying.

"I'm Detective Inspector Bragg, North Wales Police, Major Crimes Unit," Bragg said quietly. "This is Detective Constable Evans. Do you feel up to answering a few questions? We want to get to the truth here, don't we? For his sake."

She nodded without speaking.

"All right. Sit down, or lie down if you feel more comfortable. Now take us through the morning until you came home and found your husband's body. Every little thing you can remember. You got up when?"

"I got up around seven thirty," she said. "I made some tea. Did some housework. Put a load in the washing machine."

"And your husband? What's his name, by the way?"

"Terry. Terrance William Owens like his dad." She gulped back a sob as she said the words.

"What time did Terry get up?"

"About nine thirty, maybe."

"Was he on a late shift?"

"No, he was unemployed, and it was really getting to him. He couldn't be bothered to do anything, not even get up in the mornings."

"So he got up at nine thirty."

"Maybe a little later. I told him I was going out shopping because we were out of milk and eggs, and he got a bit upset about there being no eggs because he wanted an egg for breakfast. But I told him he'd just have to have cornflakes or wait until I got back from the shops. He got upset really easily recently. It was the stress of being out of work, you know. It's not good for a man."

"So you went to the shops and came back when?"

"I didn't exactly look at the time, but I was as quick as possible, so that he could have his egg for breakfast, if he still wanted one. I was probably gone forty-five minutes. Not more than an hour. I came in through the side gate, put down the bags so that I could open the back door. Then as I opened it I saw Terry out of the corner of my eye and then I looked at the wall and there was red on it, and I couldn't think what it was. I thought he'd been throwing jam around . . . and then, and then I realized and I just started screaming and screaming. I couldn't make my fingers push the buttons on the phone." Her voice had been rising as she spoke and suddenly she was racked with great shuddering sobs. "He killed himself, didn't he? He shot himself. He blew his own brains out because he was so depressed. I should have done something. I should have noticed and stopped him."

Evan went over and sat on the bed beside her. "There was nothing you could have done, Mrs. Owens," he said gently, patting her hand.

"And I don't think that your husband shot himself," Bragg added. "It's more probable that somebody shot him from outside the kitchen window."

She took her hands away from her tear-stained face. "What? Who'd want to shoot Terry? That's stupid."

"This is the third such case within a week," Bragg said. "All shot in the same manner. When our forensic team gets here, they can tell us whether the same weapon was used as the other two."

"But why?" she asked. "Why would anyone do that? Is there a madman on the loose?"

"Possibly," Bragg said. "We're still trying to piece the puzzle together. Maybe you can help us. Your husband had been unemployed for how long?"

"Six months."

"And what did he do before that?"

"He worked at an assembly plant near Chester. It closed last year."

"So he hadn't been able to find another job since?" Bragg asked. "He didn't think of taking a job in fast food or something like that?"

"He had his pride, Terry did. He was a trained machinist. Besides, he made as much from the dole as he'd have got serving hamburgers."

"What about you, do you work?"

"I used to," she said. "I was a receptionist at a solicitor's office. It was a nice place to work. I liked it."

"So why did you leave?"

She looked down, studying her hands. "It was bad timing," she said, "but I got pregnant, and I wasn't feeling very well. So Terry said it would be best if I quit." There was a long pause. "Then I had a miscarriage, and I was in hospital," she said. "That was just over a month ago. I told him I'd have to go out looking for a job because one of us needed to be working, but so far I havn't found anything."

Evan looked at her with pity. She looked so young and innocent, and yet she had been through so much recently. "Do you have friends or relatives nearby you can go to?" he asked.

"My mum doesn't live far away," she said.

"That's good, isn't it?" Bragg said. "You can call her to come and get you then."

"I suppose so." She sounded unsure.

"You don't get on well with your mum?" Evan asked.

She shrugged. "She didn't like Terry. There was always a scene when we went over there, so Terry didn't like me going. She thought he was lazy for not getting a job."

"Why didn't she like Terry?" Evan asked.

"They never hit it off from the start. Terry could be—prejudiced, you know. My mum is overweight. He couldn't stand overweight people. He used to say just looking at her made him sick."

"Was Terry prejudiced about other things too?"

"Yeah. He and his mates—they were always bad-mouthing other races, you know. They blamed immigrants for coming here taking jobs away from local men."

"Did he get into any fights about this? He wasn't a skinhead or anything was he?" Bragg asked.

"Oh no, nothing like that. They got into a few shouting matches down the pub, and he got upset when he saw immigrant families moving in around here. He used to tell terrible jokes. When I tried to stop him, he'd say it was only in fun and I had no sense of humor."

"Can you think of anyone who might have been angry enough with your husband to want to kill him?"

"My mum," she said instantly, then laughed. "But she'd never be able to shoot anybody. You should see how crooked she throws darts. And where would she find a gun?"

"What about the neighbors?" Bragg asked. "Did Terry get on all right with them?"

"We don't see much of them on either side," she said. "The Smiths have got two little kids and they both work, so they're gone early in the mornings, and all weekends it's football and gymnastics and that kind of thing."

"And the other side?"

"They're a snooty couple. Hardly say two words when you pass them. I think they're both supposed to be very brainy. She's a librarian, I know that, and he's in some kind of research. Not our kind at all."

"Mrs. Owens," Bragg said quietly, "I want you to think back to when you went out this morning. Did you notice anything unusual on your street? Any strange cars parked; anybody standing around watching?"

Megan Owens screwed up her face in concentration. "No," she said. "The street was deserted, except the lady who has twins was pushing them in a stroller. She waved when I went past. She seems nice."

"So no strange cars?"

"Wait a minute. There was some kind of van, parked down at the other end of the crescent. TV repair, maybe?"

"What color?" Evan asked.

"Gray? With bright green letters? I'm sorry, I really didn't pay too much attention to it. You don't, do you?"

"And when you returned?" Bragg asked. "Did you see any cars driving away? Anything unusual then?"

"No, but I wasn't paying attention. All I could think of was getting home with those eggs so that Terry wouldn't yell at me."

"He did a lot of yelling, did he?" Evan asked.

"These days. Like I said, he was so stressed that the least little thing upset him. So I tried to make everything run as smoothly as possible."

"Right, Mrs. Owens." Bragg straightened up. "I think that will do for now. Do you want to call your mother and go over to her place? It would probably be best. Just as long as you give us the address and phone number so that we know where to find you."

She nodded passively. "All right. I'll phone her," she said, chewing on her lip like a small child. "I'll come down. The phone's in the front hall."

Chapter 22

"What do you think, lads?" Bragg asked, as they regrouped back at headquarters with a cup of coffee and a sandwich. It was from the canteen this time, pale gray liquid that could be described at best as sweet and hot. "Three murders in one week. As far as we can tell, all three victims shot with the same weapon. Is it possible that we're dealing with a serial killer?"

"If so, it's an odd kind of serial killer," Wingate said. "Not the sort of person we hear about usually."

"Why is that, Wingate?"

"I don't think I've ever come across a serial killer who targets men, for one thing," Wingate said. "I mean a true serial killer, not a hit man who kills who he's paid to kill. Don't they always kill women? Like a sexual fantasy?"

"Not necessarily," Evan said. "Remember that bloke in America? He lured young gay men to his place and then killed them. What was his name? Dahlmer?"

Bragg's eyes lit up with interest. "Is that the connection, do you think? That all of these men were secretly gay?"

The four men stared at each other, digesting this suggestion.

Evan opened his mouth to say that this theory was ridiculous. Luckily Wingate voiced it first.

"It would have to be very secretly gay," Wingate said, "because there's been no hint of it from anyone we've talked to."

"Well, in the case of Martin Rogers, he had his reputation to consider, didn't he? And both Luigi Alessi and Terry Owens were blustering types who came across as one of the lads." Bragg slapped his hand on the table. "Right, so we've got a new line of inquiry. Wingate—gay bars, gay clubs in the area. List of members. Take photos with you—see if anyone recognizes any of our three victims."

"I wouldn't mind going back to the university again," Evan said. "We've got three men on that faculty who are unmarried. There's just a possibility that one of them is that way inclined and could have had a relationship with Professor Rogers."

"Just because a young man is unmarried, doesn't mean he's gay, Evans," Bragg said. "Look at Wingate and Pritchard here, healthy, red-blooded males, the two of them. Even I am not married. I can assure you there is nothing queer about me!"

"I wasn't hinting that they were necessarily that way," Evan said, feeling his hackles rising. "It just occurred to me that if one of them were gay, then they'd know whether Martin Rogers also had those sort of tendencies."

"Worth a try, I suppose," Bragg said. "God knows, anything is worth a try at the moment. You want to tackle that then? Think you can be tactful enough?"

More tactful than you, Evan thought. "I think so, sir," he said.

"So let me get this straight," Wingate said. "These weren't in any way killings done by somebody with a lust to kill. That sort of killer takes his time, enjoys his victim's panic. Shooting through an open window is an impersonal way to kill. Almost execution style. So I'm wondering if we're looking for someone who targets gay men because he abhors homosexuals? A righteous and overly moral crackpot?"

"That's possible too. Ex-military type, still has a Japanese pistol from the war." Bragg nodded.

"In which case," Wingate continued, "that type writes letters to newspapers and may well have made a nuisance of himself before.

He may have tried to get a gay club shut down. Someone should check through newspaper files."

"Job for you then, Pritchard," Bragg said. "But I have to tell you, in my gut, I don't feel this is heading in the right direction. Martin Rogers—yes, I suppose he could have been a closet gay. But the other two--don't seem the type. Terry Owens is newly married. Why get married? You don't have to be secret about sexual preferences these days. Why not be openly gay?"

"And Megan Owens was recently pregnant," Pritchard chimed in, "so that shows he was doing his stuff."

"Unless he wasn't the daddy," Wingate said.

Bragg chuckled. "Assuming he was. That pretty much rules him out, in my opinion."

"So you don't want us to check out these things after all?" Wingate asked, with a touch of annoyance.

Bragg shrugged. "Might as well. It's not as if we've got a stronger lead or a stronger connection between the three. We should follow up on that TV repair van that was parked nearby, I suppose. I'll do that. And I think I'll go and have a chat with Megan's mum. She'd probably love to dish any dirt she has on Terry. Meet me back here at two thirty. We should have forensic reports by then."

Evan hurried in the direction of the car park. If he got through his interviews at the university quickly enough, then there was nothing to stop him from checking in with Watkins and seeing how the search for Jamila was proceeding. He had scarcely driven out of the car park when his cell phone rang. He answered it, praying it wasn't Bragg, having changed his mind and wanting Evan to be his page boy again.

"Evan, it's me," said Bronwen's soft melodious voice into his ear. "Sorry to ring you when you're working but this is important. I did borrow a car and go to Jamila's school at lunchtime. I spoke with several of her friends, and they are all extremely worried about her. Apparently she actually told one of the girls that her brother had threatened to kill her if she ever tainted the honor of the family. Would you let Inspector Watkins know this?"

"I will. I'll go over there right away," Evan said.

"I'm so worried about her, Evan," she said. "I can't think straight. It's torture sitting in a classroom when I want to be out looking for her."

"I feel the same way, love. But we both have jobs we have to do."

"I just feel there would be a better chance of finding her quickly if you were on the case."

"Come on, Bron." Evan laughed uneasily. "You know Watkins is a good man. And Glynis Davies is top-notch. If they're on the case, they'll be doing their best."

"But what if their best isn't good enough?" Evan heard the catch in her voice.

"I'm on my way to speak to them right now. Don't worry. I'll make sure they're doing everything possible. See you tonight then. I've no idea what time."

Instead of turning off to the university, Evan put his foot down and kept going. There was no sign of DI Watkins, but Glynis was just coming into the police station front door as Evan was leaving.

"Hello, what are you doing here, stranger?" She gave him her dazzling smile.

"Came to check on you, actually," Evan said. "I wanted to know what news there was on Jamila."

Glynis's face grew serious again. "Nothing yet, I'm afraid. We've had the parents bugging us all morning. I went to her school first thing, and nobody there knows where she might have gone. We've got the Leeds Police asking around her old neighborhood, in case she's gone back there. We've shown her picture at the railway station and on the buses, and so far no luck."

"All of these are presupposing she's run away," Evan said.

"What do you mean? Of course she's run away."

Evan shook his head. "Bronwen says that Jamila's school friends agree with her, that Jamila's brother may have killed her because she disobeyed her family and besmirched their honor."

"Oh surely not?" Glynis smiled. "That's a bit extreme, isn't it?"

"Shipping someone off to Pakistan to marry a man twice her age is extreme too, wouldn't you say?"

"Yes, I suppose it is."

"And if you haven't met her brother yet, he's an aggressive and violent type. Quite capable of killing, I should think."

"Inspector Watkins said he was impossible," she said. "He went to interview him again this morning and came back foaming at the mouth."

"Rashid is anti-everything to do with Western culture," Evan said. "He's a bit of a religious fanatic. Did they search his digs this morning?"

"Not that I know of."

"He could have her imprisoned there, if she's not already dead," Evan said.

"Evan, aren't you maybe overreacting a little?" Glynis asked. "My guess would be that one of her friends is hiding her and just not telling us. I'll go and speak to their families tonight. I'll let them know that I'm a friend they can trust. I'll promise not to hand her over to her family if that's not what she wants."

"I hope to God you're right." Evan paced uneasily. "Do you happen to have Rashid's new address?"

"Are you thinking of visiting him yourself?"

"I'm going to be at the university anyway, so I thought that I might . . ."

"It's not your case, Evan," she said firmly. "Don't you think DI Watkins knows how to handle it?"

"Yes, of course."

"Well, then."

She was eyeing him coldly.

"I'm not suggesting that you're not trying hard enough, Glynis."

"That's what it sounds like to me."

"It's just that I have a rather personal interest in this case. Bronwen would never forgive me if anything happened to Jamila."

"We're doing everything we can, Evan. And I have to say it's rather presumptuous of you to hint that you can find her when we can't."

Evan looked at her in surprise. Until now they had been best mates, working well together in a close-knit team.

"I didn't mean it like that. It's just so frustrating not knowing what's going on and not being able to do anything."

"I understand." She nodded and attempted a smile. "I'll keep you up to date, I promise. If we hear anything, I'll let you know. And I'll make sure that Inspector Watkins knows about the death threats Jamila's brother made."

That was the best he was going to get. Evan drove back toward the university. It was lunch hour and students were spilling from all the academic buildings, heading for food. He tried the History Department common room and found it contained only Gwyneth Humphries.

"Badger will be out at the dig," she said. "The others are probably battling the line at the cafeteria, except for David Skinner—he usually brings his own lunch and eats it in the fresh air when it's not actually blowing a gale. He may also be out at the dig." She frowned at Evan. "What is it now, may I ask? What can you possibly ask us that hasn't already been asked?"

Evan hesitated, then he decided that there probably wasn't much that Gwyneth Humphries didn't know about the workings of the History Department.

"Is David Skinner gay?" he asked.

She looked astonished, then gave an embarrassed laugh. "To be truthful, I've sometimes suspected it, but he's not openly so. He's not living with anybody. Why do you ask?"

"Is it possible that he might have had a relationship with Professor Rogers?"

This time she laughed out loud. "You're suggesting that Martin Rogers had homosexual leanings? Oh, dear me, no. That would be barking completely up the wrong tree. Martin was a prude, as I think I mentioned. He was also very narrow-minded. He had strong ideas about what was right and wrong. And he was very outspoken about homosexuality. He tried to get the university to ban the gay/lesbian dance last year. It almost caused a campus-wide riot."

"Was there one particular student who was leading this riot? Anyone who might have been particularly upset by Professor Rogers's stance?"

She shrugged. "I didn't pay much attention, personally. Students are always protesting about something or other. You'd have to ask the gay/lesbian alliance. There's a very active group on campus. If you go to the Student Union Building, you'll see their notice board."

"Thanks," Evan said. "I'll do that."

Wingate's phrase "grasping at straws" came back to him as he battled the wind across the main quad to the Student Union Building. Students were trying to put up banners and stringing lights, and were having a tough time of it. Some kind of Celtic festival, he noted.

Just what did he possibly hope to gain from pursuing this? If Martin Rogers wasn't gay, then that whole theory was shot—bad choice of words, he chided himself. A member of a campus gay revolution would have had no interest in assassinating either a pizza parlor owner or an unemployed machinist.

Still, he had learned before now that sometimes the leanest of clues, the smallest of hints, could point a detective in the right direction to unlocking the case. He was about to join the swarm of students lining up to enter the Union Building when he spotted a figure crossing the quad—a swarthy fellow with a dark beard, dressed in the traditional Muslim dress, white robes billowing out around him as he strode out.

Rashid, Evan thought and changed direction. He didn't pause to consider the ramifications of following Rashid when he had clearly been told to stay off the case. He dodged around groups of students coming up the steps from the road. Rashid was moving fast, almost running now. Evan ran too. Down the steps, down the street, toward the town. Then he turned into one of the Victorian houses on College Road. Evan sprinted to catch up with him before he shut the front door.

"Rashid, wait!" he called and sprinted through the traffic.

The person spun around, and Evan saw that it wasn't Rashid at all.

"I'm sorry," he said. "I thought you were somebody else."

"That's okay. I suppose we all look alike to white people," the young man said with heavy sarcasm.

"Do you happen to know Rashid Khan?" Evan asked.

"Of course. There aren't too many of us who walk around looking like freaks, are there?" The young man stared at him coldly. "He lives here. Why do you want him?"

"I'm a policeman," Evan said.

"I thought as much. You're too late. The police have already been here and questioned him."

"Is he here now?"

"No, he's at a lecture."

"He just moved in yesterday, didn't he?" Evan asked. "Did he bring a lot of luggage with him?"

"Yeah. Quite a bit. Why?"

"Heavy, was it?"

"Why are you asking me stupid questions?"

"I wonder if I could take a look at his room," Evan said.

"Take a look at his room? What for?"

"In case you haven't heard, his sister is missing," Evan said. "Rashid has already threatened to kill his sister if she went against her family. For all I know, he's kidnapped her or killed her."

"Listen, mate," The boy stepped forward wagging a finger menacingly, "if you want to know the truth, Rashid was really upset about his sister. He drove around like crazy looking for her. It's the job of Muslim men to protect our women."

"And sometimes kill them when they disobey."

The young man looked amused. "In case you haven't realized, this is supposed to be a civilized country. We're all raised in Britain, you know. It's not an Afghan village."

"Then you won't object to letting me see Rashid's room."

"Do you have a search warrant?"

Evan laughed. "You've been watching too many American movies. I can search anything I like with just cause, and a girl who might have been killed or spirited away is just cause, I believe."

They stood there for a moment, eye to eye.

"What's your name, Copper? I don't believe you introduced yourself, or showed me your warrant card."

"And I don't believe you introduced yourself either."

"I'm Saleem Mohammed. Third-year engineering student. And you are?"

"DC Evans. Major Crimes Unit."

The boy's lip curled with scorn. "A constable? I'm wasting my time with a bloody constable? You go away, mate, and come back with someone with authority, and we'll let you in."

What might have happened next was avoided by the arrival of two other bearded men in traditional Muslim dress.

"What's going on?" one of them asked.

"This bloke, this police constable, wants to take a look at Rashid's room. He thinks Rashid might have cut his sister up into little pieces and brought her here in his trunk."

"I carried that trunk upstairs." This man was older, with more rounded features. "I can verify that it was bloody heavy and full of books. But if he wants to take a look for himself, then let him."

"Let him see Rashid's room?"

"Certainly. Why not?"

Evan caught the rapid glances between the men. He wasn't sure what vibes he was picking up, but it did cross his mind that they might be quite happy to lure him into the house alone and then dispose of him. And he'd have only himself to blame. The basic rule of conducting searches in pairs was a sound one. His father hadn't obeyed it, and he had been gunned down. Evan decided not to push it this time, not only because it was taking an unnecessary risk, but because it might make things more difficult if Watkins needed to search the house later.

"It's all right. Forget it. The detective inspector in charge of the case will probably want to see for himself anyway. If you're so willing to let me inside, there can't be much to see."

Saleem didn't quite manage to hide the smirk. Evan felt like a fool as he walked away. He knew his face was red, and he was furious with himself. He shouldn't have let them get the better of him like that. Now they'd think that North Wales Police were soft.

Once across the street he stood and looked back at the house, noting the street number. They had been tense enough, that was for sure. Those glances that flickered like electricity between them as they answered his questions. Was it possible that Jamila was being held a prisoner there? He could hardly call Watkins or Glynis without admitting that he had been poking his nose into their case, and yet he couldn't walk away and do nothing. At the risk of being yelled at, he dialed Watkins's cell.

"Any news yet on Jamila?" he asked. "I had to question some faculty members at the university, and I encountered a group of young Muslim male students. I asked them some questions about Jamila, and they were definitely cagey."

"Well, they would be. They don't exactly have fond feelings about the police, most of them," Watkins said dryly.

"But then I noticed they went into a house on College Street, and I believe it's where Rashid Khan is now living. I know you've questioned him, but I just wondered if they could be holding her there. Have you searched the place yet?"

"Listen, boyo, you know how damn careful we have to be about barging into a racially charged situation like this."

"Not even if it's likely he's got his sister locked up there, or even lying there, dead?"

"You really think something bad's happened to her, do you?" Watkins asked.

"I'm trying not to, but I'm dreading the worst," Evan said. "Look, I know it's none of my business and it's your case."

"Your instincts aren't often wrong," Watkins said at last. "I suppose I can go and have another chat with Mr. Khan, and take a look at the place while I'm there. It's not as if anybody else has seen her. Now, could you leave me in peace for two minutes and go back to annoying DI Bragg?"

"I'll try." Evan managed a laugh.

Chapter 23

Frustration boiled over as Evan drove back to Colwyn Bay, wanting to drive fast, but hampered by afternoon traffic. Someone should be watching that house right now. Someone should be searching Rashid's room before he had a chance to hide anything.

He tried to make himself take deep breaths and calm down. It was not his case. He should be leaving things to Watkins and channeling his energy to catching a murderer. Yet again he would be returning to his boss empty-handed, with no new clues and no new insights. His mind went back over the incidents of the morning—the blood-spattered kitchen, Megan Owen's tear-stained face. How many more grief-stricken families would there be before this cold-blooded killer was caught? Because one thing was sure—the killer had to have nerves of steel. Shooting Rogers in a respectable street during the morning commute hour, shooting Alessi on a Friday night when people would still be coming out of the pubs and clubs, and then shooting Terry Owens in broad daylight on a housing estate. All highly risky procedures. The term "hit man" came to him again. These were all hits. The quick dispatching of someone who needed to be dispatched. Maybe their team should focus more on the North Wales underworld after all.

Why would a professor, a pizza parlor owner, and an unemployed machinist run afoul of organized crime, he asked himself? Drugs were the most obvious answer, but there had been no hint of drug use. What they hadn't yet checked was whether any of the victims was in trouble financially. They should also find out whether any of them had borrowed money or had a gambling problem.

Then he had to smile at the absurdity of these thoughts. Missy Rogers would know if her husband took drugs or gambled. So would the other wives. Ridiculous. He felt especially bad about Megan Owens. She'd gone through a lot recently for one so young and frail looking. Poor kid, she had lost a child and a husband within a month of each other. Barely recovered from one before she had to go through this. He hoped her mother was being nice to her. There had been a definite coldness between the two as Evan watched them go off in the mother's car.

Then suddenly he broke off in midthought. "Wait a minute," he said out loud. There was a connection at last. He couldn't see how it might impact the three murders, but it was a connection. He put his foot down and zigzagged in and out of the traffic.

"Listen, I think I've got something," he gasped, out of breath from taking the stairs two at a time. The other men looked up expectantly.

"Megan Owens had a miscarriage a month ago. Missy Rogers went into hospital a month ago. Pamela Alessi had been under the care of a doctor."

"So?" Bragg asked.

"We've been looking for a connection. All three women have been ill. Is it possible they met in hospital?"

"And decided to find a hit man to kill their husbands?" Bragg raised an eyebrow.

"You thought Missy Rogers had killed her husband," Evan pointed out. "You were about to charge her. What's to say the other women didn't do the same? All we have to prove is how the gun was passed from one to the other."

"And the motive?" Bragg asked. "They were all tired of their old men? Not a sound move financially in any of the cases. No big life insurance policies."

"But it is a thought," Wingate agreed. "It's the only possible link so far."

"Go for it then," Bragg shrugged. "Right now I'd believe it if you told me they all took belly-dancing lessons or turned tricks together. Let's find out where and when these women were in hospital. Talk to their doctors. Wingate, you take Rogers, Evans you can take Alessi, and Pritchard, you get Owens."

Evan hurried back to his car. The blinds were drawn at Papa Luigi's, and the sign said CLOSED UNTIL FURTHER NOTICE. But Pamela Alessi answered the door after peeping out from behind one of the blinds.

"Oh, it's you, Constable Evans. Any news?"

"Not yet, I'm afraid, Mrs. Alessi," he said. "So you're still living here then? I thought you might have moved in with a friend or gone to a hotel."

"I don't have any friends living close by that I choose to go to right now," she said, "and hotels cost money. Besides, I'd like to get the restaurant up and running again as soon as the police will release my kitchen from being a crime scene. I need to make money, or I won't be able to pay next month's rent."

"So Luigi didn't leave you well provided for?"

"Luigi wasn't good with money," she said angrily. "If he had it, he spent it. He thought nothing of blowing twenty pounds on drinks for the lads. And those TV sets? Always had to have the biggest and best."

"But didn't Luigi do all the cooking?"

"Yes, but the lads and me can probably muddle through. That's what I'll be doing for a while, I expect, muddling through."

"Have you seen your doctor since it happened?" Evan asked cautiously.

"What would he do—just give me more pills that make me dopey half the time."

"The illness you spoke about," Evan went on. "Is it serious? I know you mentioned something about your nerves, but it isn't a serious condition that put you in the hospital, is it?"

"What are you implying—that I'm a nutter?"

"Of course not. So it's just a case of stress and depression then, is it? The normal difficulties of life?"

"That's about it. The normal difficulties."

"And you haven't been in hospital recently for any condition?"

"What's this about hospitals?" she asked sharply.

"Just following up on something we've heard."

"Hang about. You don't suspect me of murdering Lou, do you? Shooting my husband? What, because I'm really off my head? Oh, that would wrap it up nice and conveniently for you, I must say."

Evan raised a protesting hand. "Nobody's accusing you of anything, Mrs. Alessi. We have to follow up on all the leads we've been given, however absurd they seem. I'm sorry to have troubled you."

With that he made his exit. A visit to the regional hospital nearby did not show that she had been admitted there. Neither did a phone call to Ysbyty Gwyneth, the big regional hospital in Bangor. Of course there were always private nursing homes and hospitals out of the region. He'd have to see what the other two came up with.

Soon after he arrived back at HQ, Pritchard came back with the news that Megan Owens had been admitted overnight to the regional emergency center just over a month ago. Reason listed was miscarriage. She was discharged the next morning. Then Wingate arrived. No hospital in the area showed Missy Rogers as a patient. She denied ever having said that she was going into hospital—was quite indignant about it, in fact. And yet Gwyneth Humphries had insisted that she had been away getting medical treatment and Martin had been desolate without her.

"Maybe it was some kind of treatment she didn't want to admit to," Evan suggested. "Mental illness, maybe? Perhaps she went to a facility outside of the area. And it's just possible that Pam Alessi was also treated at a place like that."

"But Megan Owens wasn't. We've got records of her visits to the health clinic during her pregnancy prior to the miscarriage. She couldn't have left the area for more than a couple of days."

"So that shoots that theory," Bragg said. "Any more bright ideas, Evans? I thought you were supposed to be the whiz kid."

"I never claimed to be anything special, sir," Evan said. "I just try to do my job, like everyone else. And right now I'm as stumped as the rest of you. But the connection has to be out there. I thought that maybe we might be dealing with a hit man after all. If the men secretly gambled, took drugs, borrowed money and didn't repay it . . ."

Bragg considered this then shook his head. "I've had a bit of experience with lowlifes. They don't shoot you for not paying your debts. They'd like those debts repaid. They might bash you about a bit, break your legs, set fire to your car, just as a warning. But why kill off the goose before it can lay the golden egg?"

"That's just what it boils down to, isn't it?" Wingate said thoughtfully. "Why do it? What had anybody got to gain from it? The wives are going to be struggling financially as widows. Alessi and Owens had zero money to speak of. What was it for?"

"When we find that out," Bragg said, "then we'll have solved it. Until then let's get cracking again. So the gay angle turned up nothing, did it?"

"Quite the opposite in my case," Evan said. "Martin Rogers was so anti-gay that he tried to stop the gay/lesbian dance last year and nearly caused a campus riot."

"He seems to have been a proper killjoy," Wingate said. "Vetoing everything he didn't agree with."

"Yes, but you don't kill somebody for stopping you from having fun, do you?" Bragg sucked thoughtfully at the end of his pen.

"Especially not if you're a student," Evan agreed. "You protest. They love having something to protest about. They've got some kind of big rally going on. They were trying to put up the banners. Celtic Pride, I believe."

"Celtic Pride!" Bragg sniffed. "When I was young you were given a clip round the head and told you were lucky to be born Welsh and should feel sorry for everybody else. We didn't need bloody festivals to remind us to have pride in ourselves."

"So what else before we wrap it up for tonight?" Wingate asked wearily.

Bragg considered for a moment. "I suppose we should go back to the housing estate where the Owens lived. People who were out at work will be home by now. We can find out if Owens crossed swords with anybody there. Also telephone his mates—I've got their numbers—and find out what they've got to say about him." He got up, started to walk to the door, then looked back at them. "Well, come on. Don't just stand there."

It was after eight when Evan drove wearily back up the pass. Wind swirled dead leaves around the car and buffeted him on the turns. Winter was definitely on the way. One day soon they'd wake to find the peaks opposite dusted with snow. As he parked and got out of the car, he saw a portly figure in an overcoat running toward him. It was Mr. Khan.

"Any news yet?" he shouted. "Any news at all?"

"I'm sorry, Mr. Khan, but I'm not assigned to work on Jamila's case."

"My daughter's disappearance is not important enough that you drop what you're doing and look for her?" Mr. Khan shouted. "Because we're Asian, right? Because Pakistani people don't matter?"

"Hold on a minute," Evan shouted back over the wind. "I really wanted to look for Jamila, but I'm assigned to the Major Crimes Unit, which is investigating three murders within the past week. But I can assure you that my old boss, Inspector Watkins of Western Division, is doing everything he possibly can to find your daughter."

"But she's not anywhere," Khan said quietly now. "It's as if she's vanished from the face of the earth. Where could she have gone? She hasn't been here long. She doesn't know many people."

"There is one thing," Evan said after a moment's hesitation. "Your son, Rashid. I went to the house where he's now living, and his house mates were decidedly nervous about talking to me. So I'm asking you now, is it possible that Rashid has done something to her?"

"Done something? What do you mean?"

"Kidnapped her or even . . ." He couldn't say the words.

"You mean killed her? Killed his own sister? What do you take us for—monsters?" He was screaming now. "We should never have come to this country. I bring up my children to be good British citizens. I tell them about British justice and fair play, and what happens when I need justice and fair play? You tell me that. All we meet is prejudice."

"Mr. Khan, everybody feels very sorry for you and, believe me, we're doing everything we possibly can. Bronwen took her lunch hour to go and speak to Jamila's friends. She thought they might be more inclined to tell the truth to someone who wasn't officially with the police."

"And?"

"One of them said that Rashid had threatened to kill his sister if she stained the family honor."

"No. I don't believe this. That was just Rashid talking big," Mr. Khan said. "He says silly things sometimes. He doesn't mean them. He would never hurt Jamila. He would never—" He collected himself. "I must go back to my wife. She is almost out of her mind with worry."

"And I must go to my wife too," Evan said. "She feels almost as bad as you do."

He left the older man trudging wearily back down the road.

Bronwen looked up expectantly as he came in. "You've been working late? Any news?"

"Nothing," Evan said. "A completely frustrating day."

"She must be somewhere," Bronwen called over her shoulder, as she went into the kitchen to take out his dinner plate. "If she'd left the area, she'd have had to be on a bus or a train."

"Unless she hitchhiked. They're going to display her picture on the missing children Web site. But they can hardly show it to every long-distance lorry driver, can they?"

"Where would she go? Surely not back to Leeds. She hated it there, she told me. She hated living in a ghetto, being surrounded by only Asian families. She said she had no one to talk to. The other girls weren't interested in English or physics or any of the subjects she liked."

"I wish I knew, Bronwen," he said. "Just the same as I wish I could figure out why three very different men were shot with the same gun and apparently still no connection between them."

"What you need is one piece of luck," she said. "Now come and eat your dinner. You must be starving."

Chapter 24

During the night the wind grew in intensity. It howled down the cottage chimney. Evan held his breath, expecting to hear the crash of slates falling from the roof. But the cottage stood firm against the gale. His mind raced through all the events of the past few days. The answer had to be somewhere. Jamila had to be somewhere. Would Watkins have dared to search Rashid's house? Was her body in that heavy trunk? Where else could he have dumped it? He pictured Mr. Khan's angry face. "All we get is prejudice." And all at once he heard Megan Owens's voice. "Terry and his mates used to say terrible things about other races. They blamed immigrants for taking away jobs."

He sat up in bed. He realized that he had seen the connection all along, and it had been nagging at him. Martin Rogers had caused a near riot on campus for vetoing a speech by a radical Muslim cleric. And Luigi Alessi had been at odds with the Muslim family next door. All three men had clashed with Muslims. And Evan could imagine that young men like those he had met today might well decide to take justice into their own hands.

He got up and paced the room. Bronwen stirred sleepily. "What time is it?"

"Only three thirty. Go back to sleep."

"What are you doing up then?"

"I think I've figured something out, Bron. Each of those murders had a Muslim connection. What if extremists, like those young men I met today, decided to take things into their own hands and mete out justice to people who had insulted them and their religion?"

She sat up too. "I suppose it's possible. Extremists put out a death sentence against Salmon Rushdie for insulting the prophet, didn't they?"

"Those boys were jumpy, Bron. Two of them obviously thought the third was mad for inviting me inside the house. Does that mean they have something to hide in there?"

"Then put your case to your boss in the morning. See what he says," Bronwen said. Then she added, "Luckily it's not up to you to give the order to do something so racially charged. If you're wrong, you'll never hear the end of it."

"I know. But are we going to sit back and do nothing because we want to be politically correct? Mr. Khan said he brought up his children to be proud of British justice. Now it's about time we let British justice take its course."

"Evan the orator." Bronwen smiled. "Now come back to bed. It's freezing and there's nothing you can do until morning."

In the morning Evan presented his thoughts to DI Bragg and suggested that Inspector Watkins be invited to join them. "I would never have made that kind of connection if it hadn't been for the missing Parkistani girl from my own village, the case that Watkins is currently working on," he said.

"Right. Give him a call and ask him to join us," Bragg said wearily. "If you're right, this will require tact and strategy. I may decide to call in someone with more clout than us to help decide how we proceed. God, I hope you're right on this one, boyo. I really don't want to end up on the front page of the *Daily Mirror* for having caused a race riot."

"I'm not saying I'm right," Evan said. "I'm just saying that this is a connection we can't overlook. When I talked to those boys yesterday, I distinctly got the feeling they had something to hide. I took it to be that they might know what happened to Jamila. But maybe we've stumbled onto something more."

"That's how most things seem to happen, by stumbling on things, isn't it?" For once Bragg's tone was almost friendly. "But if you're right this time, God knows how we'll ever be able to prove it, unless we recover the weapon with fingerprints on it."

Evan went down to the cafeteria to get a cup of coffee. His nerves were as tight as a watch spring. He realized if his suggestion was wrong, he'd probably be the scapegoat. He was onto something, he was sure. He sensed he'd finally got his link. Three prejudiced men, he thought. Three men who didn't care about offending other people, who thought that they were always right, who liked to get their own way. Martin Rogers made a fuss if his egg wasn't cooked the way he wanted it. Terry Owens made a fuss because there were no eggs for breakfast. Their characters—that was what they had in common. That much was indisputable.

He was just downing the last of his coffee when his mobile rang.

"Evan, can you talk right now?" It was Bronwen.

"If it's important. But I've got to get back to work in a second."

"It is important."

"Okay then. Go on."

"I want you to promise me something." She sounded breathless. "I want you to promise that if I tell you something, you will keep it a complete secret and won't repeat it to anyone."

"What is this, Bronwen? Some kind of game?"

"It's no game, Evan. It's deadly serious. It's something you really want to know."

"To do with my work? To do with Jamila?"

"Yes. Will you promise?"

"All right."

"You'll swear on the Bible?"

"Bronwen!" He was annoyed now.

"I can't tell you unless you swear."

"All right. I swear."

"I think I know where to find her."

"Where?"

"I can't tell you, but I can take you there. But on your own. The police can't know."

"Bronwen, I can't just leave and not tell them where I'm going."

"I'm sorry. I'm not being awkward. My hands are tied, and these are the conditions I've been given."

"Somebody's holding her hostage?"

"No, she's safe, but she's being hidden. Do you want to see her?"

"Of course I do."

"Then I'll be outside your headquarters building in fifteen minutes."

The phone went dead. Evan snapped it shut and put it away. He was uneasy about the strange way Bronwen was acting and not at all sure Bragg would let him go if he asked permission. But if he didn't ask permission, then he'd be in trouble. He decided to risk the trouble. Then he had a lucky break. Just as he was leaving the building, he saw Inspector Watkins and Glynis Davies getting out of their squad car. He went over to them.

"What's this, a welcome reception?" Watkins called as Evan approached. "I have to tell you that you've stirred up a right hornet's nest—"

"Look, I need your help," Evan interrupted. "I can't tell you where I'm going, but it's important that I go there. You two know me enough to trust me. More than that I can't tell you, but it might have something to do with finding Jamila. Can you stall Bragg for me? Tell him I've got a lead that has to be followed right away, and I'll check in as soon as I can?"

Watkins stared at him for a moment then shook his head. "I hope you know what you're doing, boyo," he said.

"I have absolutely no idea what I'm doing, if you want to know the truth. And I wish I could tell you more, but I can't. Just give me an hour, okay?"

"Evan, you're not thinking of interfering in this operation, are you?" Glynis asked. "Nothing crazy like going alone to check on a terrorist cell."

"Terrorist cell? Who said anything about that?"

"Only this whole thing could turn out to be bigger than any of us imagined, and you could impair the investigation at this point."

Evan looked at Watkins for clarification. "We've been in touch with the Home Office. It appears that one of the lads we've interviewed has been making visits to Pakistan, and it's not to see his aged father. It's possible he's training young extremists right here in Wales."

"So that's why they were so jumpy. Did they let you search the house?"

"Only Rashid's room and, of course, we found nothing. We commandeered the trunk and have taken it to forensics, and that amused them."

"So you don't think I'm crazy for suggesting that these three murders may be some kind of Muslim extremists taking revenge?"

"Let's just say I'm going to recommend that we take no further action until we get more direction from the Home Office. We don't want to blow what could be a national security sweep. I don't know what you think you're going to be doing, but it better not be anything to do with those boys at the university, and that's an order."

"I understand." Evan nodded. "Bronwen's organizing it, and it's more likely to be one of Jamila's friends hiding her somewhere." He saw a car slow on the street outside and recognized Bronwen's fair hair. "There she is now. I've got to go. You will stall Bragg for me, won't you?"

He didn't wait for an answer but ran across the car park and out to the road.

Bronwen was sitting in the passenger seat. Evan climbed into the rear. The driver was a woman he had never seen before, slim, distinguished looking, gray haired.

"Evan, this is Miss Prendergast," Bronwen said. "She is Jamila's English teacher. She's prepared to take us to Jamila, but only if we promise not to reveal Jamila's whereabouts."

"Then she's safe?" Evan asked.

"For the moment, yes," Miss Prendergast said. "I'm afraid I'm going to have to ask you both to do something very strange. I want you to take these scarves and blindfold yourselves. I know it sounds ridiculous but lives can depend on it."

"Very well," Bronwen said and tied hers immediately. Evan followed suit.

"Why all the secrecy?" he asked.

"Because the address of the place I am taking you to must never be revealed," she said.

Within a Ford Escort in the middle of Colwyn Bay, it sounded overly dramatic. Middle-aged spinster were the words that crept into Evan's head. He felt the car pick up speed onto the dual carriageway, then slow into traffic again. Several stops and turns later they stopped, and she turned off the car.

"You can remove your blindfolds now," Miss Prendergast said.

Evan wasn't sure what he would see and was surprised to find they were parked outside an ordinary redbrick house with two large laurels outside the front door, on a perfectly normal suburban street. The house's name, THE LAURELS, was on the front gate.

"This way," Miss Prendergast said, and led them up the front path. As she raised her hand to knock on the front door, she turned back to them again. "I do have your word that none of this will be repeated?"

"Aren't you being a little overdramatic?" Evan asked.

"No," she said. "I'm not. You'll understand when you go inside."

"All right," Evan said. "You have my word."

The front door was opened by another middle-aged woman who frowned at Evan, listened to Miss Prendergast's whispered words, and then nodded, reluctantly.

"Very well, then. They can come in. But I hope you know what you're doing, bringing them here."

"They have given their word," Miss Prendergast said.

"There is to be no pressure put on her, they understand that?" the woman was still talking to Miss Prendergast as if Evan and Bronwen were mere observers.

"Of course. I'll be with them and I have the girl's best interest very much at heart. I believe they do too."

The woman allowed them to step into the hallway.

"What is this place?" Evan whispered, as the woman went back into an office on the right.

"This, my dear, is a safe house for battered women," Miss Prendergast said. "I volunteer here. Its whereabouts are known only to a couple of women in social services and to some volunteers like myself. You can understand the need for secrecy. Women come here when they have nowhere else to go. When their husbands have threatened to kill them, and the law can't protect them. They come here literally in fear for their lives."

"And Jamila came here?" he asked.

"Jamila sought me out, very sensibly. She had told me a little of her background when she joined my English class this year. She had obviously sensed I was a person who could be trusted. When she told me her plight, I brought her here immediately."

"May we see her?"

"On condition that you don't try to make her return to her parents."

"Absolutely not," Bronwen said. "I was all for putting her into protective custody the moment I found out what her family was going to do."

"And Bronwen was the one who tried to talk her parents out of their stupid plan," Evan said.

"I am not concerned about Mrs. Evans," Miss Prendergast said. "It's you, Mr. Evans. You are sworn to uphold the law, and you may find yourself being pressured to return her to her family if they succeed in getting a court order."

"I've already given Bronwen my word that I'd say nothing," he said. "Jamila's safety comes first with me too."

"Good. Then follow me."

They passed into a day room in which several women sat, knitting or watching TV. Some of them looked up, nervously.

"What's he doing here?" one of them demanded. "I thought there were no men allowed in the house."

"He's a policeman. Don't worry, it's okay," Miss Prendergast said, as she swept past them, then down another hallway.

"The women take care of themselves," Miss Prendergast turned back to them as they walked down the hall. "They have a roster for kitchen duty, cooking, washing up, cleaning, laundry. The one thing they don't do is the shopping. They can't risk being seen outside. We get most of our food donated by church groups. Jamila's on kitchen duty for lunch, so I'm told."

She pushed open a swing door, and they were in a big kitchen. A large, middle-aged woman was peeling potatoes, humming to herself as she worked. Another woman, this one not much older than Bronwen, was arranging chicken parts in a casserole dish, and the third person was standing at the window, washing up at a huge sink. Only her silhouette was visible against the sunlight, but the long braid down her back made her instantly recognizable She turned as she heard the door open, and her face lit up as she saw them.

"Mrs. Evans—Bronwen!"

Jamila ran across the kitchen to hug her.

"I'm sorry, I've made you all wet." She was laughing and crying at the same time, and Evan noticed that Bronwen was too.

"We've been so worried about you," Bronwen said. "We've thought terrible things. We thought Rashid might have killed you."

"I was afraid too. That's why I went to Miss Prendergast," Jamila said. "When Mummy and Daddy went out, he said some things to me that really scared me. I knew I had to escape while I had the chance." She looked up at Evan. "You haven't come to take me back, have you?"

"We want whatever is best for you, Jamila," Bronwen said, before Evan could answer.

"I don't see how I can go home," Jamila said. "but I don't know where else I could go either. And I can't stay here forever."

"We'll figure something out, don't worry," Bronwen said. "Things have a way of sorting themselves out."

"I hope so. I really didn't want to frighten Mummy and Daddy, but I had no choice, did I?"

"Of course you didn't. You did the only thing you could have done."

Evan watched them, feeling out of place and sensing the uneasy glances from the other women.

"Isn't it time for coffee yet?" the large woman who had been peeling potatoes asked suddenly. "My throat's that parched. Who's on coffee duty?"

She went over to a roster on a notice board. "It says Sally. Which one is Sally?"

"That new girl who came in the day before yesterday," the woman preparing the chicken said. "You know, the one who had her cheekbone broken?"

"Oh yes, poor thing. We won't bother her then. I can make it."

"No, I'll get her," Miss Prendergast said. "It's an important part of the healing process to make everyone feel that they are needed here and pulling their weight. Sally, you say her name is? Which bedroom is she assigned to?"

"The roster's on the wall over there," one of the women said.

Miss Prendergast went over to a large notice board and started leafing through sheets of paper. "Ah, there she is. Sally. She's in Primrose bedroom. I'll go and find her for you." She looked back at Evan and Bronwen. "You two stay put in the kitchen with Jamila, please."

Evan continued to stare at the roster sheets. He hadn't been close enough to see clearly, as she had flipped through the sheets of paper, but he thought he had read a familiar name. He tried to sound relaxed and casual as he strolled across to the notice board.

"So the rooms are all named after flowers, are they?" he asked, idly flicking through the papers. "That's nice."

He let the sheets fall again and moved away from the bulletin board. His eyes hadn't deceived him. Behind the current month's was still the sheet from the month before. And on that sheet he had seen something that set his heart racing. Surely it couldn't be a coincidence.

Chapter 25

"Bronwen—" He found it hard to speak. "Look something's come up. I've just realized something important, and I have to get back to headquarters right away."

"What is it?" Bronwen asked.

"I can't tell you. But it's nothing to do with Jamila." The words came spilling out "It's the other case I'm working on. The three murders. And now I see that I got it wrong before. I've got to call Inspector Bragg right away before he arrests the wrong people."

"What wrong people?" Bronwen's words floated after him, but he was already running down the dark hallway, making for the front door. He stood in the quiet suburban street outside and punched in the numbers, drumming his fingers on the mobile phone while he waited for the inspector to pick up. It seemed like an eternity and all sorts of horrible possibilities flashed through his mind—race riots, home office investigations, himself put on suspension . . .

"Bragg here." As usual he spat out the words

"It's Evans, sir."

"Where the devil are you?"

"I had something I had to check out, and I've got it at last. Look, I can't tell you the details, but I'd like you to bring in Missy Rogers again, right away."

"Missy Rogers? What's this now? I've just sent Wingate and a couple of uniforms to bring in your pal Rashid."

"Call Wingate immediately and tell him to come back," Evan said.

"Did I just hear you give me an order?" Bragg's voice was icily calm.

"I'm sorry, sir. It wasn't meant to sound like that, but it's very urgent. Let's just say that certain facts have just come to light that throw a whole new complexion on things. We've located that missing Pakistani girl, and she's safe and being taken care of. And her brother is in the clear at the moment. So it's quite possible those Muslim boys are guilty of nothing more than a natural suspicion of the police, and we don't want to stir up further trouble."

"So now you're telling me this whole Muslim plot idea was a load of codswallop?"

"I'm afraid so."

"You know what, Evans? You're more trouble than you are worth. I'm asking for you to be transferred out of my unit as of now."

"You do what you have to, sir. But I've only been throwing out suggestions, trying to come up with connections, not presenting you with facts. Now I'm presenting you with a fact. I'm suggesting, with respect, that you bring in Missy Rogers right away, after you've called Wingate."

"So now you're saying my first instincts were right and it was cherchez la femme after all?"

"Yes, sir. I believe you were right all along." Those were probably the hardest words he had ever had to say.

"Hmmph." Bragg gave a pleased little snort. "So do you mind telling me what has made Hercule Poirot change his mind again? What brought you back to Missy Rogers?"

"Call Wingate first, sir. We don't want a race riot around here, do we?"

"No, we bloody well don't. Let's hope I'm not too late."

Evan stood in the street and waited until the phone rang again. It seemed like another eternity while sparrows twittered in the hedge and a mother came past, pushing a pram, while a solemn two-year-old pushed a replica doll's pram beside her. At last his phone rang.

"You've got a lot to answer for, Evans," Bragg barked into the phone.

"Did you get to Wingate in time?"

"Wingate was still at the Muslim lads' house, luckily. He said he sensed they were not going to come quietly—a lot of talk about lawyers and civil rights and all that guff. He was just about to call for backup. So now we look like pansy boys, and those kids are smirking all over their faces, thanks to you."

"Look, I've said I'm sorry. And you have to admit that I did present a credible connection between the three cases. The only one we'd come up with to date."

"Only now you've got a better connection, is that it?"

"It seems that way, sir. In fact, yes, I'm sure of it."

"So do you mind telling me what great detective work you've been doing behind my back so that I don't look like a complete fool when Missy Rogers arrives?"

"I'm afraid I can't tell you anything, sir. I've been sworn to secrecy."

"Sworn to secrecy? What bloody game are you playing now? Did you always go in for this kind of dramatics?"

Evan took a deep breath. "I'm afraid I can't tell you anything more at the moment, sir. I'm just asking you to trust me."

"And why the bloody hell should I trust you?"

"No reason at all, sir, but I really think I've got it right this time."

"And you can't tell me what it is?"

"Right."

"Go and boil your head, Evans. I'm too old to play games."

"I am not playing games, sir." Evan heard his own voice rising dangerously. "I've been put in a difficult position, and I've given my word not to reveal any details."

"So exactly how am I going to interview Missy Rogers if I'm completely in the dark, Evans? Or did you plan on questioning her yourself, making me look like a fool and getting the glory for yourself?"

Evan felt the blood pounding in his temples. "Let me set one thing straight, sir. I have never wanted glory. I don't want the bloody glory now. But if you bring Missy Rogers in, and then do what I'm going to suggest, I rather think she'll tell you herself."

"And she's going to do that?"

"I believe she might, if she's taken off guard."

"Taken off guard?" Bragg was beginning to sound like a parrot. "Did you always dictate like this to your old boss?"

"Only when I was sure I was right."

"So you're sure you're right now?"

"All I can say is that I have finally come up with some proof that Missy Rogers wanted her husband dead."

Bragg sighed. "I suppose I'm going to have to trust you. If it backfires, it's your head that's going to roll, I can tell you that. And if the Chief Constable hauls me onto the carpet about picking on our Muslim brothers, you can bet your life I'll let him know that it was all your idea, based on misinformation."

"I understand that, sir. You do what you have to. I'm on my way back to HQ right now."

As soon as he had hung up the phone, he called Wingate and then Pritchard. "And don't let Bragg know where you are or what you're doing until I give the signal to come into the room," he said, the words coming out in a rush. "I can't tell you anymore right now. I'm sworn to secrecy or I would. Oh, and don't get the women alarmed. Tell them it's just something we want them to take a look at and identify." Then he hung up before they had a chance to complain or question him too deeply.

He went back into the house, his heart still racing. He couldn't be wrong this time. He had to have got it right. But he knew he was taking an enormous risk. Bronwen was sitting with Jamila on a sofa while Miss Prendergast hovered in the background.

"I'm afraid something very important has come up. Would it be possible to drive me back to police headquarters right away?" he said. "I have to be there when a suspect is brought in."

"I suppose so." Miss Prendergast gave Bronwen a look that said that men were annoying creatures. "Mrs. Evans is going to pass on a message to Jamila's parents that she is safe, and she will contact them when she is ready. Until we can assure her safety there is to be no hint of her whereabouts. I don't need to remind you that her brother presents a very real threat, do I?"

"Of course I understand," Evan said. "Don't worry. I gave you my word."

Bronwen got to her feet, still holding Jamila's hand. "I have to get back to school too, Jamila. I told them I wasn't feeling well this morning but would be in later, but I should get back as soon as I can."

"I understand, Mrs. Evans. Thank you so much for coming to see me," Jamila gave her a watery smile.

"And we will work out what is best for you, I promise," Bronwen said. They hugged again, and Jamila stood looking wistfully after them as they went back down the hall.

"That poor child," Bronwen said, as they drove away. "I promised to do what was best for her, but what can that possibly be? As long as we can't trust her family not to take her out of the country or her brother not to kill her, we can't let her return home to them. So it would have to be a foster home somewhere, and that's a miserable thing for a young girl like her. If we didn't live so close to her family, I'd want to take her in myself."

"We can't keep her in the area, that's for sure," Miss Prendergast said. "My suggestion would be a good boarding school for a while. She's a bright girl. She needs to keep up her academics, and she needs protection. But if the parents take us to court, who knows how it will end up? We may have to return her to them in the end."

"Over my dead body," Bronwen said. "I could phone my old headmistress, and we could spirit her away there for a while. They'd never find her."

"A lot depends on what Jamila decides after the initial shock wears off," Miss Prendergast said. "I know I'll fight tooth and nail to keep her safe."

Chapter 26

Evan jumped out of the car as they pulled up outside police headquarters. "Thanks for the lift," he shouted after him as he ran into the building and was informed that DI Bragg had just taken Mrs. Rogers upstairs to the interview room. Evan uttered a silent prayer that his plan was going to work as he ran up the stairs. If it didn't, he sensed that he might be back in uniform again.

He took a deep breath before he knocked and entered the interview room. Mrs. Rogers was looking more haggard than Evan remembered her—as if she hadn't slept well since her husband's death. There were dark circles around her eyes, and her hair was not as perfectly in place as when they had seen her before. This time there was no plain dress and string of pearls but an ordinary cardigan over a tweed skirt. She was also looking extremely indignant and glared at Evans and Bragg accusingly.

"This is coming close to harassment, Inspector. I can't think why you had to have me hauled in here rather than visiting me at my own home. It was quite embarrassing to have the neighbors watch me being taken away in a police car. I do hope it's not for another overnight. I've left Lucky in the garden."

"It shouldn't take long, Mrs. Rogers," Bragg said. "Only some interesting facts have come to light, and Constable Evans here asked that you be brought in again as he has something he wants to show you."

"To show me? You've found the murder weapon?" she asked.

"Just a couple of things that I've unearthed, and we'd like you to identify," Evan said.

"'Unearthed'?" She frowned as she looked up at him. "That sounds like something from one of Martin's archeological digs. Unearthed what?"

"I'll go and get them," Evan said. He left the room and went to find Jeremy Wingate, who had just arrived in the building. He explained what he wanted to happen and then went to check on DC Pritchard who was waiting in a nearby office.

"Okay." Evan nodded to Pritchard. "Let's head down to the interview room now, please. DI Bragg is waiting for us." He walked ahead along the hall, then paused outside the interview room until he heard feet approaching from the other direction. Then he nodded to Pritchard to open the door. Pritchard did so and motioned for Megan Owens to step inside first. At the same time the other door to the room opened and Pamela Alessi entered.

Evan slipped into the interview room behind them and closed the door. He saw the briefest flicker of recognition cross Missy Rogers's face, but Megan Owens let out a great gasp when she saw the other two. "Oh no," she whimpered.

"Who are these people?" Missy Rogers was still very much in control of herself.

"They know," Megan Owens gasped. "They've found out."

"Found out what? What is she talking about?" Missy Rogers said in the authoritative voice the upper classes switch on to intimidate lower-class people when necessary.

Evan stepped forward. "She's right, Mrs. Rogers. We've found out. I went to The Laurels, you see."

Missy Rogers had now turned pale too. "And they told you? They swore that they would never betray us . . ."

"Nobody told me anything. I saw your names together on the roster sheet for last month. Missy isn't a usual name around here, is it?"

"Oh well." Pamela Alessi sank onto on the nearest chair. "It was worth a try, wasn't it? I never really thought we'd get away with it."

"Of course we would have got away with it," Missy Rogers said. "We would have done now if you two had kept your heads."

"Would someone mind explaining to me what The Laurels is?" DI Bragg demanded.

"Mrs. Rogers?" Evan looked at her. "Would you like to tell the inspector?"

Her gaze did not flicker. "It's a safe house for abused and battered women. We met there a month ago." She looked from one policeman's face to the next. "I can see you're surprised. Surely not respected, cultured Martin Rogers? He was never a wife batterer? Well, he wasn't, not like Pamela's husband, or Megan's. I didn't come there with a black eye, like Pamela or having had a miscarriage because my husband had kicked me in the stomach after he knocked me to the floor like Megan. But there are other effective ways of abusing somebody, and Martin was a master at all of them. First the belittling, the humiliating, making me think that I wasn't good enough for anything, that I couldn't function without him, then the power over me—handing out the housekeeping money, making me account for every penny, flying into a rage when the least little thing was wrong, cross-questioning me whenever I dared to go out, cutting me off from everybody I loved and trusted until I had nobody."

"You could have left him," Bragg said sharply. "You didn't have to put up with that."

"I could have left him?" She looked at him and gave a brittle laugh. "I told you he had driven a wedge in between me and any friends I might have had. He had alienated me from my one sister, and if I dared to disobey him, he was frightening. He told me that if I ever had the nerve to leave him, he'd find me, wherever I was; and not only would he kill me, he'd punish those who had helped me too." She looked at Pamela. "Pamela's husband told her the same sort of thing."

Pamela nodded. "Nowhere to run; nowhere to hide," she said.

"So what gave you the courage to try to walk out on him?" Evan asked, turning back to Mrs. Rogers.

"Lucky. My dog means everything to me. Martin became horribly jealous that the dog preferred me to him, and that I lavished affection on it. So he set about torturing Lucky: teasing him, brushing him so fiercely that Lucky yelped in pain . . . that kind of thing. It was no good telling him to stop because he went on all the more savagely. I had to keep Lucky locked in the summerhouse for his own safety. Then, out of the blue, Martin announced that he had become allergic to animals and was advertising for a good home for the dog. No more hairs around the place, he said. That was it, as far as I was concerned. The straw that broke the camel's back. I took Lucky with me and called the battered women's hotline. And I moved into the shelter."

"And so you decided to kill him," Bragg said, "because he wanted to get rid of your dog." There was almost a smirk in the way he said it. Evan could hear the prosecuting barrister adopting exactly the same tone as he looked at the jury.

"Because he had abused me for years; taken away any life I might have had; and reduced me to a phantom who worked in the garden, walked the dog, and looked after Martin's needs." She glared at them, suddenly animated. "Oh, and he did have needs too, Inspector, let me tell you that. If he'd been screaming at me, frightening me, reducing me to tears, he took sadistic pleasure in forcing me into bed and then raping me. It was the ultimate humiliation, you see. Oh no, Martin Rogers deserved to die. I have no regrets at all about doing it."

She reached across and patted Megan's hand. "Strangely enough, I think that Pamela and I would have endured somehow, if it hadn't been for Megan. We're old. We should know better, but Megan—nobody should have to go through that at twenty. Her husband was out of control. Terrifying rages, especially after he'd been drinking. She'd tried to get police protection but with no success. In essence they told her it was her fault and not to upset her husband when he'd had a drop. She was terrified of going back home. 'He's going to kill me,' she kept on saying. But if she went to her mother's, he'd find her there and bring her back. I decided there and then that such men should not be allowed to live."

"So you came up with the plan," Evan said.

Missy looked at the other two and nodded. "It seemed foolproof. We'd each be the other's alibi. I couldn't see any way you could ever have connected the three of us. You should never have."

"It was luck," Evan said. "Pure luck."

"Our bad luck, as usual," Pamela said.

"So you took turns shooting your husbands with the same gun?" Bragg said.

Missy nodded. "After I had shot Martin, I sewed the gun into a small pillow I had embroidered, put it into a padded envelope I had prepared, and prestamped and posted it to Pamela on my dog walk that morning. Pamela dropped it into the post to Megan . . ."

"And Megan?" Bragg asked. "Where is the weapon now?"

"It's gone," Missy Rogers said firmly before Megan could speak. "It's gone to a place where you will never recover it. It will never be used as evidence if it comes to a trial. Your case will be all supposition."

"So it was all done just as we suspected in the beginning," Bragg said, looking rather pleased with himself. "You turned on the lawn mower so nobody would hear the shot. You opened the window, called your husband to it, and when he appeared, you shot him then closed the window."

"Not exactly like that," Missy Rogers said. "He came to the window and yelled "Turn off that bloody lawn mower while I'm trying to eat my breakfast." He looked quite surprised to see the gun pointed at him. I was too close to miss. Then I sewed up the pillow in no time and went on my dog walk, dropped off the gun at the post office, and came home to discover his body."

"And Mrs. Alessi?" Bragg turned to Pamela. "How did you manage with the sleeping pill?"

She shrugged. "I only took half, at one in the morning. It left me so groggy that I could hardly walk straight when I went to post the package with the gun in it to Megan. I said I had to go out for butter. The kind constable offered to go for me, but I needed the sub–post office at the back of the corner shop, so I convinced him that fresh air would do me good."

She gave a wistful smile. "I'm not sorry either. I'm fed up with years of lying, saying I fell down the stairs, I burned myself on the iron, to cover up for the way he bashed me around. And like Missy, he never let me out of his sight either. Always wanted to know where I'd been, who I'd spoken to. And heaven help me if I chatted to one of the customers if I was helping out in the café. If I'm going to hell for killing him, I don't really care. What I've gone through was worse than hell."

"I've been through hell too," Megan said. "But I still can't help feeling terrible about it. My Terry wasn't always like that, you know. We were in love once. He was lovely when we were going out together. Then he got laid off, and he felt angry and powerless so he just took it out on me."

"Don't make excuses for him," Missy said. "We've all spent too many years making excuses. If I had cooked the meat the way Martin liked it, if I had ironed his favorite shirt better, I wouldn't have made him angry. That's how those men operate. They want us to feel guilty for pushing them over the top."

Pamela Alessi was nodding as she spoke. "And afterward he'd be loving and sweet as if nothing had happened. He'd go out and buy me presents. Bastards, all of them. I'm staying away from men from now on."

"And the weapon," Bragg asked. "The one we'll never find?"

"It was, as you correctly established, my father's from the last war. Taken from a captured Japanese officer. A bit of a trophy. And light enough for amateurs like us to handle."

"But you're not going to tell us where it is?"

"No." She eyed him steadily. "And you haven't yet formally charged us, Inspector. So before we proceed, I think we should have a solicitor present. And while one is being found, I should like to go home and make arrangements for my dog." She saw Bragg open his mouth to speak and gave a scornful smile. "Oh, don't worry. You can send an officer with me if you like. I wouldn't dream of leaving my sisters to face this alone."

Bragg looked at the other officers with a triumphant smile as the door closed. "We did it," he said. "We bloody well pulled it off. Well done, Evans, for spotting those names. Very sharp of you. A nice open-and-shut case with a full confession, that's what I like."

"But they won't be charged with murder, will they?" Evan asked.

"Of course they will. Shot their husbands in cold blood."

"But the court will consider the extenuating circumstances," Evan insisted. "They were in fear of their lives. Their husbands had battered them and threatened to kill them . . ."

"Not at the moment they fired the gun. The prosecution will say it was premeditated murder. I reckon they'll get life."

"But we can't let that happen!" Evan banged a hand on the table. "That's not justice, is it?"

Bragg looked up in surprise. "Quite the little orator, isn't he? Listen, lad, it's not our job to decide what is justice and what is not. We bring in the guilty party, and the court takes it from there. It's over as far as we're concerned, apart from getting them to make a statement, which we'll do later today."

"But those poor women. You heard what life was like for them." Evan looked at Wingate for confirmation.

"The prosecutor will say they could have walked out at any time they liked. It didn't have to end in death," Bragg said.

"I'm sure the defense will produce psychologists who will talk about post traumatic stress and inability to make valid decisions and all that kind of stuff," Wingate said. "I know how you feel, Evan. This leaves a nasty taste in my mouth too. I had to evict a family from a house once. I felt like a heel."

"And I had to hold back local farmers while their sheep were slaughtered during the hoof-and-mouth epidemic," Evan said. "But neither of those are the same as knowing you've locked away an essentially good person for the rest of her life."

"They'll probably get out early with good behavior," Bragg said easily. Evan could see he was actually enjoying this, anticipating the pat on the back that would come from solving a tricky case. He turned away and stared out of the window. He pictured Missy Rogers, Pamela Alessi, and then little Megan Owens behind bars and felt almost physically sick. But what should I have done, he wondered. Should I have seen those names and said nothing? And let them walk free to live with their own consciences and us with an unsolved murder case? And grudgingly he had to admit that Bragg was right. The law was the law, and it wasn't up to him to play God.

Chapter 27

By that evening a statement had been obtained from each of the women, now with an elderly local solicitor in attendance. Evan found the man ineffective and wished he knew how to summon up a dynamic and forceful lawyer who might have prevented the women from saying the wrong thing. After Megan Owens had broken down in hysterical tears, it occurred to Evan that he might know where to find such a person. He excused himself from the room and called Bronwen, who gave him Miss Prendergast's number. She listened while he explained rapidly. "But this is terrible," she said. "I can't believe that you are calling me for help, Constable Evans. You betrayed those women's trust. You betrayed my trust."

"No, I didn't," he said. "My job is to solve crimes. All I did was to have the three women brought into the same room. They confessed to everything."

"But anything you saw while you were at that house was confidential information. You agreed to that."

"In Jamila's case, yes, but I'm a police officer. If I've picked up a clue to the whereabouts of a murderer, what else did you expect me to do?"

"Say nothing, as agreed."

"And let someone who has killed another human being walk free?"

There was a silence.

Evan cleared his throat uneasily. "Look, I agree it was probably a dirty trick to confront them with each other like that, but it was my job to do so. I'm paid to solve crimes, you know. And now we've solved it, but I'm feeling really terrible about it. So I wondered if you had access to a lawyer who could handle their case better. One who is experienced in litigation like theirs. I don't want them to go to prison anymore than you do."

"I'll see what I can do," she said frostily. "But you have undoubtedly blighted three lives."

"What would you have done?" he asked. "Would you have walked away after you discovered the truth and said nothing?"

She paused for a while. "Yes, I believe I would have," she said.

Evan hung up. At least now he had done what he could, and he hoped Miss Prendergast would know where to find a better lawyer who would at least give the women a fighting chance. He came back to find Bragg finishing up a report.

"Drinks all around, I think, for a job well done. I'm buying at the Queen's Head. Ready, boys?"

Evan tried to hide his utter dislike of the man as he looked at him. Actually celebrating the destruction of three decent women, women who had already suffered more than enough. There was nothing Evan wanted less in the world than to go for drinks in celebration. And yet he knew he had to go. He was part of a team. He did what he was told to do. And he was in serious need of a pint.

The bar at the Queen's Head was noisy and lively. A group of young people were huddled around a jukebox that was blasting out heavy metal music, filling the bar with the smoke from their cigarettes. Blue-collar workers from nearby factories rubbed shoulders with blokes in suits and fashionably dressed young women. It was the sort of lively scene he usually quite enjoyed, but not this time.

"Cheer up, Evans. You'll probably get a promotion out of this," Bragg said, after he had downed his first pint in a couple of slugs. He leaned closer. "Listen, lad. When you know more about women, like I do, you'll realize that they can turn on the waterworks any time they want and look you straight in the face and tell a barefaced lie. The fair sex—not bloody likely. The tricky sex, the unreliable sex, that's what they are; and to tell you the truth, I'm glad someone's going to make an example of these three."

Evan looked at him and understood. As if in answer to Evan's unasked question, Bragg went on. "Now take my ex-wife. She could play the helpless female whenever she wanted something. And she usually got it too, including enough alimony to keep me a pauper for life. . . ."

Evan could not have been more relieved when his mobile rang at that moment. He excused himself and went outside to answer it. It was Bronwen again.

"Evan, where are you?" she asked, her voice sounding sharper than her usual soft tones.

"Having a drink with Bragg and the lads in Colwyn Bay," he said. "I'll be home soon."

"No, listen, this is serious. Can you meet me in Bangor as soon as possible?"

"What is it, love? Has something happened to Jamila?"

"No, not Jamila. I've got her parents with me now. We're driving down in their van. It's Rashid they're worried about."

"Rashid—what's happened to him?"

"They don't know, Evan, but they're really worried. Apparently he went off the deep end today when he heard that Jamila was in protective custody, and they're scared he may do something silly."

"Like what?"

"They've found notes in his room on making explosives for one thing."

"Oh my God." Evan groaned. "That's the last thing we need right now. All right. Where do you want to meet?"

"We're going straight to the house where he's living now."

"I'll see you there," he said.

He ran back inside and tried to make his excuses. Bragg already had two pints inside him and was at the belligerent stage.

"What is it now, Evans. Don't tell me you've discovered it wasn't the three women after all, or are you about to solve another great crime single-handed?"

"No sir. This is a personal matter. Helping out some neighbors of ours who are in difficulties."

"Boy Scout as well as Poirot." Bragg's dislike of him was as clear as his own dislike of the man. "Well, off you go then. Can't keep the world waiting for your talents."

"Thanks for the drink, sir." Evan took a last gulp then went out into the night. It was cloudy with a threat of rain in the air, and the road surface was slick and black. Luckily there was little traffic, and Evan drove perhaps faster than he should. He arrived at College Street, parked, and waited for the Khan's van. Up the hill ahead of him the campus shone with lights, and wafts of music floated down to him—fiddles and flutes and drums beating out a lively rhythm. He remembered the banner advertising the Celtic festival. Celtic Pride celebration, he believed they had called it. He turned his attention away as he heard an elderly vehicle chugging up the hill—an ancient, dark blue van that came to a halt behind his own car. Mr. and Mrs. Khan climbed out, followed by Bronwen. Her face broke into a relieved smile when she saw Evan, and she ran over to him.

"I'm so glad you're here," she said. "I don't know whether they are overreacting or not, but it's good to have you around, just in case."

Mr. Khan refused to acknowledge Evan's presence and strode across the street to the house where Rashid was boarding. His wife flung a woolen shawl over her shoulder before she followed him. One of the young men had come to the front door. Mr. Khan let out a flood of Urdu. The young man scratched his head in embarrassed fashion.

"Sorry, pops, but I don't have the language. Born over here, you know, and my parents didn't bother to educate me properly. What can I do for you?"

He listened again. "I've no idea where he went," he said. "We don't keep track of each other, you know. He comes and goes as he pleases."

A second youth had joined them. "Rashid? He's just renting a room here," he said coldly. "His crazy notions have nothing to do with us. We thought he was just talking big. So don't go blaming us if he wants to become a martyr."

"A martyr?" Mrs. Khan shrieked. "Oh my God, what's he going to do?"

Evan glanced back up the hill where the beat of a drum had now started up again. "The Celtic festival," he muttered to Bronwen. "He wouldn't be stupid enough, would he?"

And without waiting for an answer, he started to run.

The quad at the top of the hill was strung with lights and packed with young bodies, some of whom were moving to the beat of a Celtic flute and drum in a primitive rhythm. Evan passed a booth selling mead and others selling Celtic jewelry and music CDs. Banners floated out in the wind. Students were wearing cloaks and strange head dresses. Some were dressed like Druids; some wore the Welsh tartan. A stage had been set up in the middle of the quad, and it was on this that the band was playing. The sign announced them to be CARREG LAFAR. As Evan approached, a young girl stepped up to the mike to start singing in a high sweet voice. Her hair floated out behind her in the brisk wind. The music had an ancient quality to it that added to the unreality Evan was feeling. He climbed up the steps at the side of the stage and scanned the crowd. A security man tugged at him.

"Get down please, sir."

"I'm a police officer," Evan said quietly to him. "And I'm looking for a young Pakistani man who could be dangerous. Have you see any Muslim men in the crowd?"

"It wouldn't exactly be the right night for them, would it?" The security man asked. "Not at a Celtic folk festival." He looked amused.

Evan's eyes continued scanning as the man spoke. Rashid shouldn't be that hard to pick out, not if he was wearing the traditional white robes. But then, if his plan was not to be noticed, he'd be dressed to blend into the crowd. Then he stiffened. He had spotted a glimpse of white in the midst of the sea of dancing figures. He noted the direction and came down from the stage. Painfully slowly, he maneuvered his way through the crowd. Hands grabbed at him. "Come and dance with us," one girl shouted, tugging at him. He managed to smile and shake himself free. "Spoilsport," she called after him in Welsh.

He was now where the crowd was thickest, right at the center of the quad. He hadn't stopped to think what he would say to Rashid when he reached him, but he was driven on by a terrible feeling of urgency. If Rashid did indeed have some kind of bomb, he'd have to act with extreme caution. Rashid had proved himself a volatile enough man at the best of times. Then the crowd parted, and he saw a glimpse of the white leggings. His hunch had been right. He was there . . . and he was wearing a backpack. Evan knew very little about homemade bombs. He wasn't sure what Rashid would have to do to detonate an explosive device currently carried on his back. Wouldn't he have to take it off and set the timer first? That was Evan's hope as he inched nearer, hoping to advance on Rashid from his blind side. If he merely had to push some kind of detonator button whenever he wanted, then Evan's own chances weren't too good. Neither were those of those fresh-faced, laughing kids around him.

He felt cold beads of sweat running down the back of his neck. It was becoming harder to breathe. At the last minute a group of kids in front of him joined hands and swung into a jiglike dance, laughing crazily. They broke apart and Evan found himself looking directly into Rashid's face. He saw a whole gamut of emotions flicker across that face—surprise, then fear and hate. It only took Rashid a second to register who Evan was, then instantly he turned and pushed his way through the crowd. At least he didn't have a detonator switch in his hand. Evan breathed a sigh of relief and gave chase.

"Rashid, wait," he shouted. The music seemed to have risen in intensity with the throb of a drum competing with the sounds of violins and pipes. "Stay away from me," Rashid shouted back and kept on moving. Evan caught up with him and grabbed his arm. "Rashid, slow down. We need to talk."

"What have you done with my sister?" Rashid shouted. "Where is

Jamila? What right do you have to take my sister away? Just who do you think you are?"

"I did nothing," Evan said. "My wife did nothing. It was Jamila herself who ran away. Now calm down and let's talk about this sensibly."

"Talk sensibly, you say? When did we ever get a fair deal from your sort? You despise us just as much as we despise you. Well, you're going to see. You're going to be sorry when the wrath of Allah falls upon you. Then you'll see who has the real strength, who has the real power."

He started to wrestle with his backpack, trying to take it off, shaking himself free of Evan. "Say your prayers, Copper." He spat out the words.

"Rashid, your parents are here. They are worried about you. Don't do anything stupid."

"Stupid? You call me stupid? It is you who are stupid because you are standing close to me. My parents will be proud of me. I am a martyr. A glorious martyr."

"Is that what they tell you?" Evan asked quietly. "Kill a lot of innocent kids and you go straight to Paradise? What kind of God would praise that kind of behavior? Do you think your parents want you blown to pieces? Do you think this will make them proud of you? This is a civilized country, and this isn't the way."

"Civilized?" Rashid almost spat the word. "You call this civilized? Pornography and cheating and blatant sex—then your definition of civilized and mine aren't the same. These people do not deserve to live."

The backpack slipped from his shoulder, and Rashid swung it to himself so that he was hugging it. Evan made a supreme effort and wrenched it out of his arms. He turned and ran with it, not knowing in which direction he was running, only hoping to get out of the thick of the crowd. Rashid clawed at him like a madman. In a way it reminded Evan of all those rugby games he had played, when he had run down the pitch with opposition team members trying to bring him down. He made it to the edge of the crowd and paused to catch his breath. Down the hill he picked out the shapes of Mr. and Mrs. Khan, making their way up toward him.

"Rashid!" Mrs. Khan shouted out. "Rashid, come and talk to your mummy. Let us talk quietly, Rashid. Enough of this nonsense."

"Nonsense?" Rashid screamed. Without warning he punched Evan in the face, snatched the backpack from him, turned and ran with it, back up the hill toward the crowd. Suddenly he stumbled on a slippery rock and went sprawling forward. There was a blinding flash, a boom, and Evan found himself being hurled backward with all the air sucked out of him.

"Rashid!" Mrs. Khan screamed again. Evan picked himself up, his eyes watering, his nose full of the acrid smell of gunpowder. He looked at where Rashid had been and then looked away, sickened. He picked his way back down the hill where the Khans were standing with Bronwen, openmouthed and horror-struck, behind them.

"I tried to reason with him," Evan said. "I managed to get him out of the middle of the crowd. I even got the backpack away from him, but this was something he really wanted to do."

"My boy, my son," Mrs. Khan was still screaming, rocking back and forth in an orgy of grief.

Mr. Khan looked at Evan. "I suppose you think you're some kind of hero now, don't you? First you take my daughter from me and now my son. My only son. My bright, beautiful boy. . . ."

And with that he broke down into noisy sobs. His wife put her arms around him, and they stood clinging and swaying together, overwhelmed by their misery. Bronwen came over and slipped her hand into Evan's. "You did what you could," she said.

Evan stared hopelessly up at the site where Rashid's body was not even recognizable as a human being. "But it wasn't enough," he said. "That's the problem, isn't it? You try your best, but it's not always enough."

Bronwen squeezed his hand. "You were very brave to have tackled him like that. Brave and stupid, if you want my opinion. I don't want to be a young widow, you know."

Evan looked down at her and managed a smile. "I couldn't let him detonate that thing among all those kids, could I?"

"No, you couldn't. But there are times when I wish you weren't such a bloody Boy Scout."

Chapter 28

"Would you take a look at this!" Bronwen looked up from the *Daily Post,* her eyes glaring with indignation. "Of all the cheek, Evan."

"What?" Evan was enjoying a day off and a real Welsh breakfast, neither of which happened often anymore.

"Bloody Inspector Bragg," Bronwen said. "Talk about aptly named! A whole big article about how he solved the murders single-handedly, and his stupid face grinning from a picture. He's taking all the glory for himself. Listen to this: 'I saw the wives as the primary suspects from the beginning, and it was just a question of finding the link between them. Luckily one of my team stumbled upon that link at a women's shelter.' He doesn't even name you by name, Evan."

Evan smiled as he went back to his sausage. "That doesn't worry me, love. Let him get the glory if he wants it, although personally I can't see how anyone with any feeling could get any satisfaction from solving this case."

Bronwen nodded. "Those poor women. I feel terrible for them. Evan, when we get a second car, would you mind if I signed on as a volunteer at that shelter?"

"You do what you want to, love," Evan said. "It's your life. You don't need my permission to do anything, you know that. I'm not about to turn into a domineering bully like those men."

Bronwen came over and wrapped her arms around his shoulders. "That's lucky because I don't think I'm the type who would stand for bullying. Although who can say? Those women might have started off as brave and confident and just been gradually worn down by years of abuse."

"And we've seen for ourselves that sometimes women try to be brave and stand up for themselves, and it pushes some men over the edge. Jamila was lucky to escape with her life."

Bronwen rested her cheek against his. "It sounds terrible, but in a way I'm glad that Rashid was killed. Now at least she can come back to her parents, and I don't think they'll be in a hurry to let go of her again."

"I wonder what the Khans will do now?" Evan asked. "They idolized that boy."

"What can they do? Go on with their lives without him."

But the corner grocery store stayed locked and shut the next day and the day after. Mrs. Williams, basket over her arm and needing some custard powder in a hurry, arrived to find the shop in darkness and the door locked and had some unkind things to say about unreliable foreigners.

"Probably yet another of their heathen feast days, I shouldn't wonder," Mrs. Powell-Jones commented, when she came across a very irate Mrs. Williams standing at the bus stop.

Thanks to tight police security, the nature of Rashid's real intention had not been allowed to leak out, and for once the Llanfair underground telegraph system had not picked up the true story right away. Of the other young men in the house, two maintained complete ignorance about Rashid's true intentions and his building of a bomb. The third, the one who visited Pakistan frequently, had vanished by the time the police arrived back at the house with a warrant.

But snippets of news of the Khan's tragedy eventually filtered through to the villagers, and there were mixed feelings in the Red Dragon.

"Nothing but trouble, didn't I say it from the first?" Charlie Hopkins stated. "We'd have had a terrorist cell in the village, you mark my words."

"I suppose they'll be moving away again now," Barry the Bucket said. "They won't want to stick around here after a tragedy like that."

"Good riddance, I say," came muttered from a corner.

But the women did not reflect their attitudes.

"I hope they're not thinking of moving out and shutting up shop," Mair Hopkins said to Charlie. "Just when I've become used to having eggs and baked beans on the doorstep again and not having to ride in that drafty old bus. I tell you, Charlie, if they go, you're going to have to buy me a car and teach me to drive. I'm sixty-nine years old and I've had enough of waiting in bus queues."

It was Mrs. Williams who first showed up on the Khan's doorstep with a big pot of soup and a *bara brith*. "I thought you might not feel like cooking much," she said. "I'm not sure which meats you're allowed to eat, but that soup was made with good Welsh lamb and I'm sure that's not against anybody's religion."

Mrs. Khan managed a smile. "You're most kind," she said. "Would you like to come in for a cup of tea?"

Other women followed suit, and by the end of the next week Jamila had come home and the shop had opened again.

"I suppose one can say that occasionally good things do come out of tragedy," Bronwen said to Evan as they walked together up the track to their cottage. "I think the women showing up on the Khan's doorstep with food like that really touched their hearts. Maybe it will lead to better understanding."

Evan smiled at her. "If it leads to the Welsh welcoming foreigners, it will be a bloody miracle," he said, and looked back fondly at the village nestled below, bathed in afternoon sunshine.